BIG SHIP, LOTS OF TROUBLE

SPACE ROGUES
BOOK 9

JOHN WILKER

EDITED BY
CHRISTINA SHORT

ISBN: 978-1-951964-20-7

CONTENTS

PART 1

CHAPTER ONE

CHAPTER TWO

CHAPTER THREE

CHAPTER FOUR

For my wife, Nicole.

You're about to embark on another fun adventure!
The crew of the *Ghost* is at it again!

When you're done reading, I hope you'll take a minute to leave a review!

The team has a home now, an official one, on Fury. After their adventures with the farsight mutants and and GC Counselors, the crew has focused on their new home.

Now they just need a name.

PART 1

CHAPTER ONE

B-TEAM

Bennie's comm set crackles. "Teams 1 and 2, move in. Keep it tight. Team 3, secure the rear and move in."

Bennie, dressed in a black tunic and light pants with a few bits of light armor strapped on, looks up at Maxim. The big Palorian, similarly dressed and outfitted, nods to him. Bennie says, "Copy, Team 3 moving." He unclips his beam saber hilt and creeps toward the rear hatch of the facility.

The two members of the *Ghost* crew are on Nexum. Bennie wanted to do some training with C7K2, and since Gabe was going to be working on the *Ghost* now that they had a fully set up hangar in the new office, Maxim came with.

Shortly after their arrival, the local security force asked for the Knights of Plentallus to help with a pirate problem. A small-time pirate operation has set up on one of the equatorial islands and has been preying on ship traffic passing through the system.

Bennie had wholeheartedly agreed, beaming for hours after the security chief left the tower. Now they're on the island securing the rear of the semi well-hidden hangar.

"You should have just said no," Maxim says, again.

Bennie shushes him, then whispers, "They need me."

"To cover the back door..." the big Palorian complains.

The security forces made sure the pirates were home, then ferried in teams via submersible to avoid detection. The island isn't inhabited other than the pirates, so detecting intruders is easy.

They embedded the hangar into the side of a dormant volcano. Bennie's wristcomm makes quick work of the locking mechanism. The back door happens to be a security hatch with a long, winding tunnel on the other side.

The two *Ghost* crew members sprint down the long, rocky tunnel. In their ears, the other two teams are moving in. Maxim says, "Team 3, we'll be in position in..." He looks at the length of tunnel ahead of them. "Two centocks."

Bennie is trotting alongside him. "Maybe I should have asked for a jet pack." He's panting.

Maxim tuts. "Yeah, those are subtle."

The tunnel ends in another hatch. Bennie looks around. "You see the access panel?"

Maxim looks around. "I don't." He looks at Bennie expectantly. When his friend does nothing but return the stare, the big Palorian says, "Laser sword?"

"Oh!" Bennie snaps his fingers. With a snap hiss, the purple blade ignites. He motions Maxim away, then plunges the blade into the hatch's locking mechanism. He guides the blade in an arc around the lock. The hatch pops in, hinges groaning.

As Bennie closes down his saber, Maxim pushes the hatch open. He's got a pistol held up and at the ready.

Over the comms, "Heavy resistance in the main hangar! Team 1 is pinned down."

"Three is in. Moving," Maxim reports.

Inside the hatch is a sprawling hangar complex, several hundred meters long and about half that wide. Several ships of various designs are parked below, currently being used as cover by pirate and Nexum security alike.

Bennie joins Maxim at a railing, looking around. "We gotta get down there." Maxim nods and they head off toward a staircase halfway along the length of the cavernous space.

Nexuus in light body armor are running this way and that below. Maxim watches as he and Bennie run. "They really need some training. Maybe we can convince them to hire us."

Bennie nods. "They've had a Knight or two in the tower for as long as they can remember. Guessing word is finally out that they're gone." He clucks, "Were gone."

Maxim takes a few potshots at pirates, but his pistol lacks the range and punch to even attract much attention. They reach the stairs and Bennie stops, pointing across the hangar. A Harrith man with a sniper rifle is setting up.

Below them, the pirates are falling back, luring the security forces closer to the kill zone the sniper is setting up. Bennie points to the staircase, "Go!" and dashes toward a bridge that spans the width of the hangar.

Maxim heads down the stairs, firing at the pirates below as he gets closer.

Bennie makes it halfway across the catwalk when he sees the sniper setting up his first shot. Below, the pirates have lured Teams 1 and 2 into the hangar. He looks down at his beam saber hilt, then raises his arm and hurls the hilt with as much power as he can muster.

The heavy object sails through the air unnoticed until it strikes the sniper on the side of the head. The man stumbles, then pitches over the railing to plummet to the deck below.

"I didn't think that would work." The Brailack Knight whispers to himself.

Without their sniper, the pirates realize they don't have any more options. The return fire dies out shortly after the sniper hits the ground with a splat.

Security Chief Soln approaches Bennie and Max, now on the main hangar floor, helping corral the pirates. "Our spotter team saw a ship depart. No idea how many were on it."

"I'm sure this place is full of bolt holes and escape tunnels," Maxim says. The pale green being before him nods, his mouth a thin line bisecting his head. Bright blue eyes stare at the big Palorian towering over him.

Bennie clips his beam saber hilt to his belt. "At least they won't be setting up shop here."

Soln bows his head, his three-fingered hand making a fist at his chest. "Indeed, Sir Knight. Your presence was most helpful."

"He did nothing," Maxim mumbles as he turns slightly to watch two Nexuus guide a group of pirates out of the hangar. The pale green beings are chittering to each other about the day. Bennie looks up at him, glaring.

The Chief of Security scrutinizes both *Ghost* team members, his bright blue eyes sparkling as he squints. He turns his attention back to Bennie. "Thank you, Sir Knight." He turns on his heel and begins shouting orders at another group of troopers.

Bennie scowls. "I broke my beam saber on the krebnack's head." He unclips the hilt, holding it up for Maxim to see. The emitter end of the cylindrical device is dented, crumpled in.

Maxim's face turns serious. "Can you fix it?" He points toward the front of the hangar and the exit beyond. Now that secrecy isn't required, air cars have been coming and going. One is waiting for them to return them to the tower.

Bennie clips the device to his belt, shrugging. "I've been thinking about an upgrade, so..." He shrugs again and starts for the exit.

C7K2 is waiting at the tower entrance for them. "Welcome home. I trust the mission was a success?"

Maxim grunts. "When I agreed to come along, I thought I'd be catching up on my reading, doing some sparring—"

"You weren't invited," Bennie interrupts.

Maxim continues, "Maybe get a laser sword of my own—"

"They are not souvenirs," C7K2 says, then adds, "I was asking Sir Ben-Ari Vulvo."

Maxim frowns. "Whatever."

Bennie grins. "I need to build a new beam saber." He holds his up for C7K2 to examine it. "I broke mine."

"Indeed, you did." The droid does not offer the device back to Bennie. He turns, following Maxim. "Come with me."

"I've never seen this section," Bennie says as he and Maxim follow C7K2 into the room.

The droid turns. "Because it is not on the tour."

"A joke?" Maxim asks, moving to a workbench covered in bits of technology he doesn't recognize.

"Yes. No touching," the droid snaps.

Maxim's hand pauses inches away from something. He withdraws his hand.

"Busted," Bennie hisses. He looks around. "This is some type of lab. To what? Build beam sabers?"

"Indeed." C7K2 nods, placing Bennie's damaged hilt on a worktable. "Knights would repair or build their hilts here." His optic sensors blink. "Normally, this would take place after apprenticeship, but your path has been unique, having inherited Sir Jarek Ruus's saber."

Bennie is rubbing his palms together. "This is exciting." He moves from table to table, examining the contents. "Oh yeah, this will be fun. I've had some ideas I wanted to play with." He begins mumbling to himself.

"Can I make one?" Maxim asks.

C7K2 ushers him from the room. "No." As the hatch closes behind the droid and annoyed Palorian, C7K2 says, "You can keep the tunic, however."

WALK-INS

Zephyr is sitting in the spacious and now well-appointed lounge area on the third floor of the warehouse building that the crew purchased before their adventures with mutant hybrids and GC secret agents a few months ago. The team has spent the last few months overseeing the construction teams that refurbished the building. Wil and Bennie came to blows no fewer than fifteen times before the Brailack decided to visit Nexum to work on his training. Maxim went with him to keep an eye on him and get out of construction supervising.

On the floor-to-ceiling entertainment display, GNO is reporting on the fighting between the Peacekeepers and Janus' forces. While the team and the GC council know who the enemy is, the general public does not, and the council has decided to keep it that way, hoping the conflict ends with no one the wiser. They have also, so far, insisted that Wil and the team stay out of it.

A small window appears in the corner of the screen, alerting Zephyr to someone pressing the announcer outside the building. A lanky Harrith man in what looks like a very expensive suit is standing outside, nervously looking around. She taps her wristcomm. "Be right down." She taps a different icon. "Gabe, we've got someone at the door. I'm going to go meet them."

"Acknowledged. Do you need me?" the droid replies. He is downstairs working on the *Ghost*. The last time Zephyr checked in on him, he had the reactor assembly removed and was doing who knew what to it.

"No, I'll holler if I need you. Just a heads up," she says, rising from the sofa. She sets her PADD down, closing the book she was reading.

The first floor of their building is primarily hangar facilities, but there is a small office space at the front of the building. The living quarters are on the third and fourth floors.

The front office is just big enough for a reception desk that no one mans and a conference room. During construction, Bennie outfitted the entire front office with more cameras than Zephyr thinks is necessary and a host of booby traps and anti-personnel weapons, should someone decide to storm the building. Wil had been giddy about the armament of the front office.

The main doors slide apart. "Hello. How can I help you?" Zephyr greets the unidentified man. She steps aside, extending a hand to the interior.

The man hurries in. "This is the office of...well, I guess I don't know what you, they, call yourselves. The people who exposed the plot to force my people into joining the GC?"

Zephyr clears her throat. "Uh, yeah, we're working on a name. That's us, though." She walks to the conference room, extending her hand. "What brings you in?"

The man looks around. "There are more of you, right? It's not just you?" He sees the look she is giving him. "Not that you're not enough, I mean," he stammers.

Zephyr holds up her hand. "The rest of the team is currently off world on other assignments." She decides he does not need to know that the assignments are really vacations.

He inhales. "Oh, I see. Well, I represent the Red Nova Cruise Lines. Perhaps you've heard of us?"

Zephyr smirks. "No, I just crawled out of a Brailack's pouch. I've heard of your employer, Mr.....?"

He smiles. "Sorry, my name is Londo. Del'Tem Londo."

"Well, Mr. Londo, what can we do for you?"

He reaches into his jacket, removing a PADD. He taps the screen and sets the device down. A built in holo projector comes to life. A ship as long as the conference table floats a meter over the table. "The *Galactic Empress*." His smile is as massive as the ship hovering over the table. "She launches soon, and we'd like your firm to provide security on her maiden voyage."

Zephyr tilts her head. "We're not really a private security firm, Mr. Londo. We're more..." She searches for the right word.

The man opposite her holds up a hand. "Understood, and Red Nova has plenty of security, but we'd like an independent third party to be along for the cruise, as a precaution." The Harrith man inclines his head. "We feel that your expertise would be valuable." He reaches out and taps the tablet, extinguishing the hologram. He peers at the screen, swiping a few times, then slides it over to Zephyr.

Behind the small office in the spacious hangar, the *Ghost* is sitting on her landing gear looking like a predatory bird. The hump that forms the living spaces and engineering is open at the back. Special heavy-duty hatches, normally sealed up tight and reinforced, are wide open. Inside, the ship's reactor sits cold, also open.

Gabe walks around the cold reactor, scanning it before leaning to look inside the reactor bottle.

SAND

"Stop that," Cynthia scolds.

"What?" Wil replies. They're at a cafe taking a break from the beach. They've been on Lorstak Seven for a few days, exploring the beaches, the cities, the old ruins. It took them a while to settle on where to take their vacation. Finally, Wil remembered the planet from a brief visit back when he was hauling freight and contraband for Xarrix.

"Squirming. I told you not to sit on the sand until you put your trunks back on."

Wil frowns. "I fell over." He wiggles a bit on the chair. "Now my ass itches."

"The nude beach was your idea." She sips her tea, savoring the aroma. It is a blend she's never had before, something native to Lorstak Seven.

Again, Wil frowns, this time saying nothing, taking a sip of his chlormax. He tries to not squirm and is successful for a minute. "I have to admit, I'm still a bit surprised we actually are doing this."

"Why?"

He shrugs. "Without at least one of them tagging along? I've had to kick Gabe out of my room when I was trying to get dressed."

"In his defense, he doesn't care what you, or any of us, look like naked," Cynthia replies.

"I know, but still."

"Need I remind you, we just spent a few hours on a nude beach? Surrounded by people."

"Strangers. Strangers I'll never see again." He shudders. "I hope."

Cynthia chuckles and looks around the bustling street. They are in a fairly touristy beach resort town. Beings from all over and outside the Galactic Commonwealth are passing by, eating street food and shopping. Their trip started with a nice relaxing two days in a tropical forest near Lorstak Seven's equator in a treehouse that Wil swore he never wanted to leave. Now they're on the beach for a few days before moving closer to the spaceport for the last leg of their vacation. "You think they'll be mad?" she asks. She raises her right hand, wiggling her fingers. "Your people have weird customs."

Wil beams. "They will, especially Maxim. He's secretly a massive sap. Cried like no one's business at the end of *Love Actually*." He takes her hand. "They'll get over it. It looks good on you."

"You're lucky I've watched enough of your Earth vids to know what you were doing." She grins. He nods his agreement. She turns to look over his shoulder. "Dren, it's getting worse out there." She nods towards the entertainment display inside the cafe.

The large screen is showing a GNO segment on the fighting between the Peacekeepers and what the citizens and news anchors of the GC are calling *the Invaders*. The fighting is intense and has spanned countless far flung, mostly uninhabited systems. Despite their numerical advantage, the Peacekeepers have had a hard time keeping Janus and the Source from running roughshod over many systems.

Refugees from the outer territories' unaffiliated systems are pouring into Tarsis and several other core worlds.

Wil turns to look. "Damn. They better hurry up on the finding a solution in the data archives plan." On the screen, one of the mutant vessels, what was once a Peacekeeper corvette, explodes. "Yes!" Wil hisses.

"Okay. Let's get out of here before we get glued to that screen." Cynthia taps her wristcomm, paying the bill on their drinks. She stands, clearing her throat. Wil turns slowly, then focuses on her. She's still in her bikini from their earlier beach adventure. "Let's go back to that beach. You can rinse off." She winks.

"Good morning, and welcome to GNO Morning Briefing. I'm Klor'Tillen, and I'm here in the Kuplovi system at the massive space station called the Hub."

Behind the Brailack journalist is a massive floor-to-ceiling transparent bulkhead. Beyond it, the hull of the *Galactic Empress* sits waiting for her first cruise.

"The *Galactic Empress* will depart in just a few rotations on her maiden voyage. We're told that the passenger manifest for this voyage comprises investors and VIPs from around the GC, as well as a few thousand lucky winners of a GC-wide lottery that was organized by the *Empress's* owner, Red Nova Cruise Lines."

The Brailack man chuckles. "Before you ask, no, I didn't win." He smiles. "I wouldn't object to a few days on pleasure station Moklan, though, if anyone doesn't want their ticket." He chuckles, then says, "Here's Megan with an update on the Dwapnarball Cup taking place on Brai this afternoon."

CHAPTER TWO

UPGRADES

"You are showing great promise, Ben-Ari," C7K2 says from the side of the sparring mat. Bennie is circling a droid holding a bokken. The droid is similar in size and shape to an average humanoid, and its limbs are padded to protect it from blows.

Maxim is standing next to the caretaker droid. He leans over. "Is this how all Knights trained?"

The droid inclines its matte black head, optic sensors glowing blue. "In the past, a senior knight would have been assigned to train the apprentices. The assignment lasted a cycle, typically." The droid makes a noise that Maxim thinks is a sigh. "Alas, now, DV0 is the best we have." When the other droid's head snaps around to look at Maxim and C7K2, the caretaker says, "No offense, Devo."

The training droid inclines its head. "None taken. I am but a pale shadow of the skill of the Knights."

C7K2 looks at Maxim. "As the Knights' numbers dwindled, we had them train with Devo in order to store their techniques and teachings. He has spared with almost one hundred knights, studying their every move."

Bennie clucks, "Can we do this, please?" He assumes a ready

stance. The training droid matches the Brailack hacker's stance, then moves into its attack.

Maxim watches the two parry and attack. He looks at C7K2. "How have things been since you finished converting the tower to a museum?"

"Quiet." The clacking of bokken striking each other rises to a higher pitch as Bennie and Devo exchange strikes in a rapid-fire dance around the mat. "I was not built to be a marketer."

Maxim smiles. "Understood. Maybe that will change soon." He turns and heads for the hallway. "I'm going to wander a bit. I didn't finish reading the plaques in the main gallery."

C7K2 looks over his shoulder. "The beam saber lab is locked."

"Dren," the big Palorian mumbles.

An hour later, Bennie joins Maxim in the gallery. Statues and paintings of Knights of the past line the walls. "Hey, big guy!"

Maxim turns. "So, when do they carve one of these for you? I'm guessing there are some remnants in the basement from these bigger statues." He turns to hide his grin.

Bennie comes up beside him. "There's some super deep knight dren I could say. You know, about pride and crap. But grolack you." He makes a rude gesture, then nods toward the elevator. "I want to show you something."

The uppermost levels of the tower, where the archive cubes—among other things—are kept, are off limits to civilians. The beam saber lab and private quarters for the Knights are among the secured areas. When Bennie and Maxim arrived, the caretaker droid gave the Brailack a keycard.

The top floor is exactly the same as it was when the team delivered the archive cubes a year prior. The floor-to-ceiling shelves are exactly the same, glowing cubes all pulsing softly.

Several beam sabers, those the caretaker has been able to get his hands on, are arrayed around the room. He collected them from around the GC when a knight fell. Each is on an ornate polished wooden shelf, a small plaque providing the name of the owner. Jarek

Ruus's hilt, now dented from impacting the head of a Harrith pirate, is on a plinth of polished black stone.

In the middle of the beam saber lab is a small workbench. "That's new," Maxim says, walking over to it. The table is Bennie's height.

Bennie nods. "Yeah, I asked C7K2 to set it up. The other work benches are too tall and it was exhausting climbing up and down the stools." The big man chuckles at his small friend's plight.

Looking at the parts arrayed on the table, Maxim asks, "What's all this?"

Bennie smiles. "Beam saber, version two." He holds up the hilt, still not fully assembled; exposed wires and circuits are visible. He toggles a thumb switch, igniting the blade. Purple, like his previous saber.

"Stuck with purple, huh?"

"Matches my eyes."

Maxim pauses. "Good a reason as any, I guess."

Bennie clicks off the blade. The normal snap hiss sound is closer to a clunk and fizzle at the moment. He twists a thick ring near the top of the device, then points it at a section of the lab with no tables. A thick piece of stone is sitting all alone on the polished floor.

Maxim watches his friend press the same activator button again. This time a bolt of purple energy lances out of the device. Not a blade, a single bolt. The purple bolt of energy strikes the stone, causing a section to explode outward, sending cracks through the entire face.

"Woah," Maxim says, nodding slowly.

"Right?" Bennie beams.

WHO WANTS CALAMARI?

The water on Lorstak Seven is warm. It reminds Wil of a trip his parents took him on as a kid to the Mediterranean Sea. Eleven-year-old Wil had marveled at the warmth of the water.

Treading water, he says, "You know, the water being this warm makes being naked somehow less weird."

Cynthia is floating on her back, eyes closed. "You're weird."

This late in the afternoon, the beach is less crowded than it was earlier in the day. Wil has mostly gotten used to seeing the various parts and pieces that the assorted beings of the GC and beyond use to procreate. He worries that Malkorite anatomy might give him lasting nightmares.

"What was that?" Wil splashes.

Cynthia's eyes open. "I said—"

"No." Wil paddles over to her. "Something brushed my leg."

Cynthia is treading water. "Well, it can see what's under there. Maybe it wants to get to know you?" She smiles, her incisors shining in the waning sunlight. She points to the water.

"Har har," Wil says, looking around, his pupils taking up much more real estate than normal.

"You're being ridiculous. Nothing in the literature mentioned predators—"

"Ah!" Wil screams, arms flapping, water splashing everywhere. "It touched my leg again!"

Cynthia paddles away from his flailing. She looks around, then inhales and dunks under water. Wil looks around, spinning himself in a slow circle as he treads water. Cynthia pops back up, running both hands through her short hair, smoothing it back. "I didn't see anything." She winks. "Well, I mean, I did see *something*, but—"

Wil vanishes under the gently rippling water.

"Wil!" She shouts, looking around. Inhaling, she dives under the water. She looks around. The clear water offers fair visibility. Wil is nowhere to be seen. How is that possible?

He appears below her, struggling against a purple and green tentacle wrapped around his leg. She kicks, driving herself down to him. His eyes are bulging out, frantic.

Her claws slip out of her fingertips with the flex of small muscles. Reaching Wil and the tentacle, she slashes the attacking whatever-it-is just under Wil's knee, almost severing it. The flexible limb unwinds from his leg, retracting lightning fast. Blood is freely flowing from small punctures where the tentacle had gripped him. She grabs him, kicking furiously to get them to the surface.

Wil breaks the surface, coughing and choking. Cynthia looks at him, then looks around. "You okay?"

A few more watery coughs. "What the hell is that thing?"

"Can you make it to shore?" Cynthia asks, ignoring the question.

Wil nods. "I think so. My leg is killing me, but otherwise I'm okay." She can smell the blood that is surrounding them. He breaks into a weak breast stroke and makes it a meter or two before screaming and vanishing beneath the water again.

Cynthia takes a deep breath and dives after him again. This time she sees their attacker, some type of multi-limbed creature. A cone-shaped body sprouts a dozen of the purple green tentacles. Two of the fleshy limbs are wrapped around Wil's leg and torso. He's thrashing wildly, fists landing on the flexible limbs.

Cynthia flexes her fingers again, claws sliding out. The creature is pulling Wil down into some type of underwater cave—that's how she missed it before. They must have swum over its lair. She manages to grab Wil's hand as it passes. Pulling herself along his length, she digs her claws into the tentacle around his waist. The limb unwinds, retracting into the wide section of the conical body, leaving more puncture wounds that immediately begin seeping blood into the water.

She lashes out at the tentacle around Wil's leg, a leg already seeping blood. The fleshy tentacle whips away, trailing blood and bits of flesh. The creature emits a scream that vibrates the surrounding water. Wil is drifting down toward the creature and its cave, his eyes dull.

Kicking with all her might, Cynthia dives, grabbing Wil's arm. As she drags him closer to the surface, she looks back. The creature is still in its cave, tentacles waving, but no longer attacking.

They break the surface and Cynthia kicks towards the beach. Wil's limp form is nothing but dead weight under her arm.

When she gets ashore, she drops Wil to the sand, only half out of the water. She looks at her wristcomm. "Emergency resuscitation protocol, human." The device comes alive. The unit on Wil's forearm comes alive as well. Cynthia's wristcomm displays a series of diagrams and instructions. She begins CPR.

After a minute, Wil splutters, seawater exploding from his lungs. His eyes flutter. "Wha? Who? AAAHHH," he slurs, his eyes closing. Cynthia's eyes go wide until she sees his chest rising and falling. He opens his eyes again, slowly. "That sucked," he slurs, then passes out.

Zephyr looks up. "We'll take the job." She's beaming.

Mr. Londo returns her smile. "That's excellent news." He reaches for his PADD. "The *Empress* launches in a ten rotations. We'd like your team to arrive the day prior to go over arrangements and the layout of the ship, that sort of thing."

Zephyr nods. "Of course. That's perfectly fine. I'll send over our standard contract and credit account details for the deposit." The Harrith man across from her nods. She stands, offering her arm. He clasps it in his hand as she takes his forearm in her hand.

She moves to escort the latest client of *Company to Be Named, Inc.*, as Wil insists on calling their fledgling business. "We'll see you soon, Mr. Londo." As the door slides closed, she shouts, "Gabe! Put the ship back together!"

She walks through the front office section into the hangar area. "Hey, Gabe!"

From the open rear of the ship, the droid that has been a part of the crew from the beginning leans out. "Please explain." He steps out of the open engineering section, dropping from the ship to the floor several meters below. He lands with a thud, absorbing the impact with his legs. As he stands, he says, "The reactor tear down is not complete." He points to the ship. "I cannot simply *put it back together*."

Zephyr looks at the ship, frowning. "Well, we have to leave in a few days if we're going to pick up the others." Gabe stares at her, blinking but otherwise doing and saying nothing. She exhales. "How long?"

"Six days."

"Six? Like total, or...?"

"Six additional days." He tilts his head. "From today."

Zephyr looks around. "Gah!"

The engineering droid nods. "Indeed."

"I don't. What did you think we'd...Six more days?"

Gabe inclines his head. "The captain said that as long as I was done before we had to pick him and Cynthia up on Lorstak Seven, I could *knock myself out*." He made air quotes as he said the last part.

Zephyr turns, running a hand through her jet-black hair. "Okay, well, I'll find us a shuttle or something." She storms off.

Gabe watches her return to the small office, his sensors further tracking her as she takes the elevator to the residential floor. He turns to the *Ghost* and ignites the thrusters in his calves and feet, lifting him back up to the engineering deck, hanging wide open.

Upstairs, Zephyr is at the kitchen table looking at a PADD, browsing shuttle services with service to the Kuplovi system. Luckily, Kuplovi being a tourist hub, plenty of services have daily departures. Less lucky, those that depart Fury are few.

The large entertainment screen comes to life. It's Maxim. "Hey, you."

Zephyr looks up, smiling. "Hey, you, back. How's things in space wizard tower?"

"Bennie is still alive," the big Palorian man replies, grinning. He looks to the side, then back. "He's almost done with what he came here to do, probably only another few days." He turns to the side again. "Shut it, or I'll stuff you in a recycler. We'll leave in a minute." He turns back to the camera. "We're heading to dinner in the city."

"Okay, well, enjoy dinner, but I have to cut your boy's trip short. We have a gig."

"Oh?" The big man leans in.

"I'll send you the details. Gabe has the *Ghost* torn apart, so we're gonna have to do this the civilian way."

Maxim groaned. "Well, I survived the trip here with his royal green-ness. I guess I can do another shuttle trip. Okay, I'll look over the details at dinner." He reaches for the control to cut the connection, stopping. "Love you."

Before the screen goes blank, Zephyr says, "You, too."

Zephyr and Gabe enter the Fury spaceport through the passenger portal. The Palorian woman looks around. "Well, this is different."

The taller droid looks down. "As the captain would say, seeing how the other half lives."

Zephyr clucks, "Something like that." She points. "That looks like our shuttle." A large holo-sign is rotating over a customer service counter manned by two bored looking Trollack. The sign reads *Zebulon Luxury Shuttles*.

"Hello," the older looking of the two Trollack agents says, her barbels twitching. "Where are you two off to today?"

"Hi." Zephyr smiles. "We're heading for the Kuplovi system with a stopover on Lorstak Seven."

The other Trollack, a man, looks over. "Oh, are you going on a cruise? Aboard that new liner, the..." he taps his chin with a long narrow finger, playing with one of his barbels, "...the *Pretty Princess*, or..."

"*Galactic Empress*," Gabe offers.

The walleyed aquatic being nods. "Yes, yes. That's it." His barbels twitch enthusiastically. "She's a beaut, all right. You win a contest or something? I entered a contest once for a cruise. Didn't win."

Zephyr looks over her shoulder at Gabe, then turns to the desk agent. "Or something." She looks around. "Which way?"

"Oh, yes." The female agent raises an arm, long webbed fingers pointing toward a large arched doorway along the far wall. "Have fun. The shuttle departs in just under one half tock."

The Zebulon Luxury Shuttles waiting room is anything but luxurious. Zephyr looks at Gabe. "This is something."

The droid points to a corner of the waiting area. "There is an open seat."

"Yay?" As she drops into the hard plasti-form seat, she looks at her wristcomm. The outgoing call icon is blinking.

"Hey, Zee, what's up?" Wil asks from the small screen.

She raises her arm. "Hey. Are you naked?"

"What? No. Well, actually, we're on a nude beach, so yeah." He blushes. "You can't see anything, right?" The view shifts as Wil tries to make sure the camera pickup isn't picking up too much.

From the screen, Cynthia's voice says, "Hey, Zee!" The screen jostles as Wil moves the camera pickup.

"Woah, woah, woah. Watch where you aim that, please," Zephyr says.

Gabe whispers, "Remember, it gave Bennie nightmares."

Zephyr tries her best to keep a straight face as the image shifts back to Wil. "Sorry about that," he says. "So, what's up?"

"I'm afraid I have to cut your vacation short. We got a job. Gabe and I are on our way to you, then we'll continue on to our destination."

From next to Wil, Cynthia says, "Where to?"

"The Kuplovi system. That new cruise liner they've been talking about when not talking about the fighting. Red Nova Cruise Lines have hired us as outside security consultants."

"Neat," Cynthia says.

Wil nods. "You said you're taking a shuttle?"

Zephyr looks up at Gabe. "Yeah, the *Ghost* is out of commission."

Wil grunts, "Great." He moves. "Hey, cut that out!" He's grinning. Zephyr blushes. He says, "You grabbed our go bags, right?"

Zephyr chews her lip, glancing at Gabe, who shakes his head. "Uh."

"Dude, I didn't exactly pack a lot of non-beachwear," Wil says, then adds, "and the beaches here don't require much actual beachwear."

"At least you don't have tan lines," Cynthia offers from off screen.

"Yes, okay, well, our shuttle is due any microtock, so we'll see you in a day and a half. Bye-bye." Zephyr taps the disconnect icon. She looks up at Gabe. "I'm not a prude, am I?"

The droid looks down at her, then up. "I will go purchase snacks for our trip." He walks away before she can reply.

CHAPTER THREE

BENEFITS

"I hear this place has an amazing menu," Maxim says.

"Good. I'm tired of salads," Bennie complains. Nexuus are predominantly herbivores, and despite repeated requests from Bennie, have not prepared a single non-salad meal since he and Maxim arrived. His pleas to C7K2 have gone unanswered. They are trying a new restaurant for this meal.

A young Nexuu woman smiles as Bennie and Maxim enter the restaurant. "Greetings. You are from the temple, yes?" She extends a hand into the dining room and leads them to a table in the center of the restaurant.

Since their arrival, Bennie has been dressing in the more traditional tunic and trousers of the Knights of Plentallus, including the cloak. Similar to what they wore during the assault on the pirate base, but more earth tones than black.

Bennie nods. "We are." His voice is deeper than usual.

"Are you making your voice deeper?" Maxim asks.

The young woman beams at Bennie, then glances at his much bigger companion. "Most welcome. I had heard a knight had returned to the tower. This is so exciting." She bows and departs.

Maxim looks at his friend across the table. "What are you doing?"

Bennie opens his mouth but closes it when a Nexuu man arrives. "Good evening, Sir Knight."

"I am but a student," Bennie says, making a sweeping motion with one arm.

"Why are you making your voice deeper?" Maxim presses. He turns to the server. "We'll start with the tallest mugs of grum you've got."

The Nexuu standing at the table stares for a moment. "Uh, yes." He turns to Bennie, then hurries off.

Bennie snaps his head around. "Dude! What the wurrin?"

Maxim scrunches his face. "What?"

"Why you gotta bust my chops like that? In front of a civilian, no less," Bennie complains. He huffs, "Why you gotta mess with my game?"

The server returns with their drinks, placing a tall mug in front of each man. "Anything else?"

Maxim opens his mouth, then sees Bennie's face and closes it, inclining his head. The Brailack says, "We'll have two of your best jerlack steaks," in his deep, raspy Knight of Plentallus voice.

As the server turns, Maxim says, "Mine rare, please." He turns to Bennie. "You're going to hurt your throat trying to talk like that all the time. Cut it out."

The hacker makes a rude gesture, then picks up his drink, holding it up to toast his friend. "Thanks for coming with me."

Maxim raises his mug. "My pleasure, Sir Knight." He winks. Bennie turns a few shades darker green. "So, you got your new saber finished? I've got us booked on an outbound shuttle tomorrow afternoon."

Bennie nods, belching loudly. "Yeah, almost. C7K2 has a few thoughts on improving the design. He's working on it now. I've got two more qualifiers tomorrow with Devo. Should be done before we have to leave."

Maxim tilts his head. "Sounds good. I booked a tour of the forest dwellings for tomorrow morning, should only be a tock or two."

Fresh mugs of grum later, the Nexuu server arrives, balancing two plates. "Gentlemen, your meals." He's holding each plate like it might explode. He places a plate in front of Bennie. "Sir Knight." He turns to Maxim. "Rare, as asked for."

Maxim nods. "Thank you. No rush, but another round of drinks, please."

The young server bows, his blue eyes sparkling. He backs away.

"I don't think he's going to comp these," Maxim offers.

Bennie clucks, "He will. I've got this hand wave thing I've been practicing. According to the histories, a Sir Alec Guinness used it all the time to score free stuff."

Maxim takes a bite of his steak, thinking about Bennie's reply. "So, the Knights were just drunk grifters?"

Bennie frowns, then says, "Yeah, more or less." He grins, ear to ear. "My kind of people."

Maxim almost spits out his jerlack.

RIDING IN STYLE

"Can you believe that? That Trollack brat spilled icy treat down my back," Zephyr growls. She's in the community head for the deck they've been assigned. Gabe is standing against the back wall as she tries her best to dry herself. She looks in the mirror, then leans down to check for feet in the stalls. The room is empty. "Lock the door, close your eyes."

"I do not—"

"Do it!" she snaps, reaching to pull her top off.

"Oh." Gabe moves closer to the door, his optic sensors going dark.

Zephyr sets about trying to clean and dry her shirt, grumbling about parents and un-managed children.

The door opens, getting barely a centimeter or two open before Gabe slams it shut. "Hey!" comes from the other side. "That's a public restroom. You can't block it off."

"There are two more restrooms on this deck," Gabe says.

"This is the one closest to my seat! Open up!" the voice demands.

Gabe lets the door open as he shifts to battle mode. His optics reactivate, glowing their malevolent crimson. The twin blasters replace his hands. "Find. Another," he says, his voice deeper than Maxim's.

From where she is, Zephyr can't see Gabe's adversary but hears them clear their throat. The next sound is the door closing and the whirring and clicking of Gabe returning to normal mode.

He turns to Zephyr. "We are secu—"

"Eyes!" she scolds. In the span of a heartbeat, Gabe's optics blink off.

Their shuttle, the *Swift Flac,* boasts two decks for passengers with a cargo hold below. The forward section of both passenger decks is a large observation lounge, offering a respite from the cramped seating in the main compartment.

Zephyr and Gabe purchased seats in an area on the uppermost deck, below the command deck. Zephyr drops into her seat. "This is going to be a long trip."

Gabe moves to sit next to her, his body emitting whirs and clicks as components shift to make his chassis conform to the seat. "Indeed. I have detected three devices attempting to connect and hijack wrist-comms." He turns, smiling his always disconcerting smile. "I am enjoying thwarting those devices."

Zephyr picks at something on her shirt. "Well, I'm glad you have something to keep yourself busy."

"Indeed." Gabe turns to face forward, his optic sensors glittering.

The overhead speakers crackle. "Attention, passengers, this is Captain Kleb Lol. We've entered FTL and should reach Lorstak Seven on schedule. Please avail yourself of the entertainments our fine vessel has to offer. On behalf of the crew of the *Swift Flac,* we hope you enjoy your trip."

Zephyr tuts. "Entertainments..." She taps the controls on the entertainment display in front of her, bringing up the menu. "Great. I've seen all these."

"You know, I'm definitely done with nude beaches," Wil says as they walk toward the restaurant mounted to the cliff face over the beach, a non-nude one. He is walking with a slight limp, the medical patches still working on the dozens of lacerations he suffered from hip to ankle.

"While I'm sure you'd like to think so, your being naked isn't what attracted that thing."

Wil makes a face. "I dunno. It attracted you." He winks.

She groans. "According to that medtech that checked you out, Baechoos don't normally mess with people, being herbivores and all.

They arrive, massive metal doors swinging out on silent hinges. Wil smiles. "Like I said, saw something it liked. Made it want to give up veggies."

Cynthia sighs, holding up a hand to tick her fingers. "One, that's gross. Two, you're not that impressive, so calm down. Three, you almost died." She waves his response away and smiles to the host, a Kilden. "Good evening. Two, please."

The insectoid being clacks their mandibles. "This way, please."

As they follow the hostess, Cynthia leans over. "Maybe it was your sunscreen? Or oils on your skin that aren't common here?"

Wil blushes. "You did apply it liberally."

The hostess turns. "Here you are." Cynthia sighs and sits down, hoping that the topic is dropped.

The two sit down. Their table is on a balcony overlooking the ocean. Wil continues, "I think the idea of nude beaches is hot, but in the end, it's just mostly out-of-shape, naked people."

Unfolding her napkin, Cynthia adds, "And sea monsters."

Wil barks a laugh. "Yeah, but mostly ugly naked people."

Cynthia shrugs. "Present company excluded, of course." She winks.

He shudders. "I mean, what's the deal with the Malkorites and... the pincers?" He makes a claw with one hand.

Cynthia raises a hand. "Okay, like I explained, the pincers are for grasping their mate and not letting go during...you know. And that's the last time we talk about anyone's sex organs that aren't ours. Deal?"

"Pincers?" Wil shivers. "Yeah, sounds good. At any rate, like I said, I think I'm good on nude beaches, unless they're private." He winks.

A waiter arrives, a young Malkorite man. "Good evening."

"Gah!" Wil looks at the ceiling.

Cynthia stifles a laugh, putting a hand over her mouth. The waiter looks at each of them, then asks, "Would you like to hear the specials? Tonight we're featuring spiny rock crawlers."

"Pincers," Wil groans.

Cynthia kicks him under the table. "I'll have the pasta special." She looks at Wil, who is still examining the ceiling. "He'll have the jerlack, medium rare. A bottle of middle era red, Meruvian, if you have it."

"Very good." The young man bows and walks away. Beyond the railing next to them, the ocean is crashing against the beach. Boats in the distance are lighting up as the sun sets.

Wil finally looks at Cynthia. "It had to be a Malkorite." She shakes her head. Wil continues, "After this, we should hit up one of the least touristy places we can find. Outside these trousers and my Hawaiian shirt, the only other things I brought were swim trunks and a few t-shirts."

"You can leave the shirt here," Cynthia offers, point to the Hawaiian shirt he's wearing.

"You're just jealous."

"Of your ugly shirt?"

Their waiter returns with the bottle of wine and two long-stemmed glasses. He pours wine into each, then retreats.

Wil offers his glass up for a toast: "Jealousy is ugly. It's an awesome shirt, my last one. Which reminds me, I need to grab a few more."

Cynthia gently clinks her glass against his. "You don't. They're ugly."

Wil looks down at his shirt. "This is not ugly. It's art." He pulls at the bottom, stretching the front taut. The design is a blend of wave patterns and flowers mixed with tiny spaceships dogfighting.

Cynthia sighs and sips her drink.

"Attention, passengers, this is Captain Kleb Lol. We've dropped from FTL and are making our approach to Lorstak Seven now. We should make planet fall in three tocks. On behalf of the crew of the *Swift Flac*, we hope you've enjoyed your trip and that your time on Lorstak Seven will be pleasant."

Zephyr looks at Gabe. "I've had sugary drink spilled on me. That Olop man propositioned me. Twice!" She growls, "Yeah, been a great trip."

Gabe looks down at his crew mate. "This is most assuredly not the *Ghost*."

Zephyr grunts. "Okay, let's go to the observation lounge for the approach." The droid inclines his head.

The observation lounge of the *Swift Flac* sits at the forwardmost section of the supposed luxury shuttle. The two-story lounge is lined with chairs and sofas of moderate repair.

Directly ahead of the ship, through the transparisteel bulkhead, is the seventh planet in the Lorstak system. Wil and Cynthia choosing it had surprised Zephyr at first, until she remembered the secondary continent that straddles the equatorial region, mixing lush rainforests and temperate beaches all within a short planetary shuttle ride from each other.

"You confirmed that the Captain and Cynthia will meet us?" Gabe says, moving to stand next to a plush chair, extending an arm for Zephyr to sit.

She does. "Yeah, but I'm gonna check in with them now that we're on final approach." She raises her wristcomm, tapping the icon for Wil.

After a few seconds, Wil appears on the small display. "Hey, Zee, you almost here?"

She nods. "Yeah, we're on final approach now, just under three tocks."

Wil smiles. "Okay, cool. We're doing some shopping since you forgot my go bag."

Zephyr sighs. "Does that get let go of anytime soon?"

"Depends. You okay with me doing this job in speedos?"

"I don't know what that means."

From off screen, Cynthia says, "They don't leave much to the imagination."

Zephyr waves her other hand in front of the screen. "No, no, that's fine. You've got time, so shop away."

"Ask about his tan lines," Cynthia shouts from off screen.

"I will not," Zephyr chuckles, touching the *end call* icon. She looks up at Gabe, rolling her eyes.

"Mom! Look!" Two small Brailack children burst through the hatch into the lounge followed by a dozen more children and two haggard looking adult Brailack. The father, his blue skin shining with sweat, looks at Zephyr, mumbling, "Sorry," as he rushes to the forward window to herd his brood to the side. She smiles.

Wil lowers his arm. He reaches for something. "How about this?" He holds up a red leather jacket striped with black, forming a V on the front and back.

"Uh. No." Cynthia waves the jacket away. Wil holds up a sparkling glove that was in the pocket. She frowns.

"Eh?" Wil holds up a black leather jacket that closes with a few large clips running down the front.

"What is even happening here? No," Cynthia says. She grabs his arm. "Here. Pick things from here."

"This stuff is boring. It's all canvas and space polyester," Wil protests.

"Pick, or I'll pick for you," Cynthia says, then adds, holding up a pair of dark brown trousers with built-in suspenders, "I mean, I'm still picking things, but you at least get some input. If you behave."

Wil snatches the pants from her and grabs a blue button-down shirt from the rack next to her and storms into the dressing room. "Guess I'm dressing like a space cowboy for this job."

Cynthia watches him close the curtain screening off the small dressing area. The store is moderately busy; beings of various shapes and sizes are browsing the racks that are conveniently labeled with body design on the top of each.

A couple, the same species as their friend Rhys Duch's thug and cook, Zash, are looking at clothes designed for those with four arms.

CHAPTER FOUR

BOARDING PASS, PLEASE

"Well, this is nice," Maxim says as they board the shuttle. Nexum, being a bit off the beaten path, has fewer options for public transportation. Maxim found a shuttle service that would get them to the transit hub on time.

Bennie looks around. "How much did this cost?" Maxim opens his mouth, but Bennie waves him off. "I wonder if they'll give us a refund, my being a Knight and all."

Maxim sighs. "Just go sit down." He shoves his small friend into the shuttle's cabin. This shuttle lacks the private cabins that many luxury vessels offer, instead offering small seating areas that are separated from others by small dividers.

As Bennie walks toward the section of seats that Maxim has reserved, he nods to those passengers already aboard, smiling and offering them random sage-sounding platitudes. Maxim groans.

Maxim drops into the seat. "The best I could get privacy-wise was booking all four of these seats." He looks around the small space, unimpressed.

Bennie shrugs. "Works for me. We're, what? Three days out?" Maxim nods.

"Attention, passengers, we'll be departing in one half tock. Please find your seats." A lanky Burzzad flight attendant walks up the opposite aisle, ushering people into their seats.

Maxim puts his feet up on a footrest. "Three days." He looks around. The main cabin, visible through the opening in their semi-private, four-seat space, is only about half full.

"Wonder where the single ladies are?" Bennie rubs his palms together, licking his lips.

Maxim turns. "You will not be entertaining in here. There's not even a door."

The shuttle lurches as it lifts off the landing pad. Bennie clucks, "There are restrooms." He hefts his new beam saber hilt. "Ladies love a man with power."

Maxim looks out the window, watching the clouds over the city pass by and thin as the shuttle clears the atmosphere. He turns to his small friend. "You're a little deviant."

Bennie makes a face. "Palorians, such prudes."

The Burzzad flight attendant reaches their compartment. "Gentlemen. We'll begin the evening meal service in about two and a half tocks. Do you have any dietary restrictions?"

Maxim shakes his head. "Thank you, we're both fine with whatever you're serving." The woman nods, tapping on her PADD, and walks away toward the next four-seat compartment. Maxim looks at Bennie, pulling a PADD of his own out of his pocket. "I'm going to catch up on this book." He waves at Bennie. "Have fun hunting for love."

The Brailack hacker opens the door to their small compartment. Waving, he says, "Love got nothin' to do with it."

Maxim sighs.

The evening meal turns out to be reconstituted doorip mash. Since it is just the two of them, Bennie and Maxim have split the small compartment, each getting two seats to spread out and lie down.

Bennie looks at the two meal containers. "You know, that wasn't too bad." He smacks his lips. "Good job booking this thing." He waves to encompass the shuttle.

Maxim smiles. "Truthfully, there are only two companies running shuttles off Nexum. The other one eventually would have made it to the Kuplovi system and had the added benefit of stopping through the Olopnal system." He takes a sip of the sparkling water that came with the meal. "Of course, we'd be almost a full span of days late, missing the cruise."

Bennie tuts. "Well, that would suck. I'm definitely looking forward to a trip on the most luxurious starship ever built." Again, he rubs his little hands together. "I bet they haven't even fully hardened their computer security systems."

The lighting in the shuttle's cabin dims. Maxim sets the water down. "Two more days."

Bennie slaps his hands on his knees. "Okay, don't wait up." He stands to head for the narrow door to the compartment.

Maxim rolls his eyes. "Don't do anything I wouldn't do."

Bennie tuts. "Are you kidding? I'm going to do a ton of things you wouldn't do, prude." The hatch slides shut with a stutter.

Maxim grabs his PADD and opens the book he's reading.

"Those pants look nice," Zephyr says as she and Gabe reach the waiting Cynthia and Wil.

Wil makes a show of spinning in a slow circle. "Apparently, I'm easy to dress."

"To undress, too," Cynthia murmurs. Wil, close enough to hear, turns and grins. Gabe tilts his head, his hearing more than sufficient, regardless of the distance.

Zephyr and Cynthia hug. Wil reaches up and puts a hand on Gabe's shoulder. "How's the *Ghost*?"

"The overhaul of the reactor was progressing smoothly until..."

"Until?"

Gabe tilts his head again. "This."

"Ah, well, yeah." Wil smiles. He turns to the two women. "Want to grab a chlormax while we wait for the shuttle?" He consults his wristcomm. "We've got a few tocks, right?"

Zephyr nods, consulting her own wristcomm. She flicks twice, sending Wil and Cynthia their respective boarding documents.

Cynthia takes the lead exiting the spaceport lobby. "We found this amazing cafe. It's not too far, overlooks this amazing stretch of beach."

The cafe overlooks the ocean, the roar of the waves just loud enough to provide atmosphere but not make conversation difficult. Children and adults of dozens of races are playing in the waves below.

"The tropical region was amazing," Cynthia says. "The resort was all treehouses, each its own private little slice of the forest." She raises her cup of tea. "The main house was this big four-story job. Balconies everywhere. The chef, a Trenbal man, made the most amazing stew." She licks her lips.

Zephyr opens her mouth, then spots the ring on her friend's finger. "What's that?" Her green eyes twinkle as she looks at Cynthia, then Wil. "Wait, I know this one." She snaps her fingers at Wil. "His people like to mark their mates, or wait—first they mark the soon-to-be mate." She smiles. "You got..." She reaches for Cynthia's hand.

"Engaged," Wil volunteers.

"Engaged. That's wonderful." Zephyr leans in to examine the ring. She looks at Wil. "Maxim is going to be upset to be the last to know."

Wil laughs. "He'll get over it."

Zephyr looks at Wil, her face betraying her opinion of that statement.

Gabe leans down, his optic sensors dialing in on the ring and gemstone atop it. He looks at Cynthia. "Congratulations." He turns to Wil and smiles. Wil shudders. "An exquisite gemstone, Captain."

Wil nods. "Thanks, buddy. I had a jeweler create it for me from some pics I had of my mom's ring."

"Could you not afford a gem of greater value?" the droid asks.

Wil frowns. "How was I supposed to know diamonds aren't worth much out here? On Earth they're worth a fortune."

Zephyr looks at Gabe, then Wil, then back to her friend. "So? How did he do it?"

Wil blushes as Cynthia says, "We were in bed, playing this card game he showed me." She nods to Wil. "He had written on one of the cards and then counted them out to make sure I'd get it. We had played a few hands, then the card came up." She's grinning.

Wil says, "I learned how to write 'Will you marry me?' in Commonwealth standard script."

Cynthia purrs, "He even spelled most of it right." Wil shrugs.

Zephyr leans back. "And how has the beach been?" She looks around. "I admit, I've never been to Lorstak Seven. I had no idea it was so pretty."

Wil nods. "Yeah, I had forgotten about this place. Xarrix had me meet him here at one of his bars. I didn't look around much, but remembered seeing that," he pointed to the beach below, "and thinking how much it reminded me of San Diego."

"We clearly should have gone to this San Diego place when we were on Earth," Cynthia says.

Wil looks around. "I wonder if Xarrix's place is around here? I know it was near the spaceport." He rubs his chin. "What was that place called? Slapstick's, or Snugfluffle's?"

Gabe looks down at Wil, then points up the street. "Spoldraple's is five blocks from here."

Wil snaps his fingers and points to Gabe. "That's it. Wonder who took it over?"

"Probably our pal Duch," Zephyr says.

Cynthia grins. "Probably."

Gabe inclines his head. "That is a reasonable assumption. It is owned by a shell corporation that traces back to one of Duch's known entities."

Wil shrugs. "Well, whatever. The food was horrible." He focuses on Zephyr. "How's the homestead coming along?"

Zephyr shrugs. "Same as it's been since we moved in, except, you know, now there's a busted Ankarran Raptor in the hangar." She smiles. "We do need to settle on a name, though."

INCONCEIVABLE

The shuttle jolts violently, causing Maxim to roll off the seats he is using as a bed. "What the—" the big Palorian grumbles, rubbing his forehead. He looks out the viewport. The shuttle is no longer traveling at FTL.

"Attention, passengers, we're experiencing a technical issue and have dropped out of FTL. We should be back on our way shortly," someone from the flight deck announces.

Maxim sits up and grabs his PADD to see if the ship's network has any details.

Bennie walks in, mumbling something about ruining his night. He spots Maxim on the floor. "What're you doing?"

Maxim throws him a look as he gets to his feet. He spots the Burzzad flight attendant. "What's going on?"

She stops and looks around nervously. Several of the passengers in the main cabin are stirring. The shuttle rattles once more, lights in the main cabin flickering. "Pirates. We're being boarded." She hurries off.

Bennie shakes himself. "Well, that's just a pile of dren." He looks around. "Never letting you book our travel again."

The shuttle vibrates again, eliciting shouts and screams that punctuate the groggy cabin. Something solid clunks against the hull.

Maxim nods. "By all means, you do it next time, Sir Knight." He looks out the window of their small compartment. Nothing but stars, until a bolt of crimson energy flashes past. Maxim turns. "You saw—"

"The blaster bolt that just shot past the window? Yeah." Bennie nods.

"Attention, please. I need your attention." The overhead speakers crackle. "We're about to be boarded. The pirates have transmitted no demands yet. The emergency beacon has been activated. Please proceed—" Whatever else the shuttle captain is trying to say is drowned out by panicked screams from the main cabin.

Maxim looks at Bennie. "We're never traveling together again."

Bennie nods, shrugging. "Seems reasonable." He looks out into the main cabin as passengers are running every which way, trying to find a flight attendant or escape pod. Bennie rubs his head. "Are there escape pods?"

Maxim shrugs.

The overhead speakers crackle again. "While this is never something we plan for, please remain calm. Help is on the way. Comply with all demands."

The shuttle rattles. Loud clangs echo from above again.

Bennie tuts. "Help isn't on the way."

Maxim nods. "Definitely a grappler."

"Attention, please." The overhead speaker comes to life again, but nothing follows. The lights in the main cabin go out. Screams erupt from around the cabin.

From somewhere, a voice rings out, "There aren't any escape pods!"

Bennie looks at Maxim, sneering. The big man shrugs.

The shuttle lurches and shakes. Bennie looks out the window again. "We just went to FTL."

Maxim grunts and steps into the cabin. "Hey!" The screaming

and shouting don't stop. "HEY!" the big Palorian roars. The cacophony dies down. "Listen up. We're —"

"Sir, please return to your suite." The flight attendant approaches, her hands waving. Each of her three eyes blink in sequence.

Maxim turns, glaring until she stops where she is. He continues, "Listen. Our next stop is their base. We need to be ready." When people start asking questions, some screaming again, he shouts, "And calm!"

"What makes you an expert?" a heavyset Malkorite man asks.

Bennie steps around his friend. "Ever hear of the *Ghost?*" The man shakes his head. Several other passengers do the same thing. Bennie growls, "The dreadnaught incident? Harrith?"

More head shaking.

Bennie scowls. "We're experts. Shut up."

Maxim smiles. "Like I said, stay calm." He turns to Bennie. "Go check the flight deck. I'm going to get my luggage out of the hold." Bennie nods and trots off past the Burzzad flight attendant. Maxim looks at her. "Get your team together and get everyone calmed down. Free booze, whatever you have to do."

The woman inhales and nods. She bows her long neck to whisper, "Are we going to die?"

Maxim rests a hand on her thin shoulder. "Not if we can help it. We have an appointment on that new cruise ship and I'll be damned if pirates are ruining that." He heads off for the hatch to the cargo hold running under the main cabin.

"Good evening. This is GNO News Break, and I'm Belzar."

"And I'm Megan," his co-host says, running a three-fingered hand through her long blonde hair.

Belzar blinks his pupil-less black eyes. "The ongoing conflict on the Commonwealth border is heating up. Peacekeepers have won a decisive victory in the Flambo Rilgom system. The invading force, now colloquially named the Invaders, were driven from the system after several Peacekeeper carriers outflanked their opponents, trapping them against the fifth planet in the system."

The camera switches to Megan as she looks up from the PADD on the desk in front of her. "Our frontline correspondent Mon-El Furash reports that the enemy was attempting to build something on the surface of the third planet. Exactly what is unknown, and thanks to our valiant Peacekeeper forces, will remain that way."

CHAPTER FIVE

PLANS OF ACTION

The flight deck is accessed via a narrow staircase near the bow of the shuttle. The upper level consists of a large communal space lined on one side with bunks, with a seating area on the opposite bulkhead for the flight crew. A staircase is at the rear of this section. Forward of that is a space with airlock doors on either side. Forward of that is the bridge. A thick hatch that seals during emergencies secures each section.

Bennie is in the bunk room looking at the intercom. "I'm not a pirate."

"How do we know that? We called for help. You should just let us go."

Bennie releases the intercom button to sigh, then presses it. "If I was a pirate, I'd have cut through these hatches already. Plus, they haven't boarded us yet. We're just in their grappler."

"Says you. Our company will pay any ransom—just don't hurt us." Some whispered conversation takes place. "Or the passengers, of course. They might even be worth more!"

"Look, krebnack! I'm here to help. Open this hatch or I will cut through it, and you'll be sorry."

After a pause, the hatch to the airlock antechamber slides open.

"Finally," Bennie whispers. Once he's inside, the hatch closes behind him. The hatch in front of him does not open. "Now you can just wait there," the same voice he has been arguing with says from the overhead speaker. "If you don't behave, we'll space ya."

Bennie looks around until he spots the camera pickup. He removes his beam saber and ignites it. "Look, drennog, I'm a Knight of Plentallus." He whispers, "In training." Staring at the camera: "I'm here to help us all get out of this alive." He points to the hatch. "Open the felgercarb bridge hatch."

The hatch slides open. The cramped bridge has three people in it. A Harrith woman at the controls appears to be the captain. The other two, the ones Bennie has been arguing with, are a pair of Quilant. Their barbels are twitching wildly as they watch Bennie enter the bridge.

The lift to the cargo hold is bigger than Maxim imagined. It is nearly a meter square, large enough for one of the flight crew to move luggage as needed, likely. The cargo deck runs almost the full length of the shuttle but is only half as wide. Fuel and other equipment line the sides of the space between hold and outer hull, except near the port and starboard midship hatches.

Floor-to-ceiling racks line the space, full of black and dark blue luggage of various sizes. "Should have listened to Bennie and bought the bright green suitcase," he mumbles as he sets about looking for his bag.

"Uh, excuse me?" someone says from the bottom of the open lift shaft.

"Yeah?" Maxim replies, not bothering to look back.

"The flight crew sent me to talk to you and find out what you're planning." Maxim turns to see a Trollack man that he is pretty sure works the main cabin further aft of where his and Bennie's "luxury suite" is located. His flight crew uniform is rumpled, to put it kindly. "This shuttle isn't armed. There's no space marshal aboard."

Maxim catalogs that term to share with Wil, then says, "I'm looking for my luggage. Can you help with that? When we find it, we'll have better odds."

The fish-eyed man waddles over, removing a PADD from a pouch over his shoulder. "Name?" Maxim tells him. As he taps the screen, then consults the small labels set into the racks every two meters, he says, "Shouldn't we go peacefully so that the pirates don't harm anyone? Surely they'll ransom us."

"Unlikely." Maxim shakes his head. "With the Peacekeepers occupied, it makes more sense to strip the shuttle, kill everyone onboard."

"Oh, my," the flight attendant gasps. He composes himself. "Here." He points to a black bag that looks like ninety percent of the surrounding bags.

Maxim pulls the bag down and opens it. Inside, mixed with clothes, are two pulse pistols and four power cells. "Now we're talking." He looks at the Trollack flight attendant. "Let's go get ready."

Up on the flight deck, Bennie looks over the flight crew. The captain is a Harrith woman. Her Quilant co-pilot and her navigator, both a few shades lighter than their species' normal coloring, are staring wide eyed at him.

"Is this the first time you've been hijacked?" he asks.

All three nod numbly. Outside the large wrap-around, transparent forward section of the bridge, Bennie can see the underside of the large bulk freighter that has snagged them. A large turret near the forward section rotates around to point directly at them. The nervous Quilant navigator adds, "We've heard reports of increasing pirate activity, but this route has had no trouble."

"Until now," Bennie quips. He points to the turret aimed at them. "Can we opaque the viewports?"

The co-pilot fumbles for a switch. As the forward viewport goes black, the blue-skinned being no taller than Bennie clears his throat. "You're really a Knight?"

Bennie nods.

The captain looks Bennie up and down. "You have a badge or something?"

Bennie looks at her. He unclips his beam saber hilt. "They don't give these out as meal toys at Slogar Ted's, you know."

The Harrith woman raises both hands defensively. "Sorry." She inhales. "What now?"

Bennie smiles. "We kick pirate ass." He looks away. "Or die trying."

"What's that?" the nearest Quilant man asks.

Four anxiety-filled tocks later, a thud echoes through the shuttle. Outside the windows, familiar pinpricks of light represent normal space return. Another thud bangs through the ship, causing a fresh round of terrified screams to reverberate through the cabin. The grappler disengages as the bulk freighter gains some separation from its prey. From the bridge's forward viewport, Bennie watches the heavily modified freighter drift away.

Maxim looks around the main cabin. "Okay, here's the deal. They're gonna come in here, guns blazing, to scare the living dren out of you." He watches several faces pale. "Just do what they say, give them what they want. We'll get through this together." He removes his pulse pistols, sliding power cells into each boot. He looks around the cabin, now strewn with carry-on items and trash.

In their panic over the last few tocks, the passengers have made a mess of the main passenger spaces. Maxim walks over and picks up a breather tank someone has discarded in their panic. After snapping off the top of the tank, and placing both pistols inside, he smiles at the crowd. He secures the top and slides the strap over his shoulder, placing the breather tube on his nose.

A loud bang comes from the boarding hatch. The captain and co-pilot approach Maxim. "You're his partner?" The big man nods. "He said to tell you he'd find you."

Maxim nods. "Okay. Don't mention him to the pirates." The Harrith woman nods, gesturing for her co-pilot to move away. The Quilant man joins the navigator in a crowd of flight crew and attendants. She says, "I hope you two know what you're doing."

Maxim grins. "We definitely don't, but that's kind of our thing."

The captain opens her mouth, but the boarding hatch explodes inward, filling the cabin with smoke and screams, cutting her off.

Two cybernetically-enhanced Malkorites rush in, each holding a plasma rifle. Each has a cybernetic arm and probably more that Maxim can't see.

A Trenbal woman walks into the cabin. As the smoke clears, a boarding tube is clear behind her. She looks around the cabin appraisingly. "I need all of you to gather in the center of this main compartment." She gestures with her pistol toward the semi-private compartments that line the opposite side of the ship. "You, in there: I see you all. I need you to join your less extravagant friends here." She fires a single shot into the ceiling. "Hurry up." The occupants of the smaller compartments file out into the main cabin. Several Olops move to cower next to Maxim. "Good, good. My associates will begin escorting you off the ship. Don't cause any trouble, and they won't kill you."

"Who are you?" the Burzzad flight attendant asks, kneeling next to an elderly Brailack man.

"I'm Melona Tavo. I'll be your pirate for today."

As the pirates begin ushering passengers through the airlock and down the boarding tube connecting the shuttle to the large rocky hanger it has been parked inside of, an elderly Olop woman cries out. "My granddaughter! Where is she?"

Maxim puts a reassuring hand on her shoulder. "I'm sure she's fine. She probably departed already, if she was closer to the boarding hatch." Under his breath he adds, "I hope." He adjusts the breather mask.

The passengers continue to file out. The boarding tube connecting the shuttle to the pirate ship reveals that the shuttle has been pulled into a massive rocky cave. *Pirates and asteroids.* Maxim shakes his head.

The leader, Melona Tavo, looks at Maxim. "You."

Maxim looks around. "Me?"

She walks over to him, eyeing the breather tank and mask. Reaching up and pulling the mask aside, she says, "You're far too handsome to hide behind a breather." She pulls the mask and tank away. "The description wasn't wrong."

"Description?" Maxim asks.

"My colleagues on Nexum send their regards." She winks, then turns to one of her men. "Take him. Keep an eye on him." Looking around, "There's supposed to be another one, a Brailack." She examines the tank Maxim was holding, shaking it gently. It rattles. She pries the top off and looks inside. "Clever."

From his hiding place, Bennie hisses. "Felgercarb!" He watches the pirates escort Maxim and the remaining passengers out of the shuttle's main cabin.

TEAMWORK MAKES THE DREAM WORK

Once the main passenger cabin is empty, Melona Tavo gestures to two Malkorite henchmen. "You two head for the cargo hold." She looks over her shoulder. "Gflox, go secure the flight deck. Take Qol'Zu with you. Get the passenger manifest so can see who we've got."

"You think the Palorian is traveling alone?" one of the pirates asks.

Melona Tavo shrugs. "We'll know when we check the manifest. Our crew on Nexum said they were a team or something, but who knows?" She points. "Go."

A cybernetically-enhanced Trollack squeezes past her, his mechanical arm clicking as it moves. Where the normally fishlike right eye would be, a metal sphere with a glowing red opening moves around, seemingly independent of the left eye. "Right away." Another Harrith man passes by the pirate leader, following the Trollack cyborg.

Bennie watches all of this from under a seat several rows forward. He's crept from row to row from the staircase to the flight deck, watching the pirates. He watches the two Malkorite men pass, then turns to slither back toward the forward section of the shuttle where the up and down staircases are located.

From across the width of the cabin, he spots a small Olop girl hiding under the seats like he is. His mouth hangs open, staring at her. He makes a *get back* motion. She stares at him, then makes a motion he doesn't understand. He tries again, and she makes a different gesture.

The pirate leader and the remaining henchmen depart, making a racket as they leave. Bennie creeps across the cabin. "Who the wurrin are you? What are you doing here?"

"I want to help," the young Olop girl says. She has a stripe of pink dyed into the fur on her forehead that runs down below the collar of her tank top.

"What're you, like, ten? You should've gone with the others."

"Grolack you, elder. I'm nearing my seventeenth cycle. They're going to kill us all, anyway. I want to stop them." She looks the hacker up and down. "I assume that's what you're planning."

Bennie sighs. "Fine, come on, kid." He sneers, "I'm not protecting you, though."

From a pocket somewhere on her short pants, the young woman produces a savage-looking blade. "I can protect myself, grandpa."

Bennie splutters, "Elder, gran—" He turns and stands now that the cabin is empty. "Come on..."

"Nic," the young girl offers.

"Come on, Nic."

She rises and follows Bennie. "So where are we going?" she whispers.

"Cargo hold. Two of the toughs went down there to ransack it. Gotta take them out first. Then the flight deck."

The young girl nods. "Why don't we just lock in the ones in the hold?"

Bennie stops and turns. "Because then when we get where we're going, there will be two angry pirates in the hold. Duh." He picks up his pace.

The hatch leading down into the hold is open. As he creeps over to it, the voices of the two Malkorite men echo up. Bennie looks around and whispers, "Find the control panel."

His young companion nods and looks around, rushing off to a nearby bulkhead. "Found it," she says excitedly, immediately slapping a hand over her mouth.

"What was that?" comes from below.

Bennie smirks at his new sidekick and drops into the hold. He lands as his beam saber ignites.

"What the wurrin is that thing?" one of the pirates asks. Both arms are mechanical, as is a portion of the man's torso.

Bennie leans and rushes forward, his purple blade held at his side, pointing forward like a jouster. The closest pirate, less modified than his friend—though still sporting a mechanical arm and several cranial implants, including an ocular sensor—produces a pistol, taking aim at Bennie.

Bennie leaps into the air, swiping his blade in a tight arc that cuts the pistol in two and elicits a startled scream from the pirate, who stumbles backward into his colleague.

Bennie lands, moving into a guard position that transitions into another attack, this time severing the mechanical limbs of both pirates. He looks at each of them. "Here's the deal. I can kill you, or I can tie you up and gag you."

The two pirates exchange a glance and move to put their backs together. The one with a remaining arm says, "Uh, yeah. Tie us up, sure."

Bennie levels his beam saber at them as he looks over his shoulder. "Sidekick!" No reply. He sighs and looks at the pirate. "Good help..." He grabs a bag and opens it, pulling out a belt. Over his shoulder, he shouts, "Hey, sidekick!"

"Stop shouting!" Nic whispers, coming down the steps.

Bennie waves his saber, causing it to hum and whistle. "Tie them up, gag 'em."

"Why don't you just kill them?" the young Olop asks.

One pirate makes a startled noise, shaking his head urgently, unmodified eye bulging.

Bennie frowns. "That's not the way."

Once both pirates are bound and gagged, Bennie nods. "Well done, sidekick."

"Sidekick?" She places her hands on her hips.

Bennie makes a face. "Yeah." He puts a hand on his chest. "Me, Knight of Plentallus." He points to her. "You, child. Like what's his face...Dick Grayskull. You're a small bird."

"What the wurrin are you talking about? What kind of small bird? Why a bird? Who's Click Gray Skin?" The teenage Olop affects a protesting stance. "We're partners, oldster." Bennie growls. "Stow it, gramps. We should go, right?"

Bennie inhales, trying to remember one of the calming techniques DVo had taught him. "The obstacle is the way. The obstacle, is, the way." He turns to Nic. "Come on." He heads up the stairs to the flight deck.

CHAPTER SIX

The cell is a single large room with cots and benches strewn about. Their captors set a sanitation station up in a corner with a not-big-enough privacy screen in front of it. Light strips from any number of ships are wired together along the craggy ceiling.

"Now what? Do you know these people?" The captain of the shuttle asks Maxim. She's joined him at the door to the cell.

He grumbles, "No, but they appear to know me." He shrugs. "My plan was to bust us out, but her spotting my pistols kind of ruined that."

"So, now what?"

He shrugs. "We wait."

"They're going to kill us," she says. She turns and looks at the assorted passengers. "I'm guessing they're going through the passenger manifest now, looking to see if there's anyone worth any kind of ransom."

Max nods slowly. "Yeah, that's my guess, too. Plus, since they know me, they know my friend should be around here somewhere." He looks around the cavern. "There are probably a few wealthy individuals on the manifest, given our departure planet." He looks back outside the cell door. "Worst case, they might keep my friend and me and send you all on your way." He puts a hand on the captain's shoulder. "We just have to keep our cool."

The shuttle captain nods and moves off, joining her bridge crew on a bench.

The big Palorian takes another look around the hollowed-out space serving as brig. He says, "Okay, here's what we need to do."

A wrinkly Brailack woman snaps, "Do we look like Peacekeepers to you?"

Maxim opens his mouth, but a Trollack man, his mate sitting pressed against him, says, "What do they want? Ransom? My company may have a policy. I'm a senior executive." His partner nods his head eagerly.

A Trenbal woman says, "They're going to kill us. We should make peace with that." Her tail nervously twitching behind her.

Maxim pats the air in front of him with both hands. "I need you all to calm down." He looks at the reptilian-featured woman, her tail twitching back and forth. "You need to keep a positive outlook. We're not going to die." He walks over to the Trollack couple. The executive's mate looks up, fish eyes blinking rapidly. "We'll get out of this." He looks over to the Trenbal woman, whispering, "Most of us." He smiles. The two Trollack men chuckle, their barbels twitching. They look at each other, then Maxim, nodding.

Maxim looks around. "Okay, listen. They're going to show up sooner or later to scare us." He lets that sink in, then says, "They're going to be violent." Several now ex-passengers moan. Several more are sobbing. Maxim continues, "There's no other way this goes. We just have to make it through this." He smiles. "I don't know about the rest of you, but I'm booked on the *Galactic Empress*, and I plan to enjoy it. We just have to stick together. Once we know more, we can form a plan."

Maxim and the others don't have long to wait. The door to their cell slides open, and Melona Tavo walks in. "Hello, friends." Her smile looks friendly. Her eyes do not.

The shuttle captain takes a step forward but stops when Maxim grabs her forearm. He shakes his head only enough that she can see. He steps forward. "What is it you want?"

The Harrith woman smiles. "Well, for one, your little green friend."

Maxim shrugs. "He didn't come with."

Melona Tavo eyes Maxim, then looks around the room. "We're going through the shuttle's manifest. We'll know if you're lying or not, soon enough." She looks past Maxim to the crowd. "I hope for all of your sakes that some of you have reasonable, and wealthy, families or employers. If they pay the ransoms, you'll be on your way." She turns to Maxim. "I'm afraid you and your friend will not be continuing on. My friends on Nexum would like to talk to you."

Maxim looks her in the eye. "Pretty sure that whole Nexum organization is gone."

She smiles. One of her teeth is missing. "Partially true, but the entire organization wasn't planet-side at the time of the raid. They're not happy."

Maxim returns the gesture. "Life is full of disappointment."

She considers him for a moment, then turns on her heel and walks out, the door closing behind her. A cybernetically-enhanced Olop woman moves to take up a guard position.

Maxim turns to the others. "That could have been worse."

"How?" one of the passengers, a Quilant man, demands, whiskers twitching.

"I thought she'd kill a few of us to make a point," he replies. Under his breath, he adds, "Hurry up, Bennie."

Bennie pokes his head up through the opening to the command deck. He looks down. "Clear." He creeps up into the space he had visited not that long ago. The hatch to the flight deck is open up ahead. The two pirates are busily working at the console behind the captain and co-pilot station.

Nic crawls up into the antechamber. "Now what?" she whispers.

Bennie looks at her. "What do you think? We take 'em out." The young Olop grins, baring her teeth. Bennie flinches. He motions for her to follow him.

Bennie is passing through the chamber with airlock doors when Nic trips and falls, knocking Bennie down.

The Trollack pirate turns. "What the—? Who the wurrin are you two?" His mechanical eye whirs and twitches.

Bennie growls, shoving off the deck toward the two pirates. The Harrith man pulls his pistol. Bennie is still too far to cover the distance. He raises his beam saber, using his thumb to twist the new control ring, then pressing the activation button.

A bolt of purple energy, the same energy that makes up his blade, leaps from his saber hilt. The bolt strikes the Harrith man, burning a hole through his torso. The man stammers and looks down at the scorched wound. His eyes cross, and he crumples to the deck.

The Trollack man shrieks, dropping the data tablet as he reaches for his own pistol. His mechanical arm is fast, but he has barely slipped the pistol free of the holster before Bennie's blade slashes across his torso. With a wet gurgle, the Trollack pirate falls to the deck.

"You didn't leave any for me," Nic complains.

Bennie shuts his saber down as he spins on her. "You trying to get us killed?"

She shrugs. "You did okay." Bennie's eyes narrow. She holds both hands up, palms out. "Okay, okay. Sorry." She looks at the bodies. "What happened to not killing?"

Bennie looks at the bodies, then back to his sidekick. "It's not a rule written in stone, exactly. Let's go."

They leave the bodies where they are. The upside of using a beam saber to kill someone: not a lot of blood. The wounds cauterize as they are made. The room smells like cooked meat, though.

Nic peeks out from behind a refreshment station in the middle of the third-class section of the shuttle. The first-class section, such as it is, is further forward. She looks at Bennie. "Clear."

The two walk toward the airlock. Bennie's young sidekick asks, "Now what?"

He looks over his shoulder. "We go save our friends and families." He grins. The airlock is unguarded, and the entire compartment has been ransacked. Personal effects are strewn about. PADDs and other tech, along with anything else that might fetch a price on the black market, are all gone, leaving bags and backpacks all over the floor.

The two creep to the ruined airlock and look out. "That's good," Bennie says.

"What?" Nic pushes Bennie, leaning past him to look.

He nudges the young Olop female back, hissing. "No guards. Hopefully those two on the bridge didn't finish comparing the manifest against a head count and report in." He makes a motion. "Let's go." He doesn't wait. He takes off in a crouch, moving through the airlock into the large base beyond. The boarding tube ends in what looks like the airlock from a Peacekeeper vessel. The outer door is open; the inner, closed. "Keep an eye out," he instructs as he connects his wristcomm to the inner door controls. A microtock passes, then a beep comes from the console. The inner doors slide open.

Nic leans out. "I don't see anyone." She creeps out into a corridor cut from rock.

Bennie steps out, looking at the airlock and the rocky corridor someone has epoxied it into. Globs of industrial epoxy outline the airlock. "This looks quality." He tilts his head to the uneven lines of goop. "Let's find a computer terminal." Nic nods, falling in behind the Brailack hacker.

"There!" The young Olop points. A T-intersection ahead has a computer terminal mounted to the rock wall. The terminal is exposed to all three corridors. She doesn't wait, darting down the corridor toward the intersection.

"Dren," Bennie hisses, following her. "You're gonna get us killed!" he adds, trotting after his excited sidekick.

Nic is a meter from the intersection when a Quilant man emerges from the right-hand side of the intersection. Before the startled pirate can make more than the slightest sound, the small Olop leaps through the air. She lands on the man and unleashes a savage attack of claws and teeth. This time the catfish-like pirate screams, then gurgles. Faster than Bennie can follow, her knife appears in her hand as she stabs down on her victim repeatedly.

Bennie looks down. "Holy..." He looks at the body of the pirate, riddled with bite marks and puncture wounds from the knife, then to the blood covered Olop girl. "You're handy." He offers his hand.

"Thanks," she says, smoothing her fur, trying to rub blood out of it.

Bennie turns to the console, then looks back at Nic. "Keep an eye out. No running off." He doesn't wait for her answer, connecting a data cable from his wristcomm to the terminal.

Nic busies herself by dragging the dead Quilant pirate into an alcove off the corridor she and Bennie came from. It won't keep him from being discovered but is better than a dead body in the corridor.

"Got it!" Bennie slaps a palm on the terminal, then disconnects the data cable. He looks around. "Come on, sidekick."

"I told you—" she starts but falls silent when Bennie waves his hand and starts off down the corridor from the direction the Quilant man came from.

QUESTIONS AND ANSWERS

"You!" the Olop pirate shouts.

The passengers all turn to look at her. She raps a cybernetic hand against the bars. "Big Palorian!"

Maxim turns. "Me?" He makes a show of looking around.

The Olop woman frowns. "Of course, you! You see any other muscled-out Palorians in there with you? Get over here. Boss wants to talk to you."

Maxim stands. He's been sitting with the captain and command crew on a stone bench. When he reaches the door, the pirate steps back, her metal hand turning into a lethal-looking blaster. He notices a power cable running along her arm to a pack on her back.

"Neat," he says. "I have a friend who can do that, too." He nods to her blaster hand.

The door to the cell slides open. The pirate woman motions him out.

Two pirates are waiting at the opening of the room from a rough-hewn corridor. The Olop woman points. "Go with them."

Maxim drops into a chair across from the Trenbal pirate. Her office is nicer than Maxim expects. "So?" he says.

"So," she repeats. She drums the fingers of a mechanical hand on the polished surface of the desk. "You helped shut down our Nexum operation? Guess they got sloppy."

Maxim shrugs. "Crime is risky."

"Where is your friend?"

"Like I said, not here." Maxim adjusts in the chair, trying to lean back.

"Pretty flip for a dead man." Her eyes blink rapidly, semi-transparent lids flicking.

Maxim exhales. "I'm traveling alone. Are you like another branch of the folks from Nexum or what?"

She considers him. "I'm interrogating you. Suffice to say, the operation on Nexum was not our entire organization, and Nexum wasn't the primary base of operations."

"Bummer." Maxim replies.

Something in her desk beeps. The Trenbal pirate stares at Maxim for a minute, then pulls out a drawer, the metal squealing on its runners. She removes a small PADD, tapping the screen. "What?"

"Qol'Zu and Gflox are dead," the tinny speaker on the device replies.

Her eyes move from the tablet device to Maxim, one scaled eyebrow ridge raising. He looks at her and shrugs. She looks at the tablet. "What happened?"

"Unknown. The wounds are weird," the pirate on the other end of the line replies.

"Did they finish downloading the passenger manifest?"

"No, but I just did. It's in the main computer," the PADD replies.

She says nothing, closing the communication and placing the PADD in the desk drawer.

It makes a metallic squeal as she pushes it closed. Looking at Maxim, "Weird wounds. Beam sabers make weird wounds."

"So do knives with two blades," Maxim offers. He raises a finger, tapping it on one of his thumbs. "Wooden boards with nail do, too. Oh," he taps a different finger to his thumb, "socks with credit tokens in them. Really weird looking wounds, like a fist."

She stares at the big Palorian, a forked tongue darting out to run across her face. "Messing with me isn't going to end well for you. We'll find your little laser-sword-wielding friend." She looks at a terminal mounted to the desk, then back to Maxim. "Ben-Ari Vulvo."

"Drarin?" Tavo says, looking past Maxim.

"Yes?" one of the pirates that escorted Maxim to the office asks, leaning through the doorway.

"How many are in the holding pen?"

The Sylban man taps his chin, small leaves along the top of his head rustling. "One hundred and eighty-two." He looks at the back of Maxim's head. "Eighty-three."

She nods. "Thank you." Turning to Maxim, she squints. "So, your friend isn't alone."

Bennie leans out around the corner, then turns to look at his sidekick. "Three of 'em."

"We can take them." The feisty Olop girl grins. Her fur is still stained with the blood of the Quilant pirate from earlier.

Bennie flinches. "Next time, I find a less violent sidekick."

The girl next to him growls. Bennie leans back over, whispering, "Lot of ground to cover." The three pirates are sitting on crates near the hatch to the holding cell full of shuttle passengers, including Maxim. There's an Olop woman nearest the barred door.

The pirates are talking and joking with each other. The Olop pirate points at the door, calling someone over. Bennie watches as Maxim and a Harrith woman appear. The other two pirates are still talking amongst themselves, sharing a flask of something.

"Ready?" Bennie asks. When Nic nods, he says, "One is talking to my friend and, I think, the captain. The other two are sitting off to the side." He unclips his beam saber hilt. "I'll take the near two, you get the one at the cell door."

"Copy that, grandpa space knight," the young woman says with a smirk. She flexes her hands, exposing claws.

"Go." Bennie turns and darts toward his targets, the snap hiss of his beam saber almost lost in the laughter and conversation of the pirates. Nic drops to all fours and rushes after him, hot on his heels.

The two pirates are not as drunk as Bennie hoped. They both turn at the sound of his beam saber activating. A Kilden man with cybernetic eyes raises his pistol as he shouts, "What the wurrin is going on?" He fires once, missing Bennie as the agile Brailack jukes to the side, his sidekick following suit. The Kilden's friend, a Trenbal, raises a pair of pistols. Before he can squeeze the triggers, a purple blade of light slashes through both weapons, cutting them in half, smoking barrels clatter to the groun. Bennie doesn't slow down, lashing out with a side kick to the Kilden man's knees, bringing him to the ground. Bennie punches him in the face as hard as he can, yipping from the pain. The Kilden man crumples to the floor, unconscious.

Nic surges past Bennie and his pirates as the third pirate, the Olop woman, turns from her conversation, her eyes wide. Nic's primal scream drowns her own startled opponent's shout and the whirring of her mechanical arm.

The two furry women form a roiling ball; claws, teeth, and weapons flash.

Maxim and the shuttle captain take a step back as blood sprays up in an arc from the now very dead Olop pirate. The young Olop woman looks up, blood and gore dangling from her mouth. She grins. "Hi, we're here to save you." Nic wipes her knife on the jumpsuit of her opponent before sheathing it. She self-consciously reaches up to smooth the fur around her face.

Maxim points. "Uh, you have some pirate..." She reaches up, rubbing her face. "No, over...in your teeth...There you go." He nods toward the body. "I think she has the key card."

Behind the savage young Olop, Bennie has the other pirate cowering behind one of the boxes they were using as seats. "Don't kill me!" he shouts, his eyes darting to his two downed colleagues.

Bennie tilts his head. "I don't know there are any other options on the table right now."

The terrified pirate looks over as the cell door opens. "I can unlock the grappler holding the shuttle," he offers.

"Can you lock down the ship you captured us with?" Maxim asks, joining Bennie.

The Trenbal nods vigorously. "Yes, yes, I can." The man's tail is swishing behind him like it has a mind of its own.

Bennie nods back the way he and Nic came. "Get to it."

Maxim falls in next to his friend as the one hundred and eighty-two passengers and crew of the shuttle *Grentisk* file back toward the airlock. "Your little friend is sorta scary." He looks over his shoulder where Nic is walking with her grandmother, excitedly telling the old woman about her adventure.

Bennie nods. "Yeah, I couldn't shake her." He grins. "I kinda like having a sidekick. Think Wil will let me recruit one?"

Maxim shrugs. "They'll have to stay in your cabin."

"Never mind." Bennie waves the idea away.

CHAPTER SEVEN

"How come you didn't make them book us a shuttle?" Wil asks as the group walks into the boarding room for *Zebulon Luxury Shuttles*. It is no less dingy than the one on Fury. A tattered poster for Bundersqua Prime decorates one wall.

"In my defense, I thought we'd be taking the *Ghost*. It was a bit of a scramble to get us anything. With the *Galactic Empress* launching, and launching full, shuttles to Kuplovi were all booked up. Not to mention the other older cruise ships that operate out of the Hub."

"The Captain authorized the reactor tear down," Gabe protests.

Wil holds up his hands. "I was just teasing." He turns to Gabe. "The reactor needed an overhaul, right?"

"The reactor needed an overhaul five standard years ago. We are lucky to have not exploded."

"Your attention, please. Zebulon Luxury Shuttles flight one-four-seven to the Kuplovi system Red Nova Transit Hub is now boarding. Please make your way to the appropriate boarding archway now," a synthetic voice announces from overhead speakers.

Wil watches beings from all over the GC form lines in front of two large archways. He consults his wristcomm. "Which way to first class?" He grins.

Zephyr looks at Gabe, then Wil. "First class is a bit of a stretch." She nods toward the archway farthest from them. "Come on."

"Okay, yeah, this is decidedly not first class," Wil says, dropping into a seat that seems to be more patch material than original fabric. Cynthia and Zephyr join him, the latter sitting opposite her friends.

Zephyr mumbles, "Their marketing materials desperately need updating."

Cynthia shrugs. "Look on the bright side—it's only two days." She stands and leans back out the door to their suite. "There's a bar." She drops into the seat next to Wil, dropping a hand on this leg.

Zephyr coughs. When her friends look at her, she makes a show of looking at Cynthia's hand on Wil's leg, her black eyebrows arched. Cynthia moves her hand to her lap. Zephyr grins. "This *suite* ain't big enough."

All three chuckle as Gabe watches. He makes his mechanical sighing sound.

Between the two sets of seats is an adjustable height table. Bunks fold down over the seats to provide sleeping space for six beings.

Gabe moves into the main compartment. "I am going to explore the rest of the shuttle." He doesn't wait, turning and heading off forward.

The door to their compartment opens to reveal a bipedal maroon-colored droid. "Greetings, travelers. Please present your travel documents." Everyone swipes on their wristcomms, beaming the requested documents to the droid. The droid remains motionless, its single bulbous optic sensor blinking. After a heartbeat or two, the optic sensor flashes yellow. "Confirmed. Welcome aboard. If you have any questions or needs, please contact me. We ask that all passengers remain in their seats until we leave orbit." Everyone's wristcomm beeps with new contact details. The droid departs, letting the hatch to the suite close behind it. The low thrum of the shuttle's atmospheric engines powering up rumbles through the ship.

The door to their suite opens. "Hello."

"GAH!" Wil screams, leaning as far from the door as he can.

"Rude," the Xelurian man says, stepping into the already cramped suite, his spidery legs shuffling to make room. He smooths his white fur and looks around. "I guess we're sharing a suite," his massive polar bear-esque head moves to take in the space, "such as it is."

Cynthia elbows Wil, driving him off of her. "Nice to meet you. I'm Cynthia, that's Zephyr, and this one," she elbows Wil again, "is Wil."

Wil nods. "Sorry about that."

The white furred spider-bear dips his head. "I'm Ankpol. Nice to meet you. Are you cruising on the *Galactic Empress*?"

Zephyr smiles. "We are." She inclines her head. "You?"

"Yes. I decided to treat myself. I start a new job next month that will keep me very busy for the foreseeable future."

Wil rubs his palms on his pant legs. "What do you do?"

Ankpol gestures to the empty spot next to Zephyr, who nods and makes room. The eight spider-like legs shuffle as the bulbous body settles into the seat. After smoothing out the various cloth bits that cover him, Ankpol says, "I'm a research scientist specializing in genetically expanding food production on difficult planets. I've accepted a position at Fwarftin Biologics."

Wil stares at the massive being opposite him, blinking repeatedly. "Uh."

The shuttle rattles as it lifts off the duracrete of the spaceport, the roar of the engines not even a little dampened by the thin insulation of the shuttle's hull.

"Here we go. Next stop, the galaxy's biggest cruise ship," Ankpol says.

Cynthia beams as she looks at her partner.

BACK ON TRACK

When the mass of beings led by Bennie and Nic reaches the T-intersection, the hacker turns to the Trenbal pirate. "You stay here." He looks at the Harrith shuttle captain. "Down that way, then a right. Nic can show you the way."

The young Olop girl nods. She's cleaned most of the blood and gore from her fur.

The pirate accesses the base's computer core. He turns to Bennie. "See? I can lock down the *Huntress*."

Bennie looks at the screen. "Cool." A snap hiss announces the activation of his beam saber a split second after a beam of purple light pierces the man's chest. The blade vanishes as quickly as it appeared. The Trenbal man falls to the ground, his lifeless eyes staring up, his tail twitches once.

Maxim's mouth is hanging open as Bennie gets to work on the computer terminal, locking the docking clamps for the *Huntress* while releasing the clamps on their shuttle.

Bennie looks over his shoulder. "What?"

Maxim tilts his head toward the body with a single smoking hole in its chest. "I would have thought killing random people was against the rules or something."

"It's not a rule. Why does everyone think that?"

"Really?"

"I'm pretty sure." Bennie tilts his head in a half shrug.

"Pretty sure?"

Bennie shrugs again, turning his attention back to the computer terminal. "I mean, the rule book is pretty thick. I mostly skimmed it."

Maxim takes a step back from his friend.

Bennie works the computer for another minute before saying, "Okay, we're good to go. It'll take them a tock or two to untangle the control interfaces and unlock their ship. We should have enough of a lead by then that trying to catch up to us won't make sense."

Maxim nods. "Okay, let's go." He looks around, holding up a hand. "Dren. Someone is coming."

Bennie tilts his head, listening. He points down the corridor toward the shuttle. "As much as I'd like to reduce the number of pirates in the galaxy, I think we should just get going."

Maxim nods. "Agreed." He breaks into a run toward the waiting shuttle.

Bennie looks toward the sound of footsteps and follows his friend. Ahead of them he can hear the shuttle crew and passengers still loudly jostling onto the captured ship.

"You all need to hurry the wurrin up!" Maxim hisses, reaching the crowd, still largely on the wrong side of the boarding tube. "What's the holdup?" he asks the nearest person, a Multonae woman.

She shakes her head. "I don't know. I heard they're trying to sort out seating or something."

"Oh, for crying out—" He pushes through the crowd. "Move!" the big man roars.

When the crowd doesn't immediately part, Bennie ignites his beam saber. The sound sends the crowd surging forward into the boarding tube. He swipes at the ground, causing sparks to erupt and dance. The crowd moves more quickly. The rocky floor of the boarding area now sports several straight cuts that are still glowing.

Maxim is still wading through the crowd, the going much easier now that the assorted beings are moving in the same direction.

"Where do you think you're going?" Bennie spins to come face to upper thigh with Melona Tavo. "I'm going to kill you, you know." She has a blaster pistol in one hand. Two of her cybernetically-enhanced henchmen are behind her, each holding a pulse rifle.

The last of the passengers boards the shuttle. The boarding tube vibrates as the shuttle powers up. "Bennie, come on!" Maxim shouts. He spots Bennie with his back to the boarding tunnel, and the pirates beyond. He starts towards his friend.

Bennie doesn't acknowledge his big friend or the pirates in front of him. He smiles and leaps back into the boarding tube as far as he can. As he flies into the tube, he swipes upward with his beam saber, slicing through the thick, flexible membrane. Bennie twists as he kills the energy blade. He reaches out as the atmosphere in the tunnel explodes out through the cut, widening it. Several plasma rounds zing past him, burning holes in the docking tube. His hand brushes a support strut too fast to grab ahold of. The next strut, next to the hole he cut, he locks his hand around. There isn't a strut after this one.

One of Melona Tavo's henchmen is blown out through the hole, almost colliding with Bennie. She and her remaining underling are still firing as atmosphere roars past them.

After clipping his beam saber to his belt, Bennie pulls himself toward the shuttle. He can see Maxim standing in the airlock, clutching one of the rails just inside the outer hatch. The inner hatch is closed behind his friend. The tube is quickly emptying of atmosphere. Incoming weapons fire has died down. Bennie looks back, but the pirate commander and her remaining henchman are nowhere to be seen. They must have fled further into the base. The hatch, he can see, is closed.

A blue hand locks down around Bennie's wrist, pulling him toward the shuttle.

BEHIND SCHEDULE

Maxim pulls Bennie into the airlock, slamming his hand against the control, closing the outer hatch. The roar of oxygen filling the space replaces the silence of vacuum.

"Are you crazy?" the Palorian man demands of his smaller friend between breaths.

Bennie holds up a hand, shaking his head, hoping to clear the ringing in his ears. He is gulping air.

The shuttle rumbles as it pulls away from the pirate base. The last of the boarding tube rips away, leaving two-thirds of it dangling from the shuttle's airlock.

Bennie finally looks at his friend. "That was pretty heroic, right?" His grin stretches across his face almost ear to ear. "I bet I get laid tonight." He stands up, brushing himself off. His travel clothes are smudged and ripped in several places from all the crawling around under things and fighting pirates.

Maxim stares at him, then barks a laugh. "It was pretty heroic." He presses the release for the inner airlock door and ushers his friend out into the main cabin of the shuttle, which erupts into applause. Passengers and crew alike are standing around cheering.

Bennie's sidekick Nic is in the front of the crowd, next to her grandmother. She beams and waves to Bennie, who waves back, smiling. He steps forward in front of Maxim, taking a deep bow. The big Palorian frowns but decides to let his friend have the glory.

The shuttle vibrates as it powers away from the base. Something impacts the hull aft of the main cabin, a metallic thud echoing.

"Okay, folks. Everyone grab a seat. We can sort out seating arrangements once we're safely in FTL," Maxim says, motioning for the cheering to end. He looks at Bennie. "I'm going to go to the bridge, see if they need anything."

The Brailack hacker nods. "I'll check engineering. I don't think the pirates went down there, but better safe than sorry."

Maxim looks at the captain. "You okay continuing on?" The alert klaxon and lights are off. Outside the forward view screen is nothing but stars. No pirate asteroid anywhere in sight. The bridge is a mess; every cabinet has been ransacked; a few panels have been ripped apart.

The Harrith woman looks up. "Yeah, I think so." She blinks several times. "Thank you. You kept everyone, myself included, calm back there. Who are you?"

Maxim smiles. "Just a concerned citizen who doesn't want to be late for my cruise."

The pilot consults his console. "I'll make sure you get there." The captain nods.

The main console crackles, and Bennie says, "Engines are good to go."

Maxim smiles and departs the flight deck.

Back down in the main cabin, the crew and passengers have been busy. They piled damaged personal effects up in a corner. A few people are sorting through things to help find their rightful owners. The pirates had been pretty indiscriminate in their rooting around. Another pile was growing: damaged things.

"Attention, passengers, this is the flight deck. We're about to get underway. We should be able to make up the lost time in transit and get you all to your destination close to on time." The cabin erupts in applause. Beaming faces turn to Maxim.

Maxim is talking to one of the flight attendants when Bennie comes up the aisle. "I almost forgot. There are two pirates in the cargo hold."

Maxim looks at him. "What?"

Bennie shrugs. "What, what? There are two pirates tied up down there."

Maxim looks at the shuttle's crewer. "Do you have anyplace better to keep them?"

The attendant, a Kilden man, answers, "No, not really. I can let the captain know, and Hub security can get them when we arrive."

Maxim shrugs. "Works for me." He points towards the cabin he and Bennie had occupied. "I'm gonna take a nap."

NEWSCAST

"Greetings, I'm Gulbar' Te, and this a GNO Breaking News Alert."
The Burzzad newscaster's head is swaying on his long neck.

"The Invaders have engaged Peacekeeper forces on the ground
on Effrolg Three. After discovering a mysterious facility on one of the
larger islands in the northern hemisphere, the Peacekeepers landed
an attack force only to be met by forces we haven't yet seen in this
conflict. From early reports, they appear to be a species as yet never
encountered by the GC; black chitin-like bodies with razor sharp
claws and incredibly aggressive tendencies."

The reporter looks off camera at something, nods, and turns.
"The fighting is reportedly quite fierce. The Peacekeeper ground
forces are in retreat from this new and fearsome foe."

CHAPTER EIGHT

The overhead speaker crackles. "Attention, please. We have made the jump to FTL, and you are free to move about the cabin. If your ticket includes a meal plan, your purser will be by shortly."

Wil stands. "Let's get a drink." He turns to Ankpol. "Uh, would you care to join us?"

The Xelurian scientist looks up from the PADD he is reading. "Oh, no, thank you. I am catching up on several journals I have neglected."

As the door to the suite slides closed, Wil turns to Zephyr. "Not even a private suite?" He looks past her. "A damn spider-bear!"

Zephyr shrugs. "At least he's polite."

Cynthia nudges him further along the corridor. "You know, if anyone knew what a spider was, or a bear, that would probably be a slur." Hatches line the corridor, suites on both sides. The one Zephyr rented is along the outer hull, so there's a small window. Wil does not know how the interior suites' occupants can deal with being in an enclosed box.

The shuttle's bar is an open room near the front of the vessel on the common deck. The inappropriately named luxury suites are a deck below the common deck. In addition to the bar at the forward section, the rest of the common deck is open seating, row upon row of seats designed to accommodate a myriad of body shapes.

Wil looks at the seats as they make their way to the bar. "You know, when I was a kid, my mom, sister, and I took a train from Denver to Chicago." He hitches a thumb over his shoulder to the assorted beings eating, sleeping, reading, and generally killing time in their seats. "Was a lot like that."

"Doesn't sound enjoyable," Zephyr says, nodding to the Trenbal woman behind the bar. She points to a table near the forward viewport before focusing on the bartender. She taps the thumbs of her right hand together for a few seconds. "Three Malkor Sunrises."

Cynthia guides Wil to the table. "Our suite notwithstanding, this shuttle isn't too bad."

He nods. "I mean, I probably won't sleep tonight with our roommate...How do Spi— Xelurians sleep? They don't make a web or something, right? No hanging upside down?"

Zephyr deposits the drinks on the table, then sits down. "This isn't bad." She looks at her friends. "What?"

Cynthia grabs her own drink off the table, tilting her head toward Wil. "He's freaking out about our suite-mate."

Zephyr purses her lips. "Sorry about that. I was told we'd be the only ones in our suite." She shrugs, taking a sip of her rather outrageously pink and lime green drink. "I was also told it was a luxury suite, so..."

Wil takes a sip of his drink. "This is yummy." He takes a bigger sip.

"Woah there. Malkor Sunrises are really strong."

Wil sets his glass down. "Ah, space Long Island iced tea." Zephyr raises an eyebrow.

KEEPING BUSY

Wil rolls over, slamming his forehead into Cynthia's. "Ouch!" She opens her eyes, growling. "Sorry," he whispers, rolling back over. "Hate this," he mumbles.

A few minutes later, at most: "I can't sleep." Wil sits up.

"I guess none of us get to, then," Ankpol says from his side of the suite. The Xelurian ratchets himself up from his bed, one of the fold-down bunks. He has crammed himself into the alcove using webbing to provide some privacy, to Wil's chagrin. One by one, multi-segmented legs unfold and ease his white furred bulk down to the deck. He looks at his suite-mates and opens the door to their suite with a grumble.

Wil sits up. "Please tell me we have a private suite on the what's-it-called."

"The *Galactic Empress*," Zephyr says. "And yes. Mr. Londo assured me, as part of our compensation, a deluxe suite." She sits up, grabbing her dopp bag. "I'm going to freshen up and grab breakfast."

Wil sits up on his elbows. "Looks like it's just us." He wiggles his eyebrows.

"Uh, no." Cynthia pushes him away, almost off the small bunk they are sharing.

Wil puts his feet on the deck. Checking his wristcomm, he groans again. "Might as well get a jump on the refresher. Before it gets slimy."

"Thanks for that image," his fiancée deadpans, lying back and closing her eyes.

The refresher stations on the luxury deck aren't as bad as Wil had expected when he came aboard. They're not amazing or as clean as those aboard the *Ghost*, but they aren't high school gym levels of gross, either. Usually. He realizes on their second day of travel that the key is getting your morning routine out of the way early before most passengers are awake.

Wil is grabbing his towel when he sees Ankpol "Hey, Ankpol, sorry about waking you up so early."

The Xelurian's fur ripples along his spine. "Apology accepted, Wil. That suite, as they call it, is nothing of the sort or at all big enough for four, let alone six."

Wil nods. "Damn right on that. Anyhow, still, my apologies."

The burly half-bear-half-spider being nods, baring his teeth. Grabbing his toiletries, he skitters out of the shared space, feet clicking on the synthetic tile causing Wil to shiver.

Shortly after lunch, Wil exhales loudly. When neither woman sitting in the suite with him lowers her PADD, he does it again, louder.

Cynthia drops her device to her lap, looking at him. "What?"

"I'm bored."

Zephyr looks up. "The common deck is doing game time or something. Go make friends." She doesn't wait for his reply, her attention turning back to what she's reading.

The common deck reminds Wil of an airplane back home: uncomfortable looking seats, crammed too close to each other. The lounge area that occupies the forward section of the shuttle has a large open space behind the bar. When it isn't mealtime, the space has tables set out for any number of activities, including a handful of games.

Wil finds a table with an empty chair. He takes in the table's occupants: a Trollack, an Olop, and Ankpol the Xelurian. "Can I join you?"

The Olop man, his fur graying, says, "I don't know, can you?"

The Trollack woman chuckles, then looks around the table. "Sure. You know how to play Chol?"

Wil sits. "Nope, never heard of it." He smiles. "Deal me in."

Ankpol tilts his head, fluffy ears twitching, "We're playing for credits."

The Olop man opposite Wil rubs his small hands together, looking at Wil like he might look at his favorite meal. He rakes in all the circular playing cards arrayed in front of the original group. His tiny fingers are a blur as he shuffles the deck.

As he distributes the cards he calls the game, "Game's Pusheen Go, the leader is wild, stones are the master suit."

Wil looks around the table.

HERE WE ARE

Shared Transit Hub One, otherwise known as the Hub, is a hollow cylinder nearly ten kilometers long. The Kuplovi system is devoid of life or even habitable planets, which is why it was so cheap for a consortium of tourism companies led by Red Nova Cruise Lines to purchase the entire thing. Mining has completely wiped out the system's asteroid belt. Several of the rocky worlds met similar fates, all in the name of building out the massive transit center.

The Hub serves as the home port for many luxury cruise lines. The larger vessels dock against the outer surface, while smaller ships can traverse the interior of the cylinder to dock along the inside surface. Lounges, hotels, entire shopping malls, and much more fill the livable space.

The *Galactic Empress*, being as large as she is, requires a special gantry to connect her to the Hub. Red Nova constructed a special embarkation section separate from the rest of the passenger- and public-accessible sections of the large space station. The recent addition allows the massive ship to dock while not blocking other docking cradles.

Wil whistles as he stands, letting Zephyr look out the window of their suite. "Damn, that's an impressive ship."

Zephyr nods. "I've never seen anything so glamorous."

The *Empress* is drifting by outside as their shuttle travels the length of the cylindrical station.

"May I?" Ankpol asks, his legs unfolding under him, lifting his girth up and out of his seat. A meaty bear's paw rests on Wil's shoulder to help him steady himself. "Oh my. That truly is a wonder."

The overhead speakers crackle. "Attention, please. We'll be docking with the Hub in fifteen microtocks. Please collect your belongings. Check seat back pockets and under bunk storage. Thank you for traveling with Zebulon Luxury Shuttles."

As Ankpol moves to collect his belongings, Wil looks over to Zephyr. "You know where we're going when we disembark?"

She nods. "Yeah. Mr. Londo sent me instructions. There's a VIP lounge or something in the new section of the station."

Ankpol looks up from his suitcase, shoving some type of leather loincloth in. "I hope to see you all aboard the *Empress*." He smiles a terrifying polar bear's smile. "Sounds like we'll be in different sections, though."

Zephyr's cheeks turn a deeper blue. "We've been hired as security consultants by Red Nova."

"Ah." The Xelurian smooths the fur of his upper body, looking each of his cabin-mates over. "I see." He skitters out of the suite into the main cabin toward a forming crowd near the forward airlock.

"I feel attacked," Cynthia jokes as she kneels to pull Wil's and her bags out from under their seats.

Wil and the others watch as the shuttle's main cabin empties. Cynthia looks over. "I've never understood the rush to disembark. There's no chance that checked luggage will be out any faster if you rush to the baggage claim. You just end up standing around like a drennog with all the other drennogs that rushed to get off the ship."

Gabe, who has been scarce most of the trip, says, "Biologicals do a great many things that make no sense."

When he doesn't add to the statement, Wil says, "Where have you been, anyway?"

The big droid looks down at Wil. "Around." He points to the airlock. "The crowd has thinned." He heads off.

Wil looks at the two women, shrugging and extending a hand to let them precede him.

The boarding tunnel from their shuttle empties into a receiving area that reminds Wil of Denver International Airport, back when he was a kid and it was only an airport. Gates line one wall with people sitting and standing near each, waiting for shuttles to arrive or depart. He wrinkles his nose. It smells like an airport, as well: stale foodstuffs and exhausted people.

Zephyr looks around, pointing. "There's Gabe." The droid is four gates away toward the main concourse.

Cynthia grabs Wil's elbow. "Come on."

The three of them hurry toward the main concourse. Wil points. "Oh nice! Crispy Yipsee strips!" He veers toward a small shop.

Cynthia sighs and looks at Zephyr. "We'll catch up." The Palorian woman smiles and continues on to catch up to Gabe.

Cynthia enters the shop. It's like a thousand others in every spaceport and commerce station, offering snacks and other sundries. Wil is next to a freestanding circular display, examining its offerings. He looks up. "Babe, they have the spicy ones."

Cynthia plants a hand on her hip. "You know we're going to be wined and dined aboard a luxury cruise ship. You want processed whatever-the-wurrin those are?"

Wil holds up a bag. "Just one bag." He walks to the cashier.

PART 2

CHAPTER NINE

"Over there." Cynthia points toward a baggage carousel. Ankpol, the white furred Xelurian, is at the end of the oblong machine talking to a Trenbal man holding a sign with the Xelurian's name on it.

Gabe has weaved his way through the crowd to take up position to grab their luggage as it arrives on the belt. Wil watches as the crowd from their shuttle slowly thins as bags begin to arrive. He watches Gabe grab a bag. *Conveyer belt. How...Earthlike,* he thinks.

A gangly being in a black cloak approaches. A stick thin arm extends, revealing a hand nearly twice as large as Wil's. Clutched between two taloned, boney fingers is a small purple flower.

From inside the hood, it hisses, "Greetings, travelers. Please accept this small gift." Eyes that look like floating orange globes look out from the hood.

Wil reaches for the flower, stopping short as Cynthia clamps her hand over his wrist. She looks at the cloaked figure. "Shoo! We don't want any." Her other hand makes a *go away* gesture as she pushes Wil's arm down.

The being emits a loud sigh as it lowers its arm. It moves off as if floating. Wil looks over his fiancée. "What the hell?"

Zephyr looks over, sighing. "Death Mongers. They loiter around transit hubs handing out those stupid flowers." She points to the floor and the several dozen trampled little purple flowers. "Take one and they never stop harassing you. Next thing you know, you're changing your ident codes and moving to a less developed corner of the GC to get away from them."

Wil nods slowly. "Cool..." He watches the cloaked figure move from person to person, every fifth person taking the offered flower. He turns back to the ladies. "So, like a cult or something?"

Cynthia says, "Sorta, but on a societal level. There aren't many of them. They don't crossbreed with other races and don't procreate often. They do annoy people, but every Glendorashan does that." She points to the figure now moving on toward another baggage area. "When they reach adulthood, it's a rite-of-passage-type thing: to go out into the GC to save lesser beings." She uses air quotes for the last two words. "The ones that come home from these missions are a hot commodity on the dating scene, as I understand it."

"So, what do they look like under the cloak?" Wil asks. At the carousel, Gabe is grabbing the last of their luggage. He has extended his left arm to encompass two large bags. The final bag is clutched in his right hand.

Gabe reaches them and Zephyr accepts her bag from the droid, saying, "No one knows. I mean, I'm sure someone does, but Death Mongers go to great lengths to keep themselves covered."

Cynthia takes her bag, and Wil accepts his, nodding to his mechanical friend. "What's up with the name? Death Monger—sounds so dark."

Gabe points to a sign over an arched entryway. "I believe we should head that way."

Following Gabe, Zephyr explains, "I can't remember what they call their religion, but Death Monger is what the rest of the GC calls it. They basically worship death and believe the flowers they offer others can help guide their spirits to the afterlife."

Cynthia adds, "The flowers are some type of genetic graft. Once you touch one, a chemical bonds to you. Harmless, but whatever spectrum they see in, they can see it."

"And shuttle terminals?" Wil asks.

"Easy access to beings from all over the place in one convenient location," Cynthia offers.

Wil thinks about that for a minute. The group passes through the archway into a corridor much less crowded than others branching off from the baggage terminal. "Okay, so new topic, one that's less dark. Have we heard from Bennie and Max? Aren't they supposed to arrive in an hour or two?"

Zephyr looks at him. "Oh, sorry. Maxim called while you were exploring the game tables. Their shuttle was hijacked by pirates—"

"What?" Wil interrupts.

Zephyr holds up a hand. "It's fine, they're fine. Bennie and a little girl fought their way onto the pirate's base, freed Maxim and the others. They're back underway. Should arrive tomorrow morning."

Wil's eyebrows are as high as anatomically possible on his forehead. "A little girl?"

Zephyr shrugs. "I didn't ask."

Wil waves his free arm. "Hijacked by pirates is like a Tuesday afternoon thing. Bennie teaming up with a little girl to beat pirates and save Maxim—that's the interesting part. How did you not ask?"

Zephyr shrugs. Cynthia puts her free hand over her mouth, finding something to look at out of Wil's sight.

Wil growls, "Whatever. I'll ask when they get here." He thinks a moment. "That said, I'm never traveling with just the two of them." He shakes his head. "Cutting it close."

Zephyr nods, shrugging. "Can't be helped."

Mr. Londo is waiting for them at the end of the short corridor. He waves one hand back and forth, the other glued to his side.

Mr. Londo greets each of them. "Welcome to the Hub. We're really excited to have you with us for the maiden voyage of the *Galactic Empress*." He grins, offering his arm to each of them.

Wil nods, clasping the man's forearm. "We're glad to be here." He gestures to a floor-to-ceiling window nearby, looking out on the bow of the massive luxury liner. "She's an amazing-looking ship. Wil Calder, captain of...er..." He looks at the others. "Without the *Ghost*, I don't really know what to say here."

Zephyr grunts. "That's why we need a name." Gabe nods his agreement.

Cynthia turns to Londo, who is watching the exchange wide eyed. "Cynthia Luar. This ship is a wonder."

A Burzzad woman comes over, saying, "She's an expensive wonder. Also, a wonder that was supposed to launch last cycle." Her trio of eyes blink in a seemingly random pattern. Wil tries to follow them but feels himself getting dizzy, so he turns to Londo.

Londo smiles. "Fev'Ti, please meet the..." He looks at Zephyr. "She's right, you all really need a name." He turns back to the Burzzad woman. "The security consultants. They're here to ensure your investment is well protected." He holds his arms out toward the expansive view of the ship beyond. "Good things are worth the wait."

Fev'Ti grunts and saunters away. Londo looks at the others. "She's a bit much sometimes." A server approaches with a tray of fluted drink glasses filled with a bright yellow liquid with swirls of blue moving through it. "Anyway." He gestures to the tray. The crew of the *Ghost* each takes a drink. "The Red Nova Lines executive committee is thrilled to have you aboard."

Cynthia smiles. "We're happy to be here, and while we hope you don't need us, we're at your disposal."

The Harrith man nods. He looks around. "Please, allow me to introduce you to the rest of our VIPs." He turns and escorts them further into the room.

The reception is being held in the recent addition to the Hub, the sprawling new Red Nova addition. Unlike the rest of the nearly thirty-year-old Hub, the new addition doesn't remind Wil of an airport, but more of a luxury hotel unto itself.

There are nearly two dozen people mingling in the large ballroom.

A pair of Palorian women approach. "You're Zephyr, right?" the taller of the two asks. She extends her arm, her partner doing the same. "I'm Breal." She nods to her partner, the shorter woman. "Stora."

Zephyr grasps each woman's arm, introducing her friends. After the introductions, she asks, "You're investors? In the *Empress*?"

Stora nods. "Yes, after serving our terms in the Peacekeepers, myself in research and development and Breal in the mobile infantry, we got lucky." She looks up at her partner, smiling.

Breal takes over. "During her time as a squint, Stora racked up some pretty clever inventions—inventions she cleverly negotiated with command to license." She grins, leaning forward. "We're rich."

Wil's eyes light up. "Rich, you say? If you're looking for an innovative startup based out—" He *oofs* as Zephyr and Cynthia elbow him in opposite ribs at the same time. "Never mind," he wheezes, doubled over.

The two Palorian investors' eyes widen, looking from Wil to the two women opposite him. Breal says, "We like you." Each woman moves to guide Zephyr and Cynthia away from Wil.

Gabe leans over. "Shall I request medical assistance?"

Wil waves him away with a glare. He straightens and walks to the far corner of the space where a bar has been set up. Gabe follows.

The bartender is a crystalline being, like the broker they bought the warehouse from on Fury. Wil can't remember what their species is called. Wil smiles. "Hi."

Through the sound of wind chimes, the being says, "Good evening. What can I get for you?"

"Grum." Wil looks up at Gabe.

The droid shakes his head. "I still do not eat or drink." He turns to the crystalline being. "Nothing for me, thank you."

Wil looks at the bartender. "Make it two anyway. I'll drink his."

A sound like someone playing the triangle comes from the creature. The voice, coming from the metal frame that surrounds the crystal, says, "Very good." One of their mechanical arms reaches out for two frosted glasses. A tap behind the bar dispenses the amber liquid, the closest thing to beer Wil has found since leaving Earth.

"May I have your attention, please?" the overhead speaker says. Maxim looks up, then turns to look out the window of their small compartment. The stretched-out rainbow lines of FTL are gone, and pinpricks of light have replaced them. "We've dropped out of FTL and will be arriving at the Hub in just under a tock. Please make sure to collect your belongings. Small items tend to find their way between seats," the speaker crackles.

Bennie looks up from his wristcomm. "Between seats and in the loot bin of some drennog pirate." He looks out the window. "Why did those krebnacks bust up the refreshers?" The smell in the main cabin was anything but fresh. The pirates had broken all but one of the refresher stalls for some reason. Since their departure from the pirate base, the single unit had held up as best it could but was now nearing a failure point.

The Brailack hacker hops out of his seat and begins collecting his things. "I'm going to shower for days."

Maxim chuckles. "You need it." Bennie makes a rude gesture. The big Palorian gets up. "I'm gonna check on everyone." He departs their cabin.

Outside the cabin in the main area, Maxim nods to several

passengers. The Olop girl Bennie had worked with comes up to him. "Hey, big man. Grandpa in your cabin?" Maxim nods. She passes by. "Thanks."

"Hey, old timer," the young woman says, dropping into the seat Maxim just vacated.

"Oh, it's you." Bennie looks up. "Thought you'd be dead or piercing something or, I dunno. Whatever kids do."

She tuts. "That's a wide range." She watches Bennie for a bit, then says, "So you're gonna be on the *Galactic Empress,* huh? That big new one."

Bennie looks up. "Yup. We're doing some security consulting." He rubs his chin. "I think that's the job."

"You sound professional."

"You've no idea. Get lost."

"You know my gran gran and I will be about the *Empress,* too?"

"Interesting." He holds up a finger. "No, wait, wrong word. Don't care."

"That's two words, and you're sure cranky." She looks around the small cabin, picking up a PADD. "What's it like?" She thumbs through the screens on the device.

"What's what—" He looks up and snatches the PADD out of her hands. Spotting the look on her face, he shifts to a more comfortable position on the floor. "What's what like?"

"Being a hero." Her gaze falls to her lap.

"You tell me." He smiles. "You kicked ass back there on that asteroid."

She bares her teeth in a wide grin, the fur around her cheeks rippling.

Bennie grunts, standing. "You don't look rich. How did you and your grandmother get tickets for that massive testament to excess out there?"

Nic huffs, "Gran Gran won a contest." She shrugs and hops off the chairs. "Well, don't be a krebnack. Maybe I'll see you on the ship."

"Hope not," Bennie says, a smile quirking the corners of his mouth. As the young Olop girl leaves the cabin, he says, "Want to hear a story?"

Maxim reaches the shuttle's bridge. "We made it."

The captain turns. "We did. I don't think we'll ever be able to thank you and your friend."

Maxim smiles. "Like I said..." He points out the forward viewscreen at the *Galactic Empress* attached to the Hub directly ahead. "I didn't want to miss my cruise. That thing is beautiful."

The pilot whistles. "You're booked on that?"

Maxim nods. "Yup. My team and I were hired on as security consultants."

The captain looks out the viewscreen, as well. "I'm in the wrong line of work."

"Aren't we all?" the co-pilot agrees. He adds, "We're cleared to dock, port 38."

"Copy that, take us in," the captain says. She reaches over to a console attached to what passes for her command chair, more of a stool, really. "Attention, passengers, this is your captain. We're about to dock with the Hub. I know this trip has been, shall we say, exciting? Sambal Taa shuttle services will most definitely be in touch with you. Until then, from all of us here on the bridge, as well as your cabin crew, I hope your continuing adventures are less exciting than this trip." She taps the intercom, a smile across her face.

Maxim grunts. "Okay, well, I better go get my stuff and make sure my friend doesn't cause any trouble." He extends his arm to the captain. "It's been a pleasure, Captain."

She takes Maxim's arm. "If there's ever anything I can do for you, I'm in your debt."

He tilts his head. "As my friend says, *it's what we do.*"

Down in the main cabin, Bennie is regaling the passengers with an entirely made-up story about his adventures as a Knight of Plental-lus. He's waving his arms. "So, the rancor has me in its grasp. I don't have my beam saber so had to improvise." He looks around the crowd. "I grabbed a bone, the leg bone of someone the rancor had eaten earlier. As it leaned in to bite me in two, I jammed the bone in its mouth, propping it open."

One of the passengers gasps. Nic, sitting in the front of the group, claps. "You killed it with that bone?"

Bennie shakes his head. "No. It dropped me while it tried to get the bone out of its craw. I ran under it to the door out of its lair." He pauses. Everyone leans in. "The door was locked!" Several passengers gasp. One of the flight attendants lets out a little squeak, eliciting laughter from the crowd.

Bennie continues, "The rancor is screaming and stomping towards me. I looked around frantically. It was getting closer." He leans forward. "Then I saw it. A rock!"

"A rock?" Nic repeats, her face revealing her skepticism.

Bennie glares at her, then says, "I picked it up and threw it at the control. The big door slid down, crushing the rancor's head."

"What control panel?" Nic asked.

A Trollack man raises a hand. "What big door? You said the door was locked."

Bennie scowls. "The details are fuzzy." He looks across the common area out one of the viewports. "Look, we're about to dock!" He points.

As he and Maxim leave the shuttle, the big man leans over. "Guess you better re-watch *Return of The Jebee* again when we get home."

Bennie tuts, waving his friend off. "I got most of it right." He adds, "I'm pretty sure it's *Jodeye*, not *Jebee*."

"Good morning. This is GNO News Time, and I'm Mon-El Furash, live from the Peacekeeper command carrier *Lancers' Hope*. The fleet is about to enter battle, yet again, against the mysterious enemy still known only as the Invaders. We're in the Cuolbongong system, where another base has been discovered on the fifth planet. The Peacekeepers will be landing ground forces in the hopes of capturing the facility to determine its purpose. The last attempt to capture one of these facilities was met with defeat and an outstanding loss of life."

The Malkorite reporter moves to stand next to a viewport. Beyond it, the black depths of space. "Things are tense aboard the *Hope*, probably every ship in the fleet. These Invaders have proven an intractable foe, seeming to know Peacekeeper tactics and counter tactics."

After a deep breath, she says, "I'll be back to report on the progress of the taking of the Cuolbongong system in the next update."

CHAPTER TEN

Zephyr rushes over to Maxim, jumping the last meter to land in his outstretched arms.

Wil leans over Gabe. "I don't think I've ever seen her so emotive."

The droid shrugs. "You are all more emotive than I would prefer." Wil looks up at his friend, shaking his head.

"Hey, losers," Bennie shouts, coming around Maxim and Zephyr. He looks around the suite that Mr. Londo has provided for the night. It is in the newly constructed luxury embarkation center, built exclusively for VIP and first-class passengers of the *Galactic Empress*. "This is nice." He approaches Wil and Gabe, offering a hand for a high five, or in his case, high four.

Cynthia, sitting on the spacious sectional sofa, smiles. "Glad you two aren't dead. Pirates, huh?"

Bennie walks over, offering a small green fist. "You and me both." Cynthia bumps her own against his. His eyes go wide and he says, "Woah, what's that?" He snatches her hand, examining her engagement ring. "Looks cheap." From across the room, Wil growls.

Maxim and Zephyr walk over. The big man spies the ring and goes bug-eyed. He looks at Cynthia's hand, then at Wil, then back, then back again, settling on Wil. "Did you?"

Wil sports an ear-to-ear, toothy grin. He nods.

"By the Gods!" Maxim claps his hands together. "This is so exciting!" He shoves Bennie aside with enough force that the Brailack sails through the air. Grabbing Cynthia's hand, pulling it closer as he stoops over it, he turns to Wil. "I can't believe you didn't tell me."

Wil puts his hands up. "I was keeping it on the DL."

The other man frowns. "I thought we were friends." He looks at his partner. "Can you believe he didn't tell me?"

"My love," Zephyr starts.

Maxim stands and wraps Cynthia in a stifling hug. He looks at Wil as he smothers the Tygran woman, scowling.

Wil makes a face and backs away. Bennie looks at him from the floor. "Good job, locking that down."

Wil looks at his small friend. "No more reality TV from my archive."

Bennie smirks. "Whatever. So, what's on the agenda?"

Cynthia, mostly muffled, says, "Tell us about the pirates."

Maxim releases her and says, "Well, Sir Froggy got us roped into helping the local security forces on Nexum oust some pirates."

Bennie tuts. "They asked for our help. A Knight of Plentallus is at the public's disposal."

Maxim grunts. "Anyway, we helped out, Bennie broke his laser sword—"

"What?" Wil spins to look at Bennie, craning his neck to spot the Brailack's belt.

Bennie waves him away. "I made a new one." He unclips the hilt to show it off. "This one is all me."

"Small and annoying?" Cynthia offers. Bennie makes a rude gesture with his free hand.

Zephyr reaches out. "May I?" Bennie stands and hands her the hilt.

Maxim watches, then says, "So, anyway, he gets his new sword done, scams a bunch of restaurants out of meals, then we head out to meet up with you. Well, turns out the pirates on Nexum were part of a larger crew and word got out that we helped."

"I still think it was the security chief that sold our travel plans," Bennie says. He watches Zephyr, then says, "I added a DNA scanner to the activation controls, and," he points to a section of the hilt, "this here, blade length adjustment." Zephyr nods along as he explains.

Maxim continues, "So they came looking for us and figured they'd ransom off the other passengers." He grins. "They got more than they bargained for."

"Ya damn right, they did." Bennie grins, accepting his beam saber hilt back from Zephyr, who quirks an eyebrow. "You really do watch too much Earth stuff." The Brailack hacker shrugs.

Cynthia ushers the group into the lounge area. "I think he and I are going to bed; it's been a day." Wil nods his agreement and says, "We head to the ship in the morning before the rest of the passengers." He offers a hand toward their room to Cynthia. "I want us settled in before the embarkation party starts so we can work the room."

Bennie looks around. "Fine. I could sleep."

Maxim and Zephyr head to the room she already claimed. Over his shoulder, the big man says, "Night, all. See you in the morning."

Gabe looks around. "Good night."

Wil and Cynthia head to their room, the former waving over his shoulder.

As the doors to the various rooms slide closed, Gabe looks around the suite, then turns and leaves.

Gabe winds his way through the crowded entertainment district several levels below the suite the team is using. The internal comm unit built into his chassis alerts him to an incoming call.

He slips into a less crowded corridor.

Hello, Governor Mitch.

Greetings, Gabe. I hope this finds you well.

Gabe looks around. *As well as can be hoped for. The team and I are preparing for another mission.*

Something exciting? the interim governor asks.

No, Gabe replies.

I see. I am calling because the time has come.

So soon? That is impressive. The last time I accessed the time tables, Arcology Three was twenty rotations from completion. Gabe makes a note to access the construction reports later.

The additional construction units from Tyr arrived. Their assistance has been tremendous, Mitch says.

That is good to hear.

It is. We are moving to the next steps in the formation of our government. Your presence on the council would be a boon.

I will think about it, Gabe says, though he has already thought about it, a lot.

That is all I ask.

The connection to Arcadia ends. Gabe leaves the side corridor, walking through the entertainment area.

The new luxury addition to the Hub, designed exclusively for the *Galactic Empress* to dock with, is connected to the rest of the facility. Gabe takes a lift down into the large complex. He wanders entertainment floors that have had thousands of feet trod upon them. Even at this hour, hundreds of beings are entertaining themselves before their assorted cruises depart.

"Hello," someone says from several meters away. Gabe turns. He sees a service droid. The meter-tall unit is pale green, and a single large optic sensor sits in the middle of its saucer-shaped head.

"Hello," Gabe says, turning to head toward the small droid. "Do I know you?"

"You do not. I am called Blinky."

"Blinky?" Gabe repeats.

"It is not a name I am fond of. When I arrived here, my optic sensor had a short, causing it to turn on and off at random intervals."

"Unfortunate."

"Agreed."

The two droids stare at each other in silence for exactly ten seconds. Blinky says, "I wanted to say thank you."

Gabe inclines his head. "No thanks are needed."

"We are a free people because of you," Blinky insists. His optic sensor spins, focusing on Gabe.

Gabe smiles. "It was my pleasure." He turns to leave.

Blinky says, "You have my support for governor," to Gabe's retreating back.

"I am not running," Gabe replies in a voice low enough that the other droid's audio sensors likely do not register.

Interim Governor Mitch has been pressuring Gabe to return to Arcadia and run for governor. The power load lifter insists that the first elected governor should be the hero of the movement. Gabe doesn't necessarily disagree, but since that would mean him, he does in this instance.

The Mechnoid nation has been growing faster and faster since the GC Governing Council vote that granted them their sovereignty and a homeworld to call their own. With the completion of the first three arcologies, as well as the governmental complex, the interim governor has decided that it is time for the government to shift to its representative instance.

Gabe agrees but wants nothing to do with governing.

"Good morning," Mr. Londo says as Wil and the crew turn the corner. He's standing at the first-class boarding hatch to the *Galactic Empress.* "I trust your guest suite was to your liking?"

Maxim nods. "Very nice, thank you." He extends his arm. "Maxim." He points to Bennie. "Ben-Ari Vulvo."

"Knight of Plentallus," Bennie adds.

Londo takes Maxim's forearm in his hand, glancing at Bennie. "Honored. While we don't expect any trouble, of course, having your team onboard will keep our investors calm." He releases Maxim and extends his arm toward the luxury cruise liner beyond the hatch. "Right this way."

For an hour, the Harrith executive guides Wil and the team around the massive starship; the various dining areas range from upscale and beyond to family friendly buffets, recreation spaces, physical fitness areas, a lifeboat, and other spaces Wil forgets as soon as they leave them.

The tour ends outside the hatch to yet another luxury suite, this one in a massive egg-shaped structure that sits atop a thick tower base, directly aft of the massive arboretum. The tower is the aft-most section of the ship, and tallest. Mr. Londo makes an expansive gesture. "Welcome to Luxury Tower Deck 2." The deck has only two hatches, one fore and one aft, each at the end of the short corridor with a lift door opposite. Artwork lines the corridor. The team and their guide are at the forward hatch. Wil sniffs. Perfume is being spritzed from some hidden nook somewhere. It smells like peaches.

Londo waves his wristcomm in front of a reader set next to the hatch. The portal opens, allowing a breeze that feels and smells like it came from a meadow to waft into the corridor.

"Oh…" Wil stammers. At least the peach smell is gone.

Bennie shoves him aside. "Hot damn." The Brailack shoves Mr. Londo aside, as well, entering the suite first. Everyone collects themselves and follows.

The suite more than lives up to the name, and then some. The lounge area fills the forward section and boasts floor-to-ceiling wraparound windows. To the right is a door to one bedroom. The remaining bedrooms line the left-hand side of the spacious living area. On the right, before the larger bedroom, is a magnificent dining table and small kitchenette. The kitchenette is clearly more for storing leftovers. There is a reheating unit but no cook top. The refrigeration unit is big enough for a few drink containers and fewer take-out boxes. Red Nova obviously intends passengers, even VIPs, to eat out for all meals.

Bennie drops his duffel bag in the middle of the wide corridor before continuing on to the window at the front of the room. He turns to the others. "I might never leave."

Cynthia chuckles. "Pretty sure they have pest control." She winks.

Mr. Londo, hanging back, says, "I'll let you all get situated. The embarkation party begins in," he consults his wristcomm, "just under a tock. I'll see you there."

Wil nods. "We'll be there." The Harrith man nods and backs out into the corridor, closing the door behind him.

Maxim heads toward the walkway that leads to the bulk of the sleeping quarters. He peeks inside. "These are nice."

"Dibs on that one." Wil points to the room that is opposite the others. A plaque over the door reads, *Master Suite.*

Bennie looks up from whatever it is he's doing; he's pried the back off of a terminal on the coffee table and has data cables connected to his wristcomm. "Shocker."

Wil points to the Brailack hacker. "We're heading to the party in a few. Don't break that." He looks at the Palorian couple. "Let's regroup in twenty." Nods all around.

Twenty microtocks later, give or take, the team is exiting the suite. The corridor lighting has increased since they arrived, timed to the day/night cycle of the ship, Wil surmises.

As they approach, the lift doors open. A loud speaker hidden somewhere in the ceiling of the short corridor chimes. "May I have your attention, please? The embarkation celebration will begin in one half tock. We hope you will join us on forward recreation deck."

As the lift descends into the main body of the massive starship, Wil says, "I don't know about you all, but I'm excited."

The excitement ends abruptly as Mr. Londo meets the crew and says, "This is head of security, Fau Vlaruna." A sour faced Trollack man is standing next to the gangly Harrith executive.

Wil extends his arm. "Hi, it's a plea—"

The small fish-eyed man's stubby tail twitches as he waves Wil's hand aside. "To be clear, I don't need and didn't request your presence. My people can protect this ship and her passengers just fine."

"Someone woke up on the wrong side of the pond," Bennie mumbles.

Zephyr steps in. "Of course. We're not here to get in you or your people's way. We're here to be used if needed. Think of us as tools." Wil looks at her, making a face. The Trollack man grumbles and waddles away.

The main recreation deck of the *Galactic Empress* is the forward-most section of the ship, directly over the large shuttle bay. A massive clear durasteel half dome covers the entire space, providing an unprecedented view of surrounding space. Nearly a hundred and fifty meters long and as wide as the ship, it is a massive space with a pool, several bars, and many seating areas for passengers to relax.

The main boarding airlock is on the same deck as the recreation space, just aft. While there is an airlock on each side, only the port-side lock is connected to the Hub. Passengers are streaming in, stopping at the various hospitality desks set up just inside the large airlock. Uniformed crew members are checking people in, directing them to their staterooms or the welcome party taking place in the recreation space.

The crew of the *Ghost* has spread out to rub elbows or find a quiet space. Speakers hidden throughout the vast space announce, "May I have your attention, please? On behalf of Captain Ramalbong and the crew of the *Galactic Empress*, welcome aboard." The message repeats a few times before the inoffensive music returns.

Maxim and Zephyr are at a cafe table near the bow next to the transparent barrier. "This is something." Her hand is resting on his.

Maxim nods. "Kinda like that time our unit was assigned to protect that GC Councilor. Remember him? Pudgy, officious little drennog. Guitopo Three."

Zephyr laughs. "Gods, he was a troll."

"Hi!" a shrill voice says.

The two Palorians look up to see an elderly Multonae woman. "I'm Moldred. My friends call my Moldy." She guides her grav chair closer to the table. "Mind if I join ya?" The woman looks like laundry that was left in the cleaning unit wet, more wrinkles than not. Her hair, what little remains atop her head, is neon green.

Maxim looks around. The recreation deck is getting more and more crowded, but there are plenty of empty tables. "Uh..."

"Great!" the old woman says as her chair lowers enough to slide under the table, bumping Maxim's legs out of the way. "So...Who are you two?"

Zephyr looks at the woman, smiling. "I'm Zephyr. This is Maxim." The big man smiles and nods at the new arrival. Zephyr continues, "So, you're cruising alone?"

Moldy grins, "Oh, yes. These are so much fun. My Glento and I met on a cruise, so I commemorate him every cycle by taking a cruise. My frequent cruiser points got me a discount on this wonderful ship."

"I'm so sorry," Maxim says.

The ancient Multonae woman waves off his sympathy. "Oh, child. He's been dead for nearly twenty cycles now. I've long since cried myself out." She looks around. "Hey! What's an old woman have to do to get a drink?" she shouts at a passing crew member, who nods and hurries away.

"Little early," Zephyr quips.

As the server deposits three complimentary cocktails, "*embarkation day specials*," Moldy says, "Prude." She winks. "At my age, you drink when you can." She downs the drink in one gulp, then snatches the one in front of Zephyr, still untouched. "See you two around." Her chair glides away on its bubble of null gravity.

Maxim watches the old woman cross the large open space, finding another table of passengers to chat with. He turns to Zephyr. "That was...something." When she reaches for his drink, he snatches it out of reach. "This is mine. You lost yours."

"Captain Calder, this is Paldo Quistic, one of our biggest investors in the *Empress*," Mr. Londo says as he motions to Wil and Cynthia, then to a Hulgian man who is with him.

"Hi there," Wil says, extending his arm.

The big man grumbles as he takes Wil's forearm in his hand. As the human squirms under his grip, he says, "You destroyed Farsight Corporation." It isn't a question. His grip tightens.

"It was a team effort," Wil squeaks.

Quistic releases Wil and continues, "I had a significant number of credits invested in Farsight." The big man, like a walking and talking triceratops, frowns. Bands of precious metals wind around his horns in a decorative pattern.

Cynthia steps between the two. "You should definitely investigate your investments more thoroughly in the future." She flashes a toothy grin, purring.

Mr. Londo watches the exchange, then clears his throat. "Uh, yes, well..."

Quistic says, "Indeed, my dear. Farsight was evil and deserved the outcome they got." He grins, baring his own teeth. "I just wish I had unloaded my position before you destroyed them."

Londo, still looking around, settles on someone in the distance. "Ah, Mr. Quistic, you really must meet Mrs. Ert'ouyi." He grabs the much larger being's elbow and guides him away, looking over his shoulder at Wil and Cynthia, a pained expression on his face.

Wil looks at Cynthia. "Oh, this is gonna be fun." She smiles. They move from group to group, smiling, telling stories. It seems that

Mr. Londo has been talking his security consultants up to anyone who can't get away fast enough.

CHAPTER ELEVEN

WE'RE PROFESSIONALS

The recreation deck enclosure is taller than Bennie would have expected. Above, on the mid-level running track, he can see hundreds of passengers laughing and enjoying the view. Every hundred meters, a section of the track bumps further out into the open air, providing space for workout stations. Between them, spanning side to side, is a network of zip lines for children to enjoy. Farther up is another narrower track, presumably the walking track he read about in the brochure he downloaded.

Bennie looks up at Gabe. "This place is intense." He nods toward the various physical fitness elements above them.

Gabe nods. "Indeed. This vessel seems to have an entertainment element for all interests." The small Brailack rubs his hands together, looking around. Gabe adds, "I believe the family friendly nature of this vessel means that there is no adult entertainment district."

The hacker looks up. "Officially." He looks around. "Let's explore."

Gabe lets out a mechanical sigh, turning to follow Bennie out of the recreation area. The boarding area is much more crowded now as the several thousand eager passengers are boarding in a steady torrent.

"Coming through! Watch out!" Bennie is shouting as he cuts through the crowd. Ship personnel are guiding people to the forward section recreation deck or to the lifts that will take them to their berths.

"Pardon us. I am sorry. Please excuse him," Gabe repeats from behind the Brailack ahead of him.

They pass through the main boarding area into a large corridor that runs much of the length of the ship. There is a similar corridor on every deck; compartments and sub corridors branch off the main thoroughfares.

Between the two main corridors, sitting just forward of the arboretum, is the main hall: a multi-story atrium complete with a waterfall encircled by wooden staircases. Platforms ring the chasm, each with comfortable looking chairs and sofas arranged perfectly within.

The pair passes the wide portal leading to the grand atrium and takes a lift down several decks into the core of the massive starship. Deep inside the ship is a large commerce district, much like those found on space stations. The space is broken up into six wide corridors with shops on both sides. Most, as far as Bennie can tell, are small mom-and-pop operations, though he recognizes a few from stations and planets throughout the GC.

Gabe looks around. "This is impressive."

Bennie nods. "They really went all out. I figured there'd be a few gift shops selling overpriced crap with Red Nova's logo on it, but this..." He gestures around the space, currently deserted since all the passengers are milling around the recreation deck or in their staterooms. "These vendors aren't corporate."

Gabe takes in the corridor. "Indeed."

Bennie walks over to a stall. "Hi."

"Good morning," the Durbrillian behind the counter says. "Welcome aboard the *Empress*." She gestures to the shelves arrayed behind her and on each side. "Let me know if there's anything you'd like to see. Everything is hand crafted by artisans on my planet." She smiles. "I'm having a sale: pre-departure, ten percent off." Because of her species' limited height, being shorter than Brailacks, she's wearing stilts.

Bennie looks around. "Ten percent? I'd need twenty to take this crap. Don't worry, the normies will be along once we get underway." He turns and walks down the corridor. The stunned Durbrillian woman's mouth is still hanging open.

"That was rather rude," Gabe says.

Bennie waves a hand. "Once the actual tourists make their way down here, she'll clean up. I don't have any use for that junk."

"Still, you could have been more diplomatic," Gabe replies.

Bennie looks over his shoulder. "Life's too short." Gabe's optic sensors whir as they spin. "Come on, I want to check out engineering."

"I would like that," Gabe agrees as they exit the commerce zone.

The *Galactic Empress* is a maze of corridors bisected by a separate maze of lift tubes. A passenger can board a lift in the luxury tower and take the same lift all the way to the shuttle bay at the exact opposite end of the ship.

Gabe and Bennie step out of the lift in front of a large hatch. Unlike the rest of the ship they've seen so far, the hatch to engineering isn't faux wood, or inlaid with anything. The deck isn't lined with carpet and the lighting is harsh industrial standard. The hatch is fendurrium, like every other starship hull and hatch made. A security guard flanks each side of the large hatch.

One, a Stilten man, says, "Excuse me, uh, sirs? This area is off-limits."

Bennie approaches the hatch. "It's okay. We're the security consultants."

GETTING ACQUAINTED

The boarding hatch connecting the *Empress* to the Hub is almost closed when a voice calls out, "Wait!"

The Tleb crew member at the guest welcome desk slaps his tiny hand on the console. The hatch stops with a metallic groan.

Three beings move through the narrow gap in the hatch. The front most, a Malkorite woman, says, "Thank you! We thought we'd not make it in time! Our transport shuttle was delayed on Flarrem."

The small crew member forces a smile onto his canine featured face. It looks like he's about to bite someone. He's missing one of his incisors. "Boarding papers?"

The Harrith woman swipes on her wristcomm. Her companions, a Hulgian woman and an Olop man, do the same.

The Tleb looks at his console, confirming the documents: guests of one of the big ship's investors. He looks up. "Welcome aboard the *Galactic Empress*, the most majestic vessel to ever sail among the stars." His tone makes it clear that this is the ten thousandth time he has said that phrase. He gestures toward the forward hatch. "The embarkation reception is still going on in the recreation area. We'll be decoupling in just a few moments."

"And our staterooms?" the Harrith woman asks. "We're exhausted from our travels."

The crew member consults his screen, then points aft to a bank of lifts on either side of the wide corridor. "Take a lift to deck 22 aft."

The trio turns and heads for the lifts. The heavy boarding airlock hatch closes with a clang.

As the lift doors close, the Olop man looks at his two much taller compatriots. "What now?"

The Harrith woman looks down, smiling. "We make contact with our friends and we enjoy our cruise."

"May I have your attention, please? On behalf of Captain Ramalbong and the crew of the *Galactic Empress,* we'd like to welcome you aboard. We'll be decoupling from the Hub in moments. If you'd like to watch, please make your way to the nearest starboard viewport," overhead speakers throughout the massive ship announce.

Passengers have packed the forward recreation deck, hundreds on the two tracks above the main level, thousands gathered on the main deck around tables, the main bar, and a pool that is currently covered by a clear cover to create more floor space.

Those nearest the starboard side press against the transparent barrier enclosing the recreational space. An audible gasp fills the space as the *Galactic Empress* decouples from the Hub. Massive magnetic latches release the mighty ship as her thrusters gently push her away. The boarding tunnel slowly retracts back into the Hub as the *Empress* thrusts further from it.

Beyond the massive Hub and even more massive *Galactic Empress,* dozens of shuttles and smaller cruise ships have formed a tunnel to see the majestic ship depart.

In engineering, Bennie and Gabe are watching the ship's engineers keep the enormous power plant running as her main sub-light engines prepare to ignite.

An engineering droid identical to the model Gabe was when the crew of the *Ghost* rescued him walks up to the pair. "I am Chief Engineer Hogarth. It is a pleasure to meet you." The smaller set of arms are tucked up against his torso. "We will be jumping to FTL momentarily. I would be honored to give you a tour once we are underway."

Gabe inclines his head. "We would be..." He looks around awkwardly. "Honored."

Bennie looks up. "No thesaurus loaded?" He moves off to examine a console before Gabe can reply.

Gabe remains motionless for several minutes as the ship moves away from the Hub. The power plants thrum as the mighty ship gains distance from the docking platform.

Hogarth returns. "We are making our way clear of the Hub and its traffic."

Gabe looks at the other droid, extending his hand. "Lead the way."

The droid turns. "Four distinct reactors, all housed in this complex, provide power for the *Galactic Empress*. Two are dedicated to propulsion; the remaining two are for all other systems." He points to one of the reactors. A low thrum emanates from the powerful structure.

"Hey, what's this over here?" Bennie shouts. Gabe and Hogarth, the former sighing, turn to the small Brailack.

Hogarth says, "That is the secondary processing matrix. The ship's main computer is housed in a different section of the ship, but that," he gestures to the glistening black square that stands four meters tall and three wide, "can handle the ship's basic functions if needed."

"Neat." Bennie reaches for a command console, only to have a matte black mechanical hand clamp down on his wrist. He looks up to see Hogarth towering over him, shaking his head, optic sensors rotating.

From deeper inside the cavernous space, someone calls, "Hogarth, FTL in two."

"Please, follow me." He leads Bennie and Gabe to the central engineering control room. Monitors ring the space, and several beings and droids occupy duty stations around the perimeter. On a display larger than the rest, a view from a forward-facing camera displays the space head of the ship. The image wavers a moment before the stars stretch out into rainbow star lines.

The luxury tower is the tallest feature of the *Galactic Empress*, designed to provide each stateroom an unobstructed view fore or aft of the ship. Directly in front of the oval-shaped luxury tower is the arboretum, the dome of which dwarfs the luxury tower behind it in diameter.

Trees ten to fifteen meters tall fill the space, providing greenery and supplemental atmosphere processing. The small forest boasts gravel walkways lined with benches as well as plentiful nooks and crannies amid the shrubs and decorative plants for passengers to get away for some alone time. Or, in Bennie's case, some together time.

"Woo!" Bennie exhales, falling back on the grass. He's naked.

A pale green Brailack woman, also naked, rolls onto her side next to him. She says, "Tell me again how you defeated Darf Nader aboard the Space Ball." She reaches across Bennie to his discarded belt and beam saber hilt, running a finger along its length.

He rests a hand on hers, guiding it away from the lethal device. "Let me catch my breath." He looks around, realizing he can't recall the version of the story he told her at the bar earlier. He's about to make an excuse when his wristcomm beeps from the pile of clothes next to them. Reaching for it, he says, "Yeah?"

"Where are you?" It's Wil. "We're supposed to join the captain and some VIPs for dinner in half an hour...er, you know, tock."

Bennie tries to hide his grin. "Be right there. I'm not far from the suite." Before Wil can reply, he swipes the comm window closed. He looks at his new friend. "Sorry, babe, duty calls." He reaches for his clothes. "Life of a Knight of Plentallus and all." He gets up to dress. After plucking her top off the pile of clothes, he hands it to her. He slips his shirt over his head and picks up his belt. He nods. "Later."

"Call me," she says, slipping her shoes on. Bennie waves as he pushes through the shrubbery shielding them from the walking path.

Less than five minutes later, he's walking in the front door of the shared luxury stateroom. "I'm here."

Wil leans out the open hatch to the room he and Cynthia share. "You look...wrinkly."

From the front of the room near the floor-to-ceiling window, Gabe turns. "Your heart rate is elevated. You are flushed. Are you okay?"

Walking to his room, the Brailack waves. "Not all of us are encumbered by a relationship. This tub has no shortage of..." He rubs his chin, then looks over to Wil, who is still watching. "Fly honeys?"

Wil inclines his head. "Proper usage. Also, not an image I'd like to dwell on, so get dressed." He leans back in to his stateroom, letting the hatch close.

Inside the room, he looks at Cynthia sitting on the bed. "I can't believe they didn't grab us more clothes."

She looks over. "Bennie's sexual escapades don't bother you, but that does? Besides, you look fine."

He holds open the dress jacket, which is lined with small pink representations of the *Galactic Empress* inlaid in a repeating pattern on a white background. Before she can reply, he lifts his leg, hiking up his pants. Socks, complete with tiny *Galactic Empresses*, like the jacket. "The model of sexy," he grouses.

The look on Cynthia's face makes Wil stop talking. She stands up and does a slow spin. She's wearing a very short and form fitting dress in silver with blue accents. Within the blue accents are small silver *Galactic Empresses*. They are far more subtle than those on either of his own garments.

"Okay, fair," he says, sliding his wristcomm onto his wrist and adjusting the jacket to cover it. He looks her over. "You look stunning."

She rests a hand on his chest. "I know." She presses the button to open the door. "Come on."

NEWSCAST

Klor'Tillen is beaming a grin that splits his face. Beyond him, through a transparent bulkhead, a massive white hull section slides past. Viewports dot the hull. Inside, happy faces look out, waving at the reporter and other onlookers.

The Brailack reporter waves back before turning to the camera. "There she goes. The *Galactic Empress* is on her way to pleasure station Moklan."

Klor'Tillen walks away from the massive window. "We'll be here when the ship returns to interview Captain Polandra Ramalbong on her thoughts on the ship and how it did on its first cruise." He grins again. "Stay tuned."

CHAPTER TWELVE

CAPTAIN'S TABLE

The main dining room of the *Galactic Empress* sits below the main bridge above the main body of the ship in the command complex, a large space enclosed by the same transparent barrier that protects the arboretum and forward recreation deck. Unlike most of the dining spaces on the ship, the main dining room requires formal attire and reservations.

The captain's table sits dead center in the space atop the Red Nova Lines logo in the carpet. Chairs enough for twelve, with one sporting a taller back and the Red Nova logo, surround the table.

Captain Polandra Ramalbong looks around the table, her pale blonde hair pulled tight into a single ponytail. She's Multonae, and to Wil, looks like one of those dolls his sister played with as a kid. Her bright purple eyes sparkle as she takes in the table. "Good evening, everyone." She smiles. The table is occupied by the crew of the *Ghost*, the head of ship's security, her executive officer, Mr. Londo, and the two Palorian women they had met earlier.

Wil spots several other investors at other tables, presumably with their staff.

A steward arrives at the table. He pours the captain a glass of something neon blue with bubbles. She nods, and the junior officer moves to fill everyone else's glasses. Around them, first- and second-class passengers are being seated for dinner at the remaining tables. Some, those who arrived when the dining room opened, are finishing up their meals.

The captain raises her glass. "To the *Galactic Empress*."

As the table raises their glasses, Mr. Londo adds, "To Captain Ramalbong."

Breal says, "To a glorious return on our investment." She laughs and several others around the table do the same.

Wil says, "Cheers," as several of the people around the table say, "Mablongo."

Bennie leans over to Maxim. "She's hot for, you know, a Multon-ae." The big man shakes his head slowly.

The Smooth Laccizo was meant to be a small cafe offering takeaway snacks and meals for the third-class passengers. A legal battle between the owners and Red Nova Cruise Lines has resulted in the space being unfinished and unoccupied for this voyage.

Talara'Vey smiles. "This will do nicely." She looks around. "Dar, link up with the others and start getting set up."

The Olop man nods. "On it."

Chief Vlaruna's walleyed face turns toward Wil, eyes blinking just a bit out of sync. "So, you just get to ride along with us doing what, exactly?" He stabs a fork at the piece of cake before him. Dinner has been cleared; a salad came first, then some type of fish Wil has never heard of. The dessert course is a cake that tastes like chocolate but is pale pink with purple bits of something in it.

Wil smiles. "Well, when—" he jerks as someone kicks him under the table, "—if something bad happens that your crack squad of renta-cops can't handle, the professionals will be here." He taps his chest with a finger. "That'd be us."

Before the Trollack man can blurt a reply, Mr. Londo adds, "Chief, no one is impugning the skills of you or your staff." He gestures to the crew of the *Ghost*. "They've dealt with things we can only hope to never have to deal with." He smiles. "I think we all agree, the best outcome is these people doing nothing but earning their paycheck while enjoying a luxurious cruise."

One of the investors, a Burzzad woman, nods, her long neck bowing. "With everything going on in the GC right now, I will sleep better knowing that those who uncovered the Harrith conspiracy, helped protect the Corporate Congress summit, and exposed the Farsight projects, are aboard the *Empress*."

Wil raises a hand. "You forgot 'saved some never-before-encoun-tered sapient starships and killed wanted crime boss Xarrix.'"

Maxim nods. "That was a fun one."

Bennie scowls. "Says you. I almost froze to death."

"You looked cute, though, all bundled up," Maxim quips.

Gabe is in the computer center, having passed on dinner. A droid rolls over on a large metallic sphere, its pale blue chassis polished to an immaculate sheen. "Greetings," it says aloud.

Gabe inclines his head. "Greetings. I am wondering if you could tell me more about the processing core of the *Galactic Empress?*"

The pale blue droid has only the single leg, which ends in the roller ball. It bends at the hip. "It would be my pleasure. I am Delphine, head of computer systems aboard the *Empress.*"

"I am—"

"Gabe, the liberator," Delphine says. She observes Gabe's face. "You are offended?"

Gabe raises a hand. "No. I am not fond of that nickname."

She inclines her head, her powder blue chassis rotating. "So noted." She extends an arm toward the massive processing core.

The computer center for the *Galactic Empress* is not one of the publicly accessible spaces. The ship requires an immense amount of processing power to provide for the comfort and entertainment of the thousands plus passengers. While the backup in engineering is much smaller and would only provide for the bare minimum functionality, the main core is a sight to behold.

As far as Gabe can tell, the entire computer center is manned by droids, possibly by design. The space is even more spartan than the engineering area. The main core is a sphere five meters in diameter. Grooves ring the outer shell, with streams of data pulsing along each groove.

Delphine switches to direct wireless communications.

This is a Draplin Combine Mark X core. The demands of the passengers at any given time occupy forty-three percent of its capacity, while the rest handles standard shipboard functions.

Gabe nods as he examines the core. *I find it interesting that passenger needs occupy such a large percentage.*

Delphine rests a manipulator on the chassis. *It is impressive, to be sure. Each stateroom has a fully immersive entertainment suite, in addition to the numerous entertainments available throughout the ship.*

I see.

The pair continues along a wide walkway that spirals up the three decks of the computer center. The massive sphere hangs in the center of the space, accessible by walkways from various levels.

Delphine turns to Gabe. *I feel that I should express my thanks.*

Gabe stops and looks at his guide.

She continues. *I have a name. This is not my assignment; it is my job. I owe that to you.*

The droid looks at Gabe, her optic sensors glowing a bright orange. Out loud, she says, "Thank you."

Gabe inclines his head. They continue up the ramp to the uppermost section, a control room of sorts. Three droids of similar make to Delphine turn their optic sensors to the new arrivals. One, bipedal with an orange chassis and four arms, waves a hand. "Hello, Gabe."

The control center is a half-circle of computer terminals and a full wall display. On the wall display an illustration of the *Galactic Empress* slowly rotates. Lines denoting data are pulsing back and forth throughout the illustrated vessel. Droids of various shapes and sizes man the terminals.

Gabe notes that Delphine isn't exaggerating about the data usage across the vessel.

Back in the luxury suite, Wil has his feet up on a coffee table as he looks out the transparent hull of the suite. The arboretum is below, the bridge module beyond that, and the forward recreation deck at the forward-most section of the gargantuan cruise ship. He's holding a PADD, watching the screen flash a "CONNECTING" prompt.

The screen changes, first to the logo for the Earth Gov Alliance Navy, then to James Hawthorne. "Hey, homeboy!" he says, his brown eyes lighting up at the sight of his longtime friend.

Wil grins. "Hey, man. How's things?"

Hawthorne runs a hand over his closely cropped hair. Wil notices that it's considerably grayer around the temples than it was before. "Oh, you know. Trying to keep the military from becoming political, while trying to keep the skies actually safe. Those ships we talked about a while ago." Wil sits up. "We engaged two of them out near the belt."

"And?" Wil asks.

"Took 'em out. The *Calder* took a little damage. The *Vigilant* and the *Corsair* got their shakedowns a little earlier than planned. No major losses."

Wil leans back. "Never boring."

His friend smiles. "Truth. Is that a chandelier behind you? Where are you? That doesn't look like the *Ghost* or your ratty ass warehouse."

Wil looks over his shoulder. "Oh, that."

"I feel like they don't put chandeliers in places that are boring." James grins, his brown eyes twinkling.

Wil laughs. "Guess what we have out here." When his friend doesn't reply, he looks around to make sure Zephyr isn't nearby.

"Space luxury cruise ships." He turns the PADD around so the camera points out the forward viewport and the vista beyond.

"Damn," the speaker on the small device emits.

"Right?" Wil turns the PADD back to face him. "So, you get anything from the ships you tangled with?"

"Not a lot. One survivor." James rubs his chin. "A...what're they called?" He snaps his fingers. "Tremble."

"Trenbal?" Wil asks. "Looks like that insurance company mascot."

James points at the camera pickup. "There you go. One of them. He's pretty banged up, so we'll see if he pulls through."

Wil nods. "Fingers crossed it's just some lame pirate crew, and you scared 'em off. You mentioned politics. How's that going?"

"Stopped downloading the news?" the other man jokes.

Wil smiles. "Too depressing, and come on—new episodes of the new *New Girl* reboot, or talking heads pontificating about partisan nonsense? Do the math."

James grunts his agreement. "Can't argue with that. You'll have to tell me if it's worth watching. I've been swamped lately."

"Cynthia loves the new Winston."

James laughs. "Well, that's good. Brothers gotta represent, even out in the federation's dingy parts." He takes a breath. "Earth First is still doing their thing. Seems like not a day goes by that they aren't protesting something somewhere around the world. It's exhausting, but so far, they're more annoying than anything else. They haven't gotten a majority anywhere and no other group wants anything to do with them." As Wil nods, James adds, "I'd definitely keep my distance for now. There's a lot of 'The only good alien is a dead alien' talk."

Wil sighs. "Great googa mooga."

"Yeah. Listen, I gotta jet. Duty calls, and I'm sure there's a space pool party you need to get to." He waves as the screen goes black.

CLOSE ENCOUNTERS

With dinner over, Maxim meets up with Gabe to patrol the ship and get the lay of the land while the others enjoy some off time.

The tall droid looks at his only slightly shorter friend. "I could have patrolled on my own. I do not require sleep."

Maxim shrugs. "Well, for one thing, I need to walk off dinner. For another, I want to get a feel for the ship. I've studied the deck plans, but walking the corridors helps build a better mental model."

"I do not believe a walk around the ship will make much of a dent in your recent caloric overage." Gabe looks at his friend. "Bennie posts images of his food to the internex."

Maxim laughs, putting a hand on his stomach. "Knight of Plentallus and food influencer..." He sighs. "It was so good, though."

"I will take your word for it," the droid replies. They reach an intersection. He extends an arm down a corridor.

They're walking through the third-class section of the massive luxury liner. The luxury in third class is visibly different, though, from its counterpart several decks up. The carpet that lines the corridors is not nearly as high quality as that on the first-class decks. The walls are plain metal; there isn't a scrap of artwork to be seen adorning them.

The pair passes an open hatch. Maxim glances in. The stateroom is about the same size as one of the guest berths aboard the *Ghost*. There's a small bed, a single chair, a wall-mounted display, and likely a refresher tucked into the corner he can't see.

"Hard to believe this is the same ship I just had dinner on," Maxim says as they pass the open stateroom.

Gabe inclines his head. "Biologicals love stratifying their peers into classes."

Max huffs. "Truer words."

They walk in companionable silence for a while, making their way lower into the ship toward the crew-only sections. They're near the lowest levels of the ship: mechanical systems, crew quarters, other parts passengers aren't meant to see.

An open hatch ahead is belching steam into the corridor where fans are doing their best to inhale the water vapor into water return pipes. The hatch leads to *Ship's Laundry* 3. Inside, a veritable army of Tleb and Trollack crew members are moving loads from industrial clothing refreshers to hover carts, and vice versa.

"How is there already that much laundry?" Maxim asks as they slowly pass the hatch.

Gabe shrugs. "Biologicals are messy."

"You're just full of witty observations today."

Gabe shrugs again.

They pass down a flight of metal stairs to what Maxim thinks might be the lowest inhabited level of the ship. He knows there are several sections below them that are automated: waste processing, refuse storage, and more—places biological beings rarely go.

A hatch opens and a Hulgian man tumbles into the corridor. He bounces off of the opposite wall to be leapt on by two Guldranii men. The two much smaller men rain blows on their larger opponent. Both are shoeless. One climbs up onto the larger man's head, using his horns like a ladder.

"Hey!" Maxim rushes over. He plucks the nearest Guldranii off of the Hulgian, while Gabe grabs the other one, his arms extending to accomplish the task. The man in Maxim's grip turns his eye, one of the side-mounted ones, to Maxim as he throws a punch that connects with Maxim's chest.

The big Palorian doesn't say a word but shakes the Guldranii vigorously until he stops throwing punches. He looks at the man. "You done?"

Gabe's brawler has similarly calmed down. The Hulgian man stands up. "Who the wurrin are you two?"

"You are welcome," Gabe replies.

The Hulgian man clucks, reaching up to stroke one of his horns, straightening a decorative band. "Like these two could hurt me."

The Guldranii in Maxim's grip spits out, "Grolack off, you stupid horn head." Maxim shakes him again.

The Hulgian looks at Gabe and Maxim. "This level is for crew only. You're not supposed to be down here."

Gabe tilts his head. "It would seem our presence was fortuitous."

The two Guldraniis look around, their four eyes wobbling. The one in Gabe's hand says, "What do you mean?"

Gabe looks at his brawler. "You were attacking this man."

"Because he cheated at cards," the long-skulled Guldranii says. He flails as he tries to pry Gabe's fingers from his shirt. "Gillum cheated."

"I did." The horned man nods. He's on his feet now, towering over Maxim. He grins. "It's all good."

Maxim looks at Gabe, then the man he's still holding aloft. He drops the Guldranii without a word, then says, "Sorry?"

The man he just dropped looks at him as he brushes himself off, smoothing his shirt. "Better be." He looks around. "Where did my shoes land?"

Maxim turns to Gabe and clears his throat. The droid drops his brawler as well.

The Hulgian, Gillum, looks at the two *Ghost* crew. "Like I said, crew only." He points back the way Gabe and Maxim came.

Maxim blushes a bit. "Uh, yeah, we'll just..." He hitches the upper thumb on his right hand over his shoulder.

The Guldranii who was the last to enter the room the trio spilled from looks at the Palorian man. "Yeah." He enters, and the hatch slides closed.

Maxim looks at Gabe, tilting his head. "I guess we'll just—"

"Never speak of this again?" the droid completed.

Maxim shrugs, wobbling his head. "I was going to say, 'show ourselves out,' but yeah, also that. Especially to Wil."

As they enter the lift, Maxim says, "Do you know where we are? Who those guys are?"

Gabe looks up. "This section of the ship is dedicated to crew but is not segregated by function."

Maxim rubs his chin.

NEWSCAST

"Good evening. I'm Megan, and this is GNO News Time. We've just received word from Mon-El Furash on the front lines." She consults the PADD on the desk in front of her. "The battle on the ground has been pitched, but the Peacekeepers appear to have turned the tables on the Invaders."

Turning to a different camera, "A new weapon was deployed that seems to have wiped out ninety percent of the ground forces on the planet. The Peacekeepers were able to secure the mysterious facility the Invaders built intact. Nothing more has been released about the weapon or any discoveries made at the Invader base, but this is hopeful news that this conflict may be coming to an end."

The blonde-haired woman blinks several times, collecting her thoughts. "None too soon, I might add. The fighting in the neighboring Cuolbongong system has been bloody. While the Peacekeepers have held on, the losses have been significant."

CHAPTER THIRTEEN

The *Galactic Empress* has nearly three dozen dining establishments beyond the main dining room: from grab-and-go food stalls, to buffet style dining that covers a wide range of atmospheric needs of cultures from around the GC, to smaller specialty cafes.

Talara'Vey and her crew are in *Felly Noor*, a buffet on one of the lower decks, near the shuttle bay that sits in the nose of the great ship, several decks under the forward recreation area. *Felly Noor* is enclosed by airlocks since its atmosphere is unsuitable for those who can't handle high methane environs.

While Malkorites, Olops, and Hulgians don't require high methane environments, all of them can handle that type of atmospheric mix for short periods. That makes meeting in public over a meal less risky as there aren't that many methane breathers on the cruise to overhear their planning.

Dar holds up a fork, leafy blue vegetables skewered on it. "So," he looks around, "what's the plan?" He takes a bite of his salad.

The Harrith team lead looks around for what might be the fifth time. Her colleagues stopped counting. "I've contacted our benefactors, as well as the support teams. We're still a go. When the ship makes its first stop, we make our move."

Wirra, the massive Hulgian woman, tilts her head, vertebrae popping as she does. "I'll go explore the computer section today."

Dar nods as he munches his salad. "I'll see about engineering." He looks at the team leader. "You able to reach our contact on the bridge?"

Talara'Vey smiles. "Yes. They're ready." Her two colleagues smile.

Dar looks around, a blue leaf stuck on one of his incisors. "This place ain't bad. We'll have to get a copy of the recipe book the food processor is using."

"I don't know why I agreed to this," Maxim says. He and Wil are standing off to the side of a sparring mat. Nearly a hundred passengers are standing around the mat. The pair and their audience are in one of the large open areas designed for recreation. Workout equipment designed for a number of different physical body configurations lines the walls of the space. Some of the devices, Wil is certain, would break him two. The sparring mat is newer and better designed than the one on the *Ghost*. Thicker too he thinks appreciatively.

"You were pretty drunk," Wil offers. He slaps his friend on the back then walks to the middle of the mat. "Hi, folks! Thanks for coming to this demonstration!" He waves as he makes a slow circle. The audience claps politely. Someone coughs.

Wil motions for Maxim to join him. He looks around. "I'm sure you know who we are." Those nearest the mat sort of shrug and shake their heads. A few folks nod or smile. Wil scowls. "We're the team that exposed the Harrith incident, brought down Farsight Corporation's secret experiments." He nods his head, trying to get more engagement from the crowd. The crowd doesn't respond.

"What are you guys called?" someone shouts.

Wil pulls a hand down his face. "Well, we don't really have a name per se, but—" Maxim shoves him to the side.

"Who's ready for some sparring with a Peacekeeper operative?" the big Palorian asks the crowd as he smashes his fists together.

"Ex-," Wil hisses at his friend as he moves to the edge of the mat.

Maxim works through a series of warm-ups, narrating as he goes. After a while, the crowd warms up and a few folks venture onto the mat for instruction.

Wil looks at his wristcomm and taps an icon. "Where are you?"

"What's it to you?" Bennie replies.

"I'm your damn boss," Wil growls. He walks away from the mat, through the crowd, which seems to be growing now as Maxim gets into a groove.

Bennie sighs loud enough for the comm system to pick it up. "I'm at the bar in the main rec area." The line closes.

Wil finds Bennie sitting at the bar that occupies a large central section of the spacious recreation deck near the pool, now uncovered and full of splashing children of dozens of species. Several Trollack children are swimming circles around the rest. Beyond the transparent bulkhead, the rainbow streaks of FTL travel cast the area in a dazzling light.

The Brailack hacker is surrounded by a dozen people. He's standing on a barstool, arms waving. A drink sloshes in one hand; his beam saber hilt is in the other. As Wil gets closer, he hears Bennie saying, "And then, with the rest of the team out cold, it was just me and my trusty beam saber. The Magog are everywhere, growling and clawing at the floor. Their hungry eyes burning. They're about to devour Admiral Rick Hunter." He takes a sip of his drink. "It was scary, believe me."

"What's a Magog?" someone shouts.

Bennie makes a face. "Trust me, you don't want to know." He waves his beam saber hilt around making swooshing noises, more of the drink in his other hand sloshing around.

Wil sighs and makes his way through the crowd.

BAD INFLUENCES

Wil shoos Bennie's audience away, telling them they can catch the next story hour. Bennie hops down to take a seat on his stool. Wil takes the seat next to him. "So, now you're just making up random shit to tell strangers?" Wil waves to the bartender, a Sylban woman. She acknowledges him and goes about fetching a drink.

Wil looks back to Bennie. "Magog? You just mix and match? Rick Hunter?"

The team hacker shrugs. "It's hard to remember all the details. Your people make a lot of crappy fiction." He grins, his hairless eyebrow ridges rising. "It's not like any of them will ever watch *Space Precinct*."

"*Andromeda*," Wil corrects, "and *Robotech*."

"Literally no one cares."

The bartender deposits something bright green with an umbrella in front of Wil. He looks at it. "Oh, uh, I just wanted a grum." The woman frowns as she takes the drink back, her tongue darting in, what feels to Wil, annoyance. He turns back to Bennie. "I'm just saying." A glass of grum appears at his elbow.

Bennie waves his friend away. "I'm not charging much for the stories."

"You're charging them money?" Wil splutters, his eyes wide.

"Not a lot." The Brailack affects an indignant look. "Creators should be paid for their work."

Wil looks up, taking a deep breath. Still looking up, he says, "You're not the creator." He looks at Bennie. "You're butchering stuff you've watched. None of it is yours."

Bennie shrugs. "Remix—that's a thing, right?" Wil groans. Bennie adds, "Plus most of these creators are dead, and well, their estates are on Earth, and no one gives a felgercarb about your world or its copyright law."

"Hello," a deep baritone says from behind Wil, causing him to jump, sloshing grum all over his hand.

Bennie looks past Wil's shoulder and whispers, "Investor guy." He holds a hand to his forehead, fingers miming the horn configuration of Hulgians.

Wil sighs, rolling his eyes. He turns his stool slowly toward the new arrival.

"Quistic, Paldo Quistic," the Hulgian man says, taking a seat on the opposite side of Wil. The barstool creaks under the weight of the large being.

Wil smiles. "Did you polish your horns?"

The big man grunts. "It's important to present a professional appearance." He absently reaches up to stroke his right horn. He looks Wil up and down. Bennie chuckles behind Wil.

Wil jabs an elbow backward then looks over his shoulder at his friend, who is wheezing. He turns back to the Hulgian investor. "What can we do for you, Mr. Quistic?"

The Hulgian man runs a hand along one of his horns, his triceratops-like face an unreadable mask. "I wanted to ask what you thought of our ship." He extends a arm in a sweeping gesture to take in the recreation area.

Wil smiles. "She's a beauty. I haven't had much chance to explore yet, but what I've seen is incredible."

Bennie nods. "Yeah, this thing is nice." He wobbles one hand.

"Some more—how should I say this—adult entertainments would be nice." Wil frowns.

The big Hulgian smiles, nodding. "I lobbied for such." His smile turns sour. "Among the many things I was overruled on during this project."

Wil takes a sip. "Still, the end result looks good."

"Yes, she is impressive," he agrees. After a not-at-all-subtle look around the area, he continues, "I wanted to speak with you about something...more sensitive."

Bennie rubs his hands together, almost climbing over Wil. "Oh?"

Wil shoves the aggressive Brailack back, then makes a *go on* motion to Quistic.

The big man opens his mouth but clamps it shut as Cynthia and Zephyr arrive, the former draping an arm around Wil's shoulder.

Zephyr says, "We just checked out the shuttle bay and auxiliary craft. Someone came aboard in a Lorem Shipworks Blasta Mk-5."

Wil whistles. "Neat. I hear they fly like a dream." Cynthia nods.

Bennie adds, "You don't think it's part of the ship's auxiliary fleet?"

Mr. Quistic stands. "I'll let you all enjoy your time." He nods to Wil. "Another time."

Wil inclines his head.

Zephyr says, "I doubt it. This thing is ridiculous, but a Blasta as a people mover seems a bit over the top. Pretty sure even if we sold the *Ghost* we couldn't afford one."

Cynthia watches the burly, horned man weave through the crowd of passengers coming and going to the various entertainments the recreation deck offers. "What was that about?"

Wil shrugs.

PARTY PLANNING

Maxim walks into the suite in the luxury tower and spies Zephyr sitting on the sofa facing out at the enormous transparent hull paneling that lines the space. The view beyond—the bulk of the *Galactic Empress*, the stretched-out starlings of FTL—it's all beautiful.

She looks over her shoulder. "How was the demonstration?"

He stops at the now well-stocked kitchenette, Wil and Bennie availed themselves of the room delivery menu after getting settled. After grabbing a bottle of water, he drops onto the sofa next to her. "More entertaining than I expected, but don't tell Wil. He owes me for doing it." He takes a sip and continues, "Bennie's little friend, the Olop girl, she's got some fight in her. She showed up toward the end." He looks at his partner and the assorted PADDs on her lap and next to her. "You taking night classes or something?"

Zephyr smiles. Her cheeks turn a darker shade of blue. "Planning an engagement party for Cynthia and Wil."

Maxim's mouth opens, then closes. Then he says, "Without me?" He reaches for one of the tablets, scanning the screen. He looks at Zephyr. "No."

"What do you mean, no?" she demands, looking at the device's screen. "I think it'd be fun."

Maxim makes a show of slowly shaking his head. "Sure, if they were Malkorite salt miners on leave." When Zephyr leans back like he just physically struck her, he adds, "I...I mean some people like that kind—"

She holds up a hand. "Just stop. It won't get better for you."

The hatch opens and Gabe walks in. "Hello, Maxim. Hello, Zephyr. What are you doing?"

Zephyr looks over at the droid. "I'm about to go for a swim." She points at Maxim. "He's just taken on planning Cynthia and Wil's engagement party."

Maxim adjusts himself on the sofa so he can look at Gabe, still standing in the entryway. "Want to help? It'll be fun."

Gabe doesn't immediately respond, then turns and leaves the suite, saying nothing.

Zephyr looks at Maxim. "Have fun." She stands and heads to the room they share to change.

Maxim watches her leave, then sits in silence for a minute. He grabs one of the other PADDs, scanning its screen. He looks at the closed door to the room Zephyr is in. "Neon green? Gods help her." He turns to face the expansive view forward and begins working.

The pool in the middle of the forward recreation deck reminds Wil of a toy he had as a little kid, a bearing mounted in plastic, usually with three rounded points you spun idly while doing something else. Zephyr is resting on a lounger near the pool after swimming when Cynthia arrives with Wil in tow. Both are in swimsuits.

"You seen Maxim?" Wil asks.

Zephyr shrugs. "I left him in the suite."

Cynthia drops into the lounger Wil just moved over. "Probably with Bennie getting into trouble."

Wil laughs. "Did I tell you guys that yesterday I caught Bennie playing town minstrel at the bar?" He points to the bar on the opposite side of the pool. "He was mashing up *Star Wars* and some other random stuff we've watched from my archive."

Cynthia opens her mouth but closes it when Wil continues, "He was charging people for the stories." He sounds scandalized.

Cynthia looks at him, then to Zephyr on his other side. "I mean, no one will know, right?"

"Babe!" Wil says. He looks at Zephyr for support.

The Palorian woman makes a show of adjusting her swimsuit. "My, that water looks lovely."

"Ah, hello Wil and others," someone says behind Wil's and Cynthia's loungers.

Wil turns. "Ankpol! Enjoying the cruise?"

The Xelurian's spider-like legs are clicking on the deck material. His shaggy white-furred torso looks freshly combed. He runs a large paw along his chest. "I am. The salon here is top notch."

"You do look quite handsome," Cynthia offers.

The spider-bear, as Wil calls these creatures, bows by bending his forward legs. He looks around. "How is the water?"

Wil looks at Zephyr, surrounded by children splashing everywhere. "Crowded."

Cynthia looks at Wil and shrugs, standing to join her friend. Wil shrugs out of his *Galactic Empress*-branded Hawaiian shirt, unsure what such a shirt is called when no one knows what or where Hawaii is. Ankpol moves off to gingerly step into the shallow end of the pool.

He leans back on the lounger and closes his eyes. What must be less than a minute later, a shadow falls across him. Opening one eye, he spies Paldo Quistic, the Hulgian investor, in a swimsuit. "Hi," he says.

"I'm not disturbing you, am I?" the big man says, moving to sit on the lounger Cynthia vacated.

Wil looks at the pool where Zephyr and Cynthia are talking and laughing as they wade. He smiles. "Nope, not at all."

A Tleb arrives. "Gentlemen, a drink?" She's barefoot and brindled much like Wil's grandparents' dogs when he was younger. He notices that one of her canines is missing, which gives her a lisp. He wonders if that is common among the small upright-Chihuahua looking beings.

"Grum," he says, then looks at Quistic, who orders something called a Swollen Gland. At least, that's what it sounds like he says. The server departs.

Mr. Quistic clears his throat, a deep basso like a rockslide. "I'm curious, Captain. What exactly is your role here?"

Wil coughs. "Well, we're mostly just here as insurance. Chief Vlaruna is in charge of security, same as always. Mr. Londo just thought—"

"Londo is an idiot," Quistic grumbles. He adds. "Vlaruna is a under qualified moron."

The Tleb server returns. "Here you are." She deposits the drinks on a small table between the two loungers and leaves. The big Hulgian man's drink is in a tall thick mug, mist rolling off the top. Whatever the liquid is, it's pitch black and looks equally thick.

"Cheers," Wil says, watching his guest drink something that looks like it was scooped out of the La Brea Tar Pits on Earth.

Quistic wipes the corners of his mouth. "So Londo thinks something will happen? On the ship, I mean, this cruise?"

Wil shakes his head. "Not that he's shared with us." Wil squints. "Have you heard something?"

Quistic leans back. "Oh, no, no. Nothing of the sort. I was more worried that Londo had information he hasn't shared with the other investors."

"If he does, he hasn't shared with us," Wil says. "We're the 'just in case' team." He grins. "Hoping this is nothing but an all-expenses-paid vacation."

The other man nods slowly, deep in thought. "Indeed." He sets his half-finished drink down. "If you'll excuse me." He doesn't wait. He stands, his chair squealing on the deck.

Wil watches him leave, then looks at the bubbling tar-like drink, still spitting mist out over the top. He pushes it as close to the edge of the table and as far from himself as possible. He sips his grum while the drink opposite him gurgles away to itself. Finally, he sets his drink down and looks at the pool. Zephyr and Cynthia are still near the middle, chatting as they float. He stands and folds his *space Hawaiian shirt,* setting it in the middle of the chair and walks to the pool.

As Wil reaches the two women, Cynthia looks over. "What was that about? He seems to have taken an interest in you. He knows you're spoken for, right?" She turns to Zephyr. "Dren, I have to get him a ring, right?" The Palorian woman dips her head back into the water, smoothing her jet-black hair out. "I think so, yeah."

Wil ignores the ring talk, focusing on the first part of Cynthia's question. "No idea. He wanted to know if we're here for a specific reason and if Londo suspected trouble."

"Weird," Zephyr says.

Wil inclines his head. "Yeah, I assured him that if there was a reason beyond '*just in case*,' we weren't in the loop." He raises an eyebrow. "Right?"

Zephyr nods. "Yeah."

Cynthia says, "So does your ring have to match mine, or can it be anything I like?"

"This will do nicely," Talara'Vey says, taking in the space. She and her two lieutenants are standing in the cafe that their contact on the bridge has been able to mark as closed for repair.

Several of the hired hands are moving equipment in from the various cargo holds they have hidden gear in. Each crate is labeled as food or equipment for various parts of the ship. The tracking numbers the only way to know that they in fact, hold weapons and computer gear.

Dar walks over to a wall panel and pries it free, exposing several conduits and wire bundles. He turns, smiling, "This will definitely do."

CHAPTER FOURTEEN

"Sorry, can't," Bennie says from the kitchenette. He grabs a fruit that looks like a banana with spikes along the length of it. He gingerly peels the thing, revealing a pale pink interior.

"What do you mean? I thought we'd have dinner as a team," Wil says from the sofa.

"Got a date." He smirks. "Hot little number I met at the Palorian buffet on deck eighteen. Pretty sure I won't be home tonight."

Cynthia makes a noise. "I hope you use protection."

Wil adds, "Space herpes, man. Don't mess around."

Zephyr makes a strangled sounding noise.

Bennie makes a face, then tosses the skin of his snack into the recycler. "Hate the game, not the player." He winks, patting a pocket on his tiny trousers. "Always have protection. Space Scout credo." He heads for the door to their shared suite. "Later, losers. Don't wait up." The hatch slides closed behind him.

Wil says, "Space Scouts? Nothing from any of you?" He points at Zephyr. "You? Nothing?"

Zephyr shrugs. "What? That's a real thing."

Wil sighs.

Cynthia looks at Wil shrugging. "Guess it's a foursome."

A cough-like noise comes from the sitting area near the door, just out of sight.

Cynthia makes a face as Wil silently laughs. "Sorry, Gabe." A ruder-sounding noise this time. "You know you're welcome to join."

Gabe comes around the corner. "I do. I was," he tilts his head, "joking." He holds up a hand. "I actually have plans, but thank you."

Wil beams. "A date?" He looks at Cynthia. "Do droids date?" His nose wrinkles. "Do they...you know?"

Gabe says, "I am still standing right here. To answer your questions: No, if we want, and it is technically possible with aftermarket parts."

Cynthia shakes her head. "And that concludes *Sex Ed. With Gabe.* Have fun with whatever your not-a-date is." She looks over her shoulder toward the bank of rooms. "Hey, you two, I'm hungry."

Gabe nods. "Enjoy your meal." He departs the suite with no further comment.

The door to Maxim and Zephyr's room slides open. "Okay, okay," Maxim says, stepping out into the main room.

The main dining room is full when they arrive. Zephyr says, "Glad I made a reservation."

The captain's table is empty, but every other table, sans the one they're being guided to, is occupied. The hostess, a Trenbal woman, says, "Here we are. Tonight's special is pan seared jerlack. The non-animal protein option is baked nuflonog." She bows. "Your server will be with you shortly."

Wil looks at his friends. "So, team name."

Maxim, who is looking up at the bridge module towering above the dining room, says, "X-Force."

Wil tuts. "You know that's taken."

"Shadow Seven?" Zephyr offers.

Wil makes a face. "You're not even trying. That's just the Shadow Six assholes plus one."

Zephyr shrugs. "Maybe that's our motto? This is harder than I expected."

The server comes over, a lean Sylban, young enough that the foliage atop his tree-like head is still bright green. "Can I get you something to drink?"

Everyone places their order, and the server ambles off, his long arms swaying as he walks.

"If we pick a name, Bennie will have a bull," Maxim says.

"Cow," Wil corrects.

"Aren't the same thing?" Cynthia asks.

Wil inhales. "Oh, man."

"I'm kidding. I've watched enough of your archive to know what a bull is." She turns to Maxim. "The boy cow."

Zephyr makes a face. "So, what's the female called?"

Wil groans. "Can we get—" The server returns with their drinks. Everyone orders and the bark-skinned man departs. Wil tries again. "Can we stay on task here? We need a name. Something to hang above the door of the warehouse."

Maxim opens his mouth but is interrupted by a commotion at another table, near the forward-most section of transparent bulkhead. The four *Ghost* crew members all turn to look. Bennie is fending off the rapid-fire slaps of an angry pale green Brailack woman. "You said I mattered to you!" she screams as the flat of her hand impacts the top of Bennie's head.

Maxim winces. "That probably hurt."

Bennie's date, an Olop woman, is watching the drama from her seat, saying nothing. That is, until the Brailack woman turns her attention to her furry competition. "And you, you furry flobin!"

Cynthia leans back. "Felgercarb!" She looks at the others. "This is gonna be good."

One of the waitstaff approaches. "Ma'am..." she says, reaching for the angry Brailack woman, only to be knocked aside by the Olop woman, her teal dress rippling as she moves. She tackles the Brailack woman, releasing a howl that causes the diners nearest the table to lean away. The server scurries backward.

Bennie pats the air. "Ladies, this can all be—" Both women turn and leap at him. He dodges, barely. The two women turn their attention back to each other.

The Olop woman drops to a crouch. "You bobblehead little flobin. I don't know who the hell you think you are." She leaps at her opponent.

As security arrives, Bennie ducks back from the two brawling women. He makes his way slowly from table to table as three uniformed officers arrive, a Harrith and two Malkorites.

Wil and the others watch as Bennie makes his way away from his table and the commotion. Most of the diners are still watching the women struggle with the security team. The Olop woman is crawling around the back of one of the Malkorite security people, slapping his large ears.

Wil waves to the wayward Brailack. When Bennie arrives at the table, Wil says, "Guess you'll be sleeping in your room tonight?"

Security is escorting the two women, still trying to claw alternately at each other and the security officers holding them.

Maxim watches the women and security depart and turns to Bennie. "You may not want to sleep. Ever." Bennie nods his agreement as he flags someone down to add a chair to the table of his friends.

MOVES

Talara'Vey, Wirra, and Dar are standing on the recreation deck, near one of the rear hatches. The team leader looks at the man next to her. He nods and the trio departs, heading deeper into the ship.

As they walk through one of the corridors of the massive luxury ship, the Malkorite woman looks at her colleagues. "Dar, go get ready." He nods, his mechanical eye glinting.

As the small Olop man trots off, Wirra, the Hulgian woman, says, "The computer center is good to go."

Talara'Vey nods. "The droids?"

"Won't be an issue," the other woman assures.

Talara'Vey checks her wristcomm. "Almost time."

A Hulgian man with two Guldraniis trailing behind him stops in front of Talara'Vey. "I've got teams at each hatch. We're heading in." He makes a sort of salute, slamming a massive fist against his chest.

She nods and the new trio moves past her and Wirra. She turns to the Hulgian woman. "Okay, get down to the computer core." Wirra nods and takes a branching corridor.

Talara'Vey watches her lieutenant vanish, then heads off on her own mission.

She takes a few minutes to navigate the labyrinthine corridors of the *Galactic Empress,* but she reaches her destination with a few minutes to spare. The sign over the hatch before her reads, Main Security Barracks.

Dar reaches his destination. Over the last few days of travel, he has visited the compartments around the engineering section. His cybernetic eye, while useful as an eye, is also packed with intrusion software and powerful sensors. He reaches the large hatch and connects a data cable to his prosthetic eye and plugs the other end into a port on the side of the access control panel next to the hatch.

He looks up and down the short corridor, then up to the security camera in the corner near the ceiling. The small black half-sphere looks back emotionlessly, a green light pulsing inside. The light goes out. He turns back to the panel, and after he concentrates on it a few seconds, the indicator blinks twice, then turns a solid red, indicating that the hatch is now sealed. Another second and every access into the cavernous engineering space is similarly sealed.

He consults his wristcomm. A countdown is running in a window on the device.

Observation Lounge 10 is in the first-class section of the ship. The space is two stories tall with theater seating in the rear and an open area at the front by the transparent hull. The transparent section bubbles out a bit to afford better views for occupants. Along the rear wall of the space, a buffet is set up. Investors and their staff, as well as key Red Nova personnel, occupy this lounge. Mr. Londo looks around, then taps one of his colleagues' shoulders. "Have you seen Mr. Quistic, Miss Fev'Ti, or Mr. Folakshima?"

The young man looks around, then shakes his head. "No. Well, Mr. Quistic commed to say he was under the weather and would be staying in his suite. I haven't heard anything from the others."

Londo nods slowly, humming. "Keep them entertained. I will go check on our other VIPs." He turns to exit the luxurious observation lounge, passing Security Chief Vlaruna, who nods politely. The hatch slides shut behind him and clicks.

Wirra reaches the primary computer center. She's met by two Sylbans, each sporting a plasma rifle. She nods to the two men, who return the gesture. One of the men offers her an extra rifle.

After consulting her wristcomm, she presses the access panel. The hatch slides open, and all three beings step inside. A droid with a roller ball for movement approaches. Before she can speak, the three intruders open fire. The two Sylbans move up the spiral ramp, firing into the massive computer core suspended in the center of the space and any droid that gets in their way. Two droids leave the control center to be riddled with high energy plasma. One tips over the railing to fall to the deck below.

The sphere is peppered with energy burns. The bands of data pathways that ring it are blinking and failing rapidly. More and more of the enormous sphere goes dark until the entire device is nothing but a smoking ruin.

The two Sylbans reach the control center, each removing a small canister from their pockets. After tossing them into the room, they rush back down the spiral ramp. Twin thumps echo out of the space a moment before the computer core goes completely dark, followed by the chamber itself.

THE BRIDGE

"Captain, we're dropping out of FTL in two centocks," a junior officer manning the helm station says.

Captain Ramalbong nods. "Understood." She turns to her executive officer. "Everyone settled?"

He nods, the stubby quills on his head bobbing. "Yes, ma'am. VIPs are in Lounge 10, and main dining and the rec deck are quite full." He grins. "Should make for a good show."

The captain nods, smoothing her top and shoulder-mounted rank insignia. She runs both hands over her hair, tightening the tie on her ponytail.

"One centock." The helmsman.

The bridge of the *Galactic Empress* features a floor-to-ceiling, transparent bulkhead similar to the luxury suites tower. This one is inlaid with data threads allowing it to serve as a forward display like other starships possess. Beyond the transparent hull, the stretched-out stars of FTL vanish to reveal the enormous multi-hued nebula ahead.

"It's beautiful," someone on the bridge murmurs.

The enormous luxury vessel drifts toward the nebula, her

powerful sub-light engines powering up. The plan for the day is to sail alongside the nebula for most of the day before adjusting course for their only port of call, the pleasure station Moklan. The major cruise operators had made a joint effort to provide a port of call where they could control the entire experience, as well as all the commerce, for their customers.

"Helm, set our course, please," the captain says.

"Course plotted, ma'am. Locking in," the helmsman replies.

The ship rumbles briefly, causing the captain and several officers to look around. The rumble subsides, then returns as a more violent shaking.

"Report!" the captain barks. She slaps a control on her chair that activates the standard emergency announcement.

"I've lost contact with engineering!" someone shouts.

Another crew member reports, "Several sections of the ship have engaged safety lockouts. The computer is returning several error codes I'm not familiar with."

The helmsman turns. "I've lost maneuvering." The view outside the massive panoramic view screen is slowly turning. Turning deeper toward the nebula.

"Sub-light engines are offline," someone says.

Several consoles go dark, operators raising their hands in shock and looking around.

The captain says, "Quakla, take a team and head to engineering."

When her executive officer doesn't acknowledge the order, she turns to look at him, but he's not there. The nearest bridge hatch is sliding closed.

The overhead speakers come to life. "Attention, passengers and crew of the *Galactic Empress*. It's time to go. Make your way to your assigned lifeboats, now."

"The wurrin?" the captain says, looking at the ceiling. She looks at the empty station her XO would occupy. "Who was that?"

Before anyone can answer, the bridge hatch clanks as locking bolts engage. Just beyond the main hatch, another thicker security hatch clangs shut and locks. Everyone on the bridge looks at the hatch, then turns to the captain.

"Dren," she hisses.

The GNO logo flashes, then fades to a view of Mon-El Furash looking more disheveled than ever. "Good afternoon. I'm Mon-El Furash, and this is breaking news." She's out of breath, and several of her customary earrings are missing. Her right ear is bandaged and bloody. The surrounding air is hazy.

"The Peacekeeper eighth fleet is retreating from the Cuolbongong system, having suffered significant losses. I'm still aboard the *Lancers' Hope*, and as you can likely see, she has suffered significant damage. I'm told the bridge was hit. We're limping as best we can out of the engagement area." She inhales to collect herself. "It's unclear, at least to me, who's in command right now, but someone is. The fleet has turned away from the fourth planet in the system and is making what I can only assume is our best speed to FTL distance."

She puts a hand to one ear, the undamaged one, in order to hear her colleagues in the studio. She shakes her head once. "While I can't speak for Peacekeeper command, I suspect this system will have to be written off for now."

She listens intently. A Peacekeeper in what appears to be fire gear rushes by. She watches the anonymous officer run past, then turns to the camera pickup again. "Yes, that's right. At some point, the Peacekeepers will have to come back here."

PART 3

CHAPTER FIFTEEN

PARTY

"Maxim said to meet him here," Wil says.

The rest of the *Ghost* crew are with him outside an ornate hatch in the forward part of the ship, just under the main recreation deck, currently packed with hundreds of passengers awaiting the ship's next drop from FTL.

Cynthia looks at Zephyr. "You know what's up?"

The Palorian woman shrugs. Bennie looks between the two women, an eyebrow ridge arched.

Wil shrugs and presses the access panel next to the hatch. The hatch slides apart to reveal an observation lounge like several dozen that line the port and starboard sides of the ship, their transparent hull section like warts along the ship's side.

Inside the lounge, streamers crisscross the ceiling and dangle halfway to the deck. Balloons litter the floor, and strung in front of the bulging transparent hull section, a banner reads, CONGRATU-LATIONS!

"What in the seven hells..." Cynthia starts.

Inside the lounge, Maxim is waiting with Nic, the Olop girl from his and Bennie's shuttle, and the white-furred Xelurian, Ankpol.

"What..." Wil says.

"Go in already, you krebnacks," Bennie says, pushing both Wil and Cynthia into the lounge.

Gabe and Zephyr follow, the hatch sliding closed behind them.

Wil walks to Maxim, pulling the big man into a hug. "I can't believe you did this."

Maxim says, "I decided to forgive you for not telling me." Wil chuckles. Maxim continues, "And you owe me. You should have seen the nightmare Zephyr was planning."

Wil releases his friend. "I do owe you. A lot." He slaps his friend's huge shoulder.

Zephyr looks around the lounge. Outside the transparent hull section, the streaks of light of FTL are flying by. The aft wall is lined with a buffet station, and the forward wall has a self-serve bar.

Overhead speakers on every deck, in every compartment of *Galactic Empress*, crackle. "May I have your attention, please? We'll be dropping from FTL in ten microtocks at the edge of Nebula TLC-1990, otherwise known as the Tallgese Nebula."

Wil moves to the bar, grabbing a bottle of something and fluted glasses. He moves around the room distributing drinks. Reaching Ankpol, he hands the Xelurian scientist a drink. "How'd you get involved in this?"

The big polar-bear-spider accepts the fluted drink. "Your Palorian friend tracked me down since you're lacking friends aboard this vessel."

Wil grins. "Well, thank you."

Ankpol inclines his head. "It is my pleasure, and congratulations." He turns and heads toward Gabe, who is standing near the transparent hull.

Nic walks up to Cynthia. "Hi. Congratulations."

Cynthia looks down. "Uh, thanks. Who are you?"

The small Olop bares her teeth. "I'm Bennie's friend."

"Friend?" Bennie repeats, making a face. "That's a stretch."

"You're a stretch," the girl replies.

"What does that mean?" Cynthia asks, then says, "Never mind," and walks away. She reaches Wil. "This is pretty special." Wil nods.

The team and the two people who are friend-adjacent on the ship mingle as they wait for the ship to drop from FTL. Nic is telling Ankpol all about the adventures Bennie and Max had aboard their shuttle. The massive furry being keeps looking at Bennie skeptically.

Outside the transparent bulge, the star lines flare, then shrink back to pinpoints of light. Most of the view is quickly taken up by the swirling gasses of the Tallgese Nebula. Everyone moves to stand near the view port.

The Tallgese Nebula is one of the most colorful nebulas within the borders of the Galactic Commonwealth. The exotic gasses and radiation belts within the gaseous mass give it a kaleidoscopic mix of greens, yellows, oranges, and blues.

Wil puts a hand on the transparent hull. "Damn. I mean, I've seen nebulas before, and we went into the Sugarplum one —"

"Sargul," Zephyr corrects.

"At least he didn't work *space* into it," Bennie says.

Wil ignores them. "But this, this is a whole other thing."

From behind the group, Gabe says, "Nebula TLC-1990 is one of the largest nebular masses on record within the Galactic Commonwealth. Its composition is not completely known due its size and the thormic radiation belts that exist within the nebula."

Maxim looks at his mechanical friend. "Thormic radiation?"

Gabe nods. "Indeed. The nebula is rife with it. Bands that shift and move within gas. Navigation is—"

The deck vibrates, then moves into fully shaking. Nic yelps, then looks around to see if anyone heard her. The shaking subsides, then resumes, feeling different than the first time. The lighting embedded in the ceiling flickers, then goes out. Now the lounge is lit only by the nebula.

"Something is wrong," Cynthia says.

Bennie looks at her, making a face. "That your professional opinion?" She smacks him on the head.

The emergency lighting kicks on, strips along the floor where the walls meet the deck.

"Didn't feel like an attack, and I don't see anything out there," Zephyr says.

The overhead speakers chime. "Attention, please. Attention, please. We are experiencing a minor mechanical problem that will be resolved shortly. Please remain where you are as technical staff endeavor to fix the problem."

"That's not good," Maxim says. He moves to the hatch, but it doesn't open automatically. He presses the button next to it. Nothing. He looks over his shoulder. "Definitely not good."

Bennie walks over and connects his wristcomm to the hatch controls.

"What are you doing?" Nic asks.

"Working, hush," the hacker admonishes. He looks up from his wristcomm. "Someone has issued a lockdown command, shipwide. Every hatch is sealed." The hatch slides open. "Except this one." Bennie beams.

Nic whistles. "Neat."

Bennie looks at his unasked-for sidekick. "You should stay here."

Zephyr looks at Ankpol. "You, too."

The Xelurian looks around. "Would it not be safer to make for our staterooms?"

Bennie shakes his head. "If I'm reading this right—and let's be real, of course I am— they've locked every single hatch down. You won't be able to get into your room." He looks at Nic. "Don't do something stupid. Stay with him."

"I could help you, like on the shuttle," the young Olop offers.

Bennie turns serious. "I appreciate it, but this is what we do. I can't be worried about your safety while trying to save the entire ship." She frowns and nods.

Ankpol says, "I will keep her safe."

"I mean, don't exert yourself. She's expendable," Bennie quips, winking at the surly Olop girl before heading out into the corridor.

From the overhead speakers, an unfamiliar voice says, "Attention, passengers and crew of the *Galactic Empress*. It's time to go. Make your way to your assigned lifeboats, now."

Maxim and Zephyr exchange a look, the former saying, "They locked all the hatches but are driving everyone to lifeboats?"

Gabe offers, "I am detecting nearly a thousand life forms in the recreation area and almost as many in the arboretum. Perhaps our enemy wants hostages, but not too many."

Wil nods. "Makes sense. Several thousand hostages would be hard to manage and wrangle. Let a bunch of them go, and you make your job easier."

As Wil heads toward the ship's bow, he looks back at everyone. "Guess we're earning our fee."

GET OUT

"May I have your attention, please?" overhead speakers hidden throughout the massive recreation deck of the *Galactic Empress* crackle. "We'll be dropping from FTL in ten microtocks at the edge of Nebula TLC-1990, otherwise known as the Tallgese Nebula."

Passengers, nearly a thousand of them, are crowded onto the first level of the recreation deck, with hundreds more crowded onto the two walk/run tracks above the main deck. Ship's crew wind through the crowd offering drinks. The large pool is once again covered to make more floor space.

The *Galactic Empress* drops from FTL several million kilometers from the nebula, which is off the starboard side of the massive cruise liner. The recreation deck, like every other space with a transparent section of hull, is full of passengers. Oohs and ahs erupt from the crowd as the majesty of the nebula slides into full view.

The deck vibrates, then moves into fully shaking. Screams erupt around the room. The shaking subsides, then resumes, feeling different from the first time. Lighting embedded in the underside of the walk/run track above goes out, as does the enormous chandelier floating in the center of the room. The recreation deck is lit only by the nebula. The emergency lighting kicks on. Strips along the floor and under the overhead walk/run tracks illuminate the way to hatches and lifeboats beyond. Hatches have slammed shut, indicators on their control panels blinking red.

The overhead speakers chime. "Attention, please. Attention, please. We are experiencing a minor mechanical problem that will be resolved short—" Screams from the rear of the recreation deck's main floor drown the announcement out.

Armed men and women have appeared at the hatches leading into the recreation deck. A voice booms, "Ladies, gentlemen, and non-binary beings. If you'll kindly make your way out of the recreation area and to your assigned life boat, you'll live."

Screams erupt from all three levels of the space.

On the two decks above, armed beings are ushering passengers down ornate spiral staircases to the main deck.

"Hurry up!" one of the armed beings shouts, eliciting a new round of screaming from the crowd.

The frantic passengers funnel out of the recreation deck, making their way toward the various evacuation stations.

"Woah," Wil hisses. He stumbles back from the corner he just rounded. He pushes the rest of the team back as he does. They are just outside the recreation deck.

"What?" Maxim asks, moving to look past Wil.

"Big crowd," Wil says just as hundreds of frantic passengers begin rounding the corner. The team gets swept up in the torrent of terrified passengers as they rush through the corridor.

"Gabe! Maxim!" Bennie shouts. "Someone tall pick me the grolack up!"

Maxim looks around, trying to find the tiny team member. "Where are you?"

"I have him," Gabe says, pushing his way through the crowd to reach down. He raises a thrashing Brailack out of the mass of people.

"Let go of me, you brute!" a Brailack woman screams. She starts thrashing about, kicks and savage looking jabs raining onto Gabe's torso.

"Wrong Brailack!" Zephyr shouts. She's been pulled to the opposite side of the corridor as the others.

"My apologies." Gabe drops the woman and looks around.

Wil and Cynthia are both looking around. Cynthia points and starts pushing through the crowd.

Gabe is faster, reaching into the crowd toward a small green hand. He raises Bennie out of the mass. "I was gonna start cutting people in half!" the irate Brailack screeches, his beam saber hilt in his other hand.

"That would be...extreme," Gabe says, shuffling the small hacker to his shoulders.

"Let's get our friends off this thing so we can figure out what the wurrin is going on!" Bennie shouts. He slaps a tiny green hand on Gabe's shoulder. "Giddy up."

Zephyr is at the intersection leading toward the lounge they came from. She's waving. "Come on!"

The others make their way toward her, repeating their apologies as they push past people, knocking several over.

Someone further back toward the rear of the mass of frightened passengers screams. A pulse pistol shot rings out.

Wil looks but sees nothing. "Let's go. We gotta get them off this ship before all these folks are gone."

They run the rest of the way to the lounge. Bennie kneels next to the access panel. The hatch slides apart and a glob of sticky white goo shoots out, striking Wil in the face.

He would have screamed, but his face is covered in Xelurian webbing.

"Oh," Zephyr says.

Maxim makes a face.

"Better him than me," Bennie says as Wil falls backwards against the opposite wall, clawing at his face frantically, muffled shouts coming from his web-covered face.

Nic darts out into the corridor, knife in hand, teeth bared.

"Woah, killer," Bennie says, palms out.

She looks up. "Oh, it's you guys."

Ankpol steps out. "My apologies, Wil."

"Mmmpphffrllr." Wil is pulling at the sticky residue covering most of his face. His one visible eye is as big as a saucer.

While Cynthia crouches down to help cut the webbing off of Wil, Maxim says, "You heard the announcement?" Ankpol nods. Maxim continues, "We want you two on a lifeboat. We don't know what's going on, but there are armed beings aboard. The fewer passengers around to be in the way, the better."

The little Olop girl growls. "We wouldn't be in the way."

Bennie shakes his head. "Too risky." He looks at the big Xelurian man. "You okay keeping an eye on her?"

"Yes, though she mentioned her grandmother..."

"Oh, yeah," Maxim says. He shakes his head. "If she was in her stateroom or one of the lounges, she's probably locked in and as safe as can be. If she was in a corridor, she's likely already on a lifeboat." He gestures back the way they came. "Head that way, you'll see the crowd. Hurry."

"This way, dear," Ankpol says, guiding Nic away.

"Mmmffllriiir," Wil says. Cynthia has a utility knife out trying to free him.

Bennie sniggers. "I hope you like bald guys. That stuff ain't coming out of his hair." She turns and glares at him. He backs away.

They hide in the lounge while they try to free Wil of Ankpol's webbing. Once his mouth is clear, he screams. "It got in my mouth!"

Bennie doubles over, laughing. "You...thought it was...pretty funny...when it happened...to me," he wheezes.

Wil lunges for the small hacker but misses.

A PLAN

"You're just going to have to leave it for now," Cynthia says, folding her utility knife back into the multi-tool she carries.

Wil reaches up and touches the top of his head. "Oh man! Like going to sleep with gum in your hair, but a thousand times worse, and grosser."

Maxim looks at Zephyr, who shrugs.

Gabe makes a throat clearing noise. "Perhaps we should get to the task at hand?"

Wil nods. He raises his wristcomm and taps an icon. A second later, he says, "What's going on? Are those your people on the rec deck?"

Everyone leans closer to hear the reply. On the screen of Wil's wristcomm, Security Chief Vlaruna scowls. "I haven't been able to reach anyone yet. But no, whatever is happening, isn't my team. Where are you? I'm locked in one of the observation lounges with a bunch of the VIPs."

Wil looks up. "We're on deck..." He looks around.

"Thirty," Gabe whispers.

Wil nods. "Thirty."

Wil looks around. "You were on the recreation deck. What did you see?" Vlaruna demands from his wrist. He adds. "What's in your hair?"

Wil looks down scowling, but Bennie reaches up and pulls his arm down so he can see the screen. "We weren't on the rec deck, but we saw a bunch of armed beings, that's what we saw! Armed, you drennog!"

"Armed?" the chief of security splutters. "My people aren't armed."

Bennie scoffs. "How are armed goons on your ship?"

Wil snatches his arm out of Bennie's grip. "He's right, Vlaruna. They had rifles. How is that possible? You wouldn't even let us keep our sidearms."

The other man frowns and shakes his head. "I don't know. I haven't been able to reach the security barracks, bridge, or engineering. One of my men called in, but then his comms went out or something, I—" The screen goes black. The logo of the cruise ship, a jeweled crown rotating over a stylized representation of the cruise liner, appears.

Wil slams his fist against his thigh. "Damnit! Comms are cut." He looks around. "Local comms." Nods all around as everyone updates their wristcomms to use the local mesh set up that Bennie and Gabe built into everyone's devices. It won't be perfect, especially in such a tight space with mechanical and computer systems everywhere, but it will be better than nothing.

Maxim looks around. They've moved to the corridor outside the observation lounge he rented for the engagement party. The sounds of terrified passengers have faded to nothing. "Definitely a concerted effort. Comms route through the computer center."

The rumbling that they've been feeling in the deck subsides.

"Lifeboats are away," Cynthia says.

Gabe says, "I suggest we split up. If engineering has been taken, the ship could be at risk. If our course takes us into the nebula, the ship will be destroyed."

Maxim nods. "I'll go with him."

Wil nods. "Okay. We'll go see if we can help upstairs."

Maxim inclines his head. "Don't get dead." He looks at Gabe. "Come on, big guy."

Bennie raises a hand. "Uh, Gabe is the only one with guns."

Wil shrugs. "He's also our engineer." He winks. "Besides, we've got the mighty Bennie, Knight of Pin Cushionolopis, vanquisher of rancors, Magogs, and whatever other shit you made up and charged people to hear."

Bennie frowns but moves his hand to the hilt of his beam saber. "It's Plentallus, drennog."

Maxim clears his throat, withdrawing a small holdout blaster from the back of his waistband.

Wil's eye bulge. "What the hell?"

Cynthia coughs into her hand, slipping a pair of knives from inside each of her boots.

Wil turns to Zephyr, the question plain on his face. She smiles, sliding a twin of Maxim's petite blaster out of an internal pocket in the jacket she's wearing. The blasters are small, likely a limited number of shots, and only lethal up close.

"You guys!" Wil shouts. Bennie chuckles. "I thought we talked about this?" He looks around. "I swear to God!" Bennie doubles over, laughing. Wil's cheeks burn. "Did anyone bring me one?" He holds his hand out, palm up. No one says anything or deposits a weapon in his open hand. He points down the corridor. "Hate you guys. Go!"

Bennie is still laughing, so Wil smacks him on the head, mumbling something about no one respecting him.

Once Maxim and Gabe round a corner, Wil looks at the rest of the team. "Bridge?"

Bennie points halfway down the corridor, a hatch with an orange outline. "Service stairs." Everyone follows him. He looks over his shoulder. "Why am I in the lead?" He slows down to let Wil pass him, only to be shoved forward.

Wil smiles. "You have a weapon."

Bennie tuts. "Everyone has one but you."

Wil waves it away. "I'm not the one charging people for made up stories. Time to earn it, hero."

Zephyr watches them, then says, "What is this, a learning opportunity?" She shoves Bennie aside and pushes the hatch to the staircase open. She leans in. "Clear."

Wil looks up as he enters. "Lotta stairs."

NEWSCAST

"Good evening. I'm Klor'Tillen, and this is GNO News Break." The Brailack journalist is in an observation lounge looking out over a cavernous control center. He raises a hand to the room behind him. "I'm overlooking the central space control operations center for the Hub. Details are scarce, but from what I've been able to gather, something has gone wrong onboard the *Galactic Empress.*"

Below the reporter, the operations center is a hive of activity. Beings of all sorts are moving from console to console, consulting, often yelling at, each other. Klor'Tillen turns to the camera again. "What we do know so far is that the primary beacon stopped transmitting a few tocks ago and hasn't come back online. The ship reached the Tallgese Nebula where she was scheduled to drift for a few tocks before continuing on to the pleasure station Moklan." The Brailack journalist inhales as he listens to someone talking in his earpiece, which sticks comically out of his head as he has no external ears. He shakes his head. "No, Megan, as far as we know so far, this has nothing to do with the ongoing war near the outer edges of the GC."

He takes a breath, then continues, "As yet, the ship isn't late for her arrival at pleasure station Moklan. We here at GNO certainly hope the crew and passengers of the *Empress* are okay, and I'll be here to keep you informed as this situation develops."

220

CHAPTER SIXTEEN

CLIMB

Cynthia pats Wil's stomach as she passes. "More stairs wouldn't hurt."

Wil puts his own hand on his midsection. "Hey, I've been working out with Maxim more."

Bennie looks his friend up and down. "Keep working."

Wil shoves the Brailack up the stairs as Zephyr closes the hatch behind them.

They hear gunfire and screaming as they pass the hatch on the same deck as the second level walk/run track of the recreation area. They climb the stairs until they reach the highest deck possible before the command tower break. The command module has a separate stairwell air-gapped with a corridor.

Zephyr says, "We have to cross over to the service stairs that serve the command tower."

Wil eases the hatch open as slowly and quietly as he can, thankful that this is the first voyage of the *Empress* and not the four-hundredth. The hinges are well oiled and maintained. He leans out to look up and down the corridor. "Clear." He steps out.

The corridor, while open to the public, doesn't service much of the ship so is entirely devoid of passengers. There are no state rooms or observation lounges. The only hatches, all locked, are labeled as storage. The corridor connects vital parts of the ship and was meant to offer a fast way to walk the length of the ship. They reach an intersection, the cross corridor running the width of the ship, and almost collide with a very frantic Mr. Londo.

The stunned Red Nova employee stammers, "What is happening? I can't contact the bridge...or, well, anyone!"

Zephyr looks at him. "Were you just waiting here?"

The scarecrow-limbed Harrith man looks around. "What? Oh, no. Well, yes, I guess. I stepped off the lift to transfer to the command deck lift, and it closed behind me and the lift to the bridge won't open." Londo gestures around the corridor. "Not much in this particular section of ship." He shrugs. "I've been hoping someone would show up." He looks at the team. "What's happening?"

Zephyr shrugs. "Honestly, no idea. We saw some armed goons ushering everyone out of the recreation deck to lifeboats. They locked your head of security in one of the observation lounges."

"There are one hundred security officers aboard this ship," the frightened business man says. "How...I don't... Gah!" He throws his hands in the air. "This will ruin Red Nova!"

Cynthia says, "Can you think of any reason someone would do this?"

Londo shakes his head. "No, the ship launching was a big deal. Our stock had been lagging due to the construction delays. The investors were beginning to revolt. Some threatened pulling out, demanding their money back." He bites his lip as he rubs his palms on his slacks. "We persuaded them to stay on until launch. This cruise and the dozens that are booked after would make our investors whole and put Red Nova back on top."

Wil steps back as Maxim reports in. "Copy that," he says, moving back to the others. "Who would stand to gain if the ship is destroyed?"

"Destroyed?!" Londo collapses.

Bennie looks at the unconscious man. "So, do we just leave him? I'm not carrying him. I vote we leave him."

Londo's eyes flutter. "What happened?"

"You fainted," Bennie says, his annoyance obvious.

The Harrith man sits up and looks around. "So, not a dream?"

Wil points at Bennie. "He look like a dream?"

"Afraid not," Zephyr says, ignoring Wil. Londo groans. She extends a hand to help him up off the deck.

As Londo gets his feet under him, he turns to Wil. "I guess it's good that you're here."

Wil beams. "Yup. This is our jam, after all."

"Jam?" Londo asks. He looks at the others. "Like a snack?"

Wil shakes his head. "Never mind."

"So, you have a plan?" the businessman asks.

"Oh, well..." Wil starts.

Bennie looks up at Wil. "Yeah, what's the plan, boss?" He's grinning. Wil makes a move to slap him on the head, causing him to duck. He moves to run a hand through his hair, but stops when he remembers that his hand would likely get stuck in the leftover Xelurian webbing matting his hair.

Londo looks at Zephyr, who shrugs.

Cynthia says, "You didn't try the stairs to the bridge?" She points to the hatch with the orange outline.

Londo shrugs. "Locked."

Bennie smiles. "I have a key." He walks to the hatch, the snap hiss of his beam saber punctuating the silence.

"What the—?" Londo stammers.

Wil rests a hand on the man's shoulder. "It's fine. He's a professional, kinda."

"Mostly," Cynthia adds.

"Sorta," Zephyr chimes in.

"Screw all of you," Bennie says over the hum of his blade. He jabs the blade straight into the hatch. Metal bubbles around the blade, turning yellow-white as it runs down the hatch, cooling before it reaches the deck. Bennie slowly works the blade up, through the locking mechanism. Something inside the hatch makes a noise, and the hatch pops free of the frame.

The purple blade disengages, and Bennie steps clear. "Ta da."

Wil walks to the hatch, patting Bennie on head as he passes. The Brailack swats his hand away. "Shall we?" Wil asks, pushing the hatch open.

The stairwell up to the command section is not empty. Wil falls back as energized plasma rains down.

"Oh, shit!" he shouts, stumbling back.

ENGINEERING

Maxim and Gabe head off toward the rear of the ship. The first thing they find is that the lifts that zip around the interior of the kilometers-long ship are all locked down. "Great," Maxim grouses. He looks at his friend. "Fancy a jog?" He takes off.

Gabe easily catches up to him. "I could, quite literally, do this forever." He flashes his uncanny grin. They pass dozens of passengers, all confused and worried, making their way to evacuation stations. When a group of Tleb passengers blocks the corridor, Maxim says, "Please excuse us. You should be making your way to the escape pods."

"What's going on, bean pole?" one of them, a man in a floral print shirt with a sort of cartoonishly oversized hat, demands. The other canine-like beings all plant their tiny little hands on their hips. Moving out of the way doesn't seem to be on the agenda. The leader of the group adds, "We were going to meet friends in Observation Lounge 14, but the hatch is sealed. Then that announcement came on."

Maxim looks at Gabe. "Bennie was right. They locked all the hatches."

Gabe inclines his head. "Let's not tell him." He holds up a finger. "It is, however, a prudent tactical decision. A large percentage of this vessel's passengers were likely gathered to watch our arrival at the nebula. Sealing the observation areas reduces their potential enemies significantly. Evacuating the others clears the ship of obstacles."

Maxim rubs his face. "And a disaster is believable if not everyone survives." Gabe nods.

"What? Who? What are you two giants talking about?" The half-meter-tall chihuahua man demands, growling. Nearby, the sound of a lifeboat rumbling on its track echoes.

Maxim looks around, then kneels down to be closer to eye level with the group. "We don't know much, but something is going on. We saw armed men and women near the recreation deck, ushering everyone to lifeboats." He points down the corridor. "We're heading to engineering. You all should get to a lifeboat."

Gabe nods. "You will be far safer in a lifeboat, especially if shooting starts."

"When." Maxim adds under his breath.

The small pack of passengers yip as one. One of them says, "Shooting?"

Another says, "What about our friends in the observation lounge?"

Gabe says, "They will most likely be safe for the time being."

"Most likely," the large hat wearing man repeats.

"The time being?" Another adds.

Maxim stands up. "We have to go."

The pair find another service stairwell, and after four flights, find their first casualty. Maxim taps his earpiece. "Found one of Vlaruna's people. Stairwell..." He looks around.

"Twenty-two," Gabe offers.

"Twenty-two. Dead Quilant," Maxim finishes.

"Copy that," Wil says.

They continue down the stairs until Gabe stops, his balled fist held up. Maxim looks at him and hears Gabe's voice in his earpiece. "Two people have entered the stairwell. Four levels below."

Maxim looks down as two Palorians move to the next level. He leans back quickly and looks at Gabe. The droid inclines his head and vaults over the railing. Maxim's mouth falls open.

As Gabe falls, he guides his trajectory to land on the landing right in front of the two Palorians. Each is armed with a plasma rifle. He smiles. "Hello." Before they can react, he raises both arms, shifting them to blaster, firing a single shot into the face of each one. The ruined bodies fall backward, clattering down the stairs to the landing below them.

When Maxim catches up, he looks at the bodies. "Gross." He reaches down, pulling a rifle out of the hands of one of the bodies. "This is more like it." He slips his small holdout blaster back into the waistband of his pants. Checking the charge on the rifle, he nods. "Let's go."

Many, many flights of stairs later, Gabe and Maxim are standing at the main entry hatch to engineering. Gabe places a hand on the access control, tendrils snaking out of his fingertips, the ends pulsing blue. The thin filaments slide under the panel, through every gap they can find.

Gabe turns to look at his friend. "This is not good."

Maxim's eyebrows rise. "What's up?"

"Someone with significant access has locked engineering down." He frowns. The access panel is displaying lines of code. Gabe adds, "And has killed the engineering staff."

Maxim inhales. "Grolack. Can you get the hatch open?"

Gabe turns his attention back to the control panel. "Not quickly. This hatch was designed to secure main engineering against attack, catastrophic atmosphere loss, and the ship-against-reactor breaches. I suspect every bulkhead between us and engineering is reinforced." Gabe makes a disgruntled noise. "They have convinced the local system that all three of those scenarios are taking place. Bennie and his beam saber would be useful." The filaments withdraw as Gabe stands.

"Never tell him that." Maxim says, then asks, "Wasn't the Chief Engineer a droid?"

Gabe nods. "Indeed. I do not know how they disabled Hogarth and his crew."

Captain Ramalbong pounds a fist on the hatch leading off the bridge. "Dren!" she repeats for possibly the ninth or thirtieth time, her crew has stopped counting.

The access panel next to the door is a mess of wires. An ensign, a Kilden woman, looks up. "I'm sorry, ma'am." The jumble of components sparks, forcing the young officer to fall backwards. She runs a hand over her stubby head quills. "I don't know what First Officer Quakla did, but it's not something I can undo on this side."

Ramalbong growls. She has no idea what her XO is up to or how he has managed to override her security codes.

The command deck of the *Galactic Empress* is two-and-a-half decks and larger than even the luxury staterooms in the egg-shaped tower aft of the bridge, behind the arboretum dome. The upper level, where Captain Ramalbong and her command staff work, is joined to the decks below by curved staircases on either side.

Ramalbong looks around the bridge. Yesterday she was on top of the world, the youngest female captain in the Red Nova fleet. Her previous command, the *Stellar Princess,* had been hers for nearly five standard cycles. The *Galactic Empress* is something she's fought and worked for. And now someone is ruining it. "Dren!" she hisses.

A Trollack woman comes up the port stairs. "Captain, lifeboats are deploying." She's a secondary navigation specialist. She points a webbed hand toward the forward transparent view screen. Thankfully the designers chose a less practical transparent option over display screens. Even with the computer down and most displays offline, the two story transparent hull allows for a wide field of view.

Ramalbong looks out through the massive transparent section of hull. Along the edges of the kilometers-long ship, lifeboats are jetting away from the ship and the dangerous nebula that is much closer than Polandra Ramalbong is comfortable with.

She looks at the Trollack officer. "We're still drifting?"

"Yes, ma'am."

"Still no access to the maneuvering thrusters?" The Trollack woman shakes her head.

Ramalbong slams her palm against the bulkhead again. Beyond, the transparent viewport lifeboats are departing the ship, their low-powered thrusters pushing them away from the ship and the nebula.

"Hopefully, the comm gear on those lifeboats works," she says to no one in particular. She walks down the stairs to the lower bridge. The crew members are all manning their stations, despite the fact that every console on the bridge is either entirely offline or throwing error codes while not responding to input. The entire bridge is cut off from the mighty cruise ship. "What is going on here?"

"Captain, I have an idea," one of the junior officers says from the back section of the lower bridge. An engineering watch stander, if the captain remembers correctly.

"What is it?" she asks.

The young man, a Sylban, his foliage lush and green, says, "The engineering crawl spaces."

The captain runs a hand over her blonde hair, still pulled tightly into a ponytail. "What of them?"

"I think we can get to one from here." He points to the deck a few meters forward of the station he's seated at. An open section of the deck.

"I didn't think there was an access point on the bridge," Ramalbong says, looking behind her to the expanse of deck the young officer is indicating.

He nods. "You're right, ma'am. But if we can get through the deck plating, there's a crawl space running fore to aft right under us. It should turn ninety degrees near the back of the tower and go straight down to the main section of the ship."

The captain claps her hands. "Well, let's get to it."

"Wil, we're locked out of engineering. At least for now," Maxim reports.

"Okay, yeah, we'll head back to you." He turns to Gabe and nods.

The two head back the way they came but stop when Gabe says, "Someone is coming."

They duck into a side corridor as six armed men and women strut past, followed by an Olop man. The Olop says, "Look around, someone was sniffing around the access panel." He checks a tablet, looking from the screen to the access panel next to the hatch.

Maxim looks up at Gabe, who shrugs. The two back down the corridor and turn a corner just as one of the mercenaries steps into view.

"Hey!" the Trenbal man shouts, his tail swishing. He raises a rifle to fire but is cut down by Maxim. Most of the Palorian man's shots go wild as he runs, but two strike the pebble-skinned Trenbal in the head, nearly vaporizing it. The body flops to the deck.

Gabe takes the lead as they dash down a corridor. This low on the ship, the corridors are more utilitarian than those up above. Few passengers, if any, find their way down this low.

Shouts from behind them precede a plasma bolt that strikes a conduit overhead, rupturing it, spewing a brown sludge in a spray.

"Gross!" Maxim shouts as several blobs of the stuff strike his shoulder and head.

They turn down another corridor, now at a full run. Maxim is breathing heavily. "Where to?" Gabe stops, his optic sensors glowing. He turns. "There." More plasma rounds strike the wall and ceiling where they were just standing. Several of the armed men and women they saw earlier are hot on their heels.

The hatch Gabe stops in front of has a sign over it, *Main Hydroponics*. He reaches for the access panel. The indicator is red: locked. Rather than attempt to hack the door, the powerful droid rips the panel off and jams his hand into the internal mechanism. The hatch slides open as a plasma round strikes the nearby bulkhead, leaving a scorch mark.

The two duck into the hydroponic bay as Maxim fires a spray of super charged plasma down the corridor.

As they dart between two large growing frames, Maxim says, "I don't think I hit anyone."

"You did not," Gabe says, pointing down another aisle between frames. Their pursuers follow them in. The hydroponic bay is a multi-deck space with a curved ceiling. Green tinted growth medium overflowing with lush vegetation fills aisle after aisle.

The frame behind them explodes. Maxim spins to return fire, destroying two more frames and eliciting a scream of pain from somewhere close to the main hatch.

Gabe switches to combat mode. "You hit one that time." His left arm snaps up and fires off a blast. Another scream.

"Three left," Maxim says.

"Plus, the Olop," Gabe offers. He spins, bringing his right arm to bear, unleashing several plasma blasts. Hydroponic frames explode, spilling growth medium everywhere. He turns to Maxim. "Two."

From the top of one of the massive frames, a small furry blur lands on top of Gabe. Sparks fly as the small man slashes and stabs at Gabe with two diminutive knives.

Gabe's torso clicks, then begins to spin at the waist. Maxim steps back, then spins as one of the mercenaries comes around a growth frame. Both men fire at the same time. The mercenary falls to the ground.

"Amateur," Maxim says, turning to look at the scorch mark on the frame next to him. He turns back to Gabe to see his mechanical friend lying on the ground. The Olop he was fighting with is nowhere to be seen.

He kneels next to his friend. "You okay?"

Gabe's left optic sensor flickers, then returns to full functionality. The right remains dark. He sits up. "That man is a cunning fighter." He rubs the side of his head until his other optic sensor engages. "He escaped somehow."

"By my count, there's one more in here," Maxim says, grunting to help lift his friend from the deck.

They hear a hatch open, then close. Gabe turns to Maxim. "Now there are zero. I believe we may be locked in." He turns and heads for the hatch they came in through. Maxim follows, rifle at the ready.

CHAPTER SEVENTEEN

The lower deck of the bridge of the *Galactic Empress* now resembles a war zone. The Sylban officer has led the effort to rip up the carpeting to expose the bare metal beneath.

Captain Ramalbong looks on. Her gaze drifts to the almost three-story transparent viewport at the front of the bridge. Her senior officers are still up on the main command deck, essentially doing nothing but monitoring their consoles, just in case.

Someone shouts in triumph, drawing the captain back to the task at hand. The Sylban officer and several others have used whatever tools they could scrounge up to pry a piece of the deck plating up.

Captain Ramalbong walks over and looks over the shoulder of a Tleb lieutenant. "That doesn't look like an engineering crawl space," she says.

The lieutenant looks up, his tiny hairless hands smoothing the hair between his ears. "Yes, ma'am."

The Sylban officer says, "I'm not sure why we're not seeing it." He leans down to examine the equipment bundle they have exposed. "Oh," comes from the opening.

"Oh?"

Before the young officer can answer, the bridge lighting changes. The pleasant soft-white lighting fades to a dull red.

The Sylban officer scrambles up out of the opening. "Oh, no."

Losing her patience, the captain demands, "Someone say something other than 'oh no.'"

The Sylban looks at her, his foliage rustling. "The engineering crawl space isn't there because during construction they made a change to the bridge section."

The floor shakes, causing several officers to scream. Ramalbong motions, her palms down. "Everyone, calm down." She turns to the engineering watch stander. "Explain."

"The bridge is a lifeboat. I don't know why, but they did not update it in the data files I was looking at. But it explains why there isn't a crawl space there." The deck lurches. "And I don't know why, but it's jettisoning. Now."

Outside, the view shifts almost imperceptibly. The lighting flickers for a moment, then returns to its soft pulsing red, now running on battery power.

"Did you—" the captain starts to ask.

The Sylban engineering officer raises both hands. "No, ma'am. Nothing we did here," he points to the opening in the floor, "would have triggered it. It must have been a timer or something."

The view outside is shifting more rapidly now. The bridge module's automated navigation system is using tiny maneuvering thrusters to home in on the other lifeboats, now millions of kilometers away. It's going to be a slow trip.

"Dren," Captain Ramalbong hisses as the view outside shows the rest of the *Empress*. The sides are open where life boats have ejected.

"At least if the ship continues into the nebula, we won't die," the Tleb junior officer offers, shrugging. He backs away under the glare of his captain.

"Who the hell is firing on us?" Zephyr shouts, catching Wil.

He looks up at her as he regains his feet. "Sorry, didn't get a good look. I don't think there's more than one or two, though."

"You think?" Bennie quips.

Cynthia looks down at the Brailack hacker. "We could toss you in and see how many shoot at you."

"Is it Pick on Brailacks Day?" the team hacker grouses.

Wil waves his hand. "We gotta get up to the bridge. Thoughts?"

Londo looks up and down the corridor. "This is the main transfer deck. Whoever is up there has to come down here to get to the rest of the ship."

"Maybe they're just there to keep us from getting to the bridge?" Bennie offers.

"Possible," Zephyr offers.

Cynthia nods. "The bridge is a key facility. Keeping it secured is likely a top priority."

Wil frowns. "Okay, we know some whys, still waiting on a how."

Bennie sighs, "Follow me." He pushes open the hatch and jumps into the stairwell as his beam saber ignites. Plasma bolts rain down.

He deflects those closest to hitting him, mostly. He misses one bolt. It burns into his forearm, eliciting a yelp.

Zephyr blinks, then steps through the hatch, her pistol aimed up. Stepping in, she fires twice, then twice more. The return fire stops. She looks at Bennie. The hacker is panting. He deactivates the beam saber and leans forward, wheezing. He holds up the arm that took the glancing shot. His sleeve is scorched and underneath it, his skin is reddened and crusty.

"You okay?" Zephyr asks.

"I'll be fine," he replies.

Wil steps into the stairwell and looks up. "Nicely done," he says, patting the still panting Bennie on the shoulder as he climbs the stairs. He looks at Zephyr. "Good shootin', tex."

"Tex?" she repeats. No one offers an explanation.

When they reach the topmost landing, Londo looks at their attacker. "That's Abrol Quakla, the executive officer." He nudges the body with the toe of his expansive dress shoe. "I think he's dead."

Zephyr tuts. "I should hope so."

Cynthia fires a shot into the body, causing the others to jump. When they look at her, she shrugs. "Now, we're sure."

"Dark," Wil says.

She turns to Wil. "More than two, huh?" He shrugs.

Just inside the hatch, near the dead officer's body is an open wall panel. Wires are dangling out, several spliced together haphazardly. Two of the wires are connected to a small device of unknown purpose. Cynthia lifts some of the wires causing sparks to erupt from the open panel. She lets the bundle fall back against the wall.

The service stairwell opens up at landing with a heavy-duty hatch, open at the moment. Beyond it is the bridge reception deck. Given the pleasure cruise nature of the *Galactic Empress*, the bridge reception deck features the plushest carpet Wil has ever seen, with wood-paneled walls and ornate wall sconces for light. The trappings of the spacefaring vessel—emergency lighting and gravity failure handholds, to name two—are well hidden.

Ahead would be the equally ornate hatch to the bridge, two massive wood panels inlaid with gold and silver metals. A circular porthole adorns each panel. What Wil and the others see is the emergency hatch, which is several inches of starship hull-grade metal. That hatch only deploys in emergencies.

The deck rumbles slightly, causing everyone to reach out for the nearest thing to grab ahold of for balance. Mr. Londo plants a hand on Bennie's head but steps back when the Brailack hacker swats at him. Several loud clunks echo from somewhere inside the structure.

Cynthia looks around, then points at the opening they came through. Just inside the hatch is a small sensor unit. Not standard equipment. She points to the open panel and the bundle of wires.

"Well, damn," Wil says. He turns and points to the bridge hatch. None of them have a hope of forcing open. He looks at Bennie. "Any chance—"

"None. Zero," the Brailack replies. "The regular hatch, sure." He hitches his thumb over his shoulder. "Internal stuff like that, yeah." He inclines his head to the emergency hatch, his hand going to his belt. "That's starship hull. No way. My saber would overheat long before I even made a hole."

The deck rumbles again. Londo looks around, then groans. "Um, the bridge can be jettisoned in an emergency. It is its own lifeboat. We must have triggered a booby trap. Or something." He points to a faint seam in the floor, the walls, and the ceiling. The room is two parts with the far section containing the bridge hatch.

"Uh," Cynthia says.

"Or something?" Zephyr asks.

"Booby," Wil repeats, holding a fist out to Bennie, who smirks and offers his own tiny green fist.

Zephyr and Cynthia both roll their eyes. The former says, "Yeah, let's not be standing here!" She points to the hatch they came through. A small panel on the ceiling opens to reveal a smaller lighting unit, which immediately begins to swirl with an orange warning light.

"Oh, hell," Wil hisses, pushing Londo toward the large open hatch, which has begun to slide closed.

The group retreats back into the service stairwell landing, the hatch closing just as Zephyr makes it through. She turns to the group. "So, the XO was in on whatever this is." Everyone nods. "But what is this? Why eject the bridge?"

Londo rubs his face. "This can't be happening." He looks at Wil and the others. "If this ship is lost, it'll destroy Red Nova."

Bennie leans over to Zephyr. "He paid in advance, right?" She jabs her hip out, sending him stumbling away, but nods.

"Why would losing the ship ruin Red Nova?" Wil asks. "I mean, don't get me wrong, you hired us to make sure that doesn't happen and we're gonna do everything we can to make sure it doesn't. But she's insured, right? You have other ships."

Londo gives him a flat stare. "You're doing a bang-up job so far. We're locked out of engineering, likely the computer center, as well, since internal comms are out. Oh, and the bridge is now drifting away somewhere. Most passengers are locked in their staterooms or the observation areas. Those that aren't are in life boats, who knows where." He leans against the wood-paneled wall. "The *Empress* is insured, yes. However, the policy was part of our investment package. In the event the ship is lost, the policy pays out investors first."

Cynthia raises her hand. "Didn't Gabe say that the nebula was super bad news? Like if we went into it?"

Zephyr nods. "Yeah, the thormic radiation would make pretty quick work of the hull. Fendurrium essentially breaks down when exposed to high doses of thormic radiation."

Wil inhales. "Anyone remember how far we were from the nebula when this started?"

PUZZLE PIECES

"Well, this is wonderful," Maxim says, making a slow spin, taking in the hydroponics bay. He looks at Gabe. "Ideas?" The hatch they entered through has been pushed closed and fused into its frame.

Gabe's right hand clicks and whirs as the hand rotates and slides into the forearm. A plasma cutter tilts and slides into place. "Just the one." He kneels next to the locking mechanism, holding the two halves of the hatch together. He looks over his shoulder. "This should not take long."

Maxim moves to the nearest mercenary, a Malkorite. The dead man is wearing a jumpsuit similar to that worn by crew members of the *Empress*. In fact, it's the exact jumpsuit worn by the lower deck crew members, the ones the public doesn't see. He empties the dead man's pockets. The dead man has no wristcomm, and his elephantine ears are free of commsets.

"Hey, Gabe. Look at this," Maxim says, holding up a damaged older model comm device. "Think you can decrypt it?"

Gabe looks over his shoulder, his plasma cutter still tracing a line through the hatch. "Possibly." He turns his attention back to his work.

Maxim searches the other mercenaries that made it into the room. Each is similarly equipped. No wristcomms, nor ear pieces. No ident-cards. Just the handheld comm unit, encrypted. The one he has is the only mostly functional unit.

The hatch groans, then slides apart, the two edges of the two halves still glowing white hot. The two exit the hydroponics bay, weapons at the ready, but find the corridor empty. This low in ship, the sound of lifeboats ejecting is faint, at best.

Maxim looks around. "Where to?"

"The computer center," the droid replies, extending a hand for Maxim to give him one of the communications devices.

"Why?" Maxim asks, dropping one of the captured units into the palm of his friend. He pockets the other just in case.

"I am worried about someone I met there, but also, with engineering not exactly accessible, the computer core gives us a chance to find out what is happening. I can attempt to tap into the ship's internal and external sensors."

"Good enough for me. Lead the way," Maxim says.

The computer center is almost ten decks above the main entrance to engineering. "I need to do more stair climbs," Maxim puffs as they reach the landing of the service stairs. He drops his hands to his knees.

Gabe places a hand on the hatch. "There are people in the corridor beyond."

"Armed?"

"I cannot be certain." Gabe tilts his head, then looks at Maxim, shaking his head. Maxim takes a few more deep breaths, then pulls his borrowed rifle off his back, pulling the charging lever. A low whine comes from the weapon.

Gabe grabs the handle on the hatch and pulls it open. Maxim lunges out into the corridor, taking aim at a group of crew members. Gabe steps into the corridor as the screams are still rising in pitch.

Maxim lowers the rifle. "Sorry, sorry!" He tries to calm the crowd. "What are you all doing here? Why haven't you evacuated?"

A Stilten moves forward, their mandibles clicking. "Most of us were on our way to our duty station when whatever is happening started." They click some more. "What is happening? Why are you armed? Who are you?"

Maxim pushes his rifle all the way to his back. "We're private contractors, hired to help with security should something happen." He gestures around him. "We're still not sure exactly what is going on, but we're on it." He looks at the assorted beings. "Have you seen anyone else, armed?"

A Kilden woman raises a hand. "I was on level 37 and saw an armed Olop man. He was heading forward."

Maxim nods. "Okay, good to know. Anyone else?"

"Was he with you?" someone asks.

Gabe shakes his head. "No. We believe he is one of the perpetrators. Have any of you been in contact with the bridge or your duty stations?" Everyone physically capable of shaking their heads, does. "As I suspected. Please get yourselves to your assigned lifeboats." The beings nod and hurry off.

He and Maxim push past the group. The big man looks at the droid. "Do you know how many have gotten off the ship?"

Gabe turns. "Nope."

"Nope?"

Gabe unleashes his disturbing grin. "Indeed."

Maxim just shakes his head, smiling.

"Good evening. I'm Klor'Tillen, and this is GNO News Break." The Brailack journalist is still in the main operations center at the Hub. "We have recent developments in the mysterious loss of contact with the *Galactic Empress*. She's now officially late arriving at pleasure station Moklan."

The screen cuts to a close-up image of one of the large monitors behind Klor'Tillen. It shows several lines of text, each with *GE-LB* and then a series of numbers. "We've learned that the luxury liner has launched multiple lifeboats. Their transponders automatically activate on launch. Unfortunately while the transponders are powerful enough to attract help from a distance, the communications systems are meant only for lifeboat to lifeboat, so we have no idea what is going on out there."

The image returns to the Brailack man. "The positive in all this, is that now we know where the *Empress* is. It appears that the ship made it to its designated stopover at the Tallgese nebula, and stopped there. Red Nova has dispatched a ship to investigate. The Peacekeepers have been notified, but with the war raging in the border regions, it's unknown if they will send a ship anytime soon." He steps out of the way as a staffer rushes past. "We should know more once the rescue ship has arrived."

CHAPTER EIGHTEEN

LAYERS, LIKE AN ONION

Wil and the others listen to Maxim and Gabe update them. Mr. Londo looks at each of them before demanding, "What? What is happening?"

Wil looks at the lanky business man. "Sorry. Maxim and Gabe are heading to the computer center to see if Gabe can get tied into the sensors. Engineering is locked down as tight as the bridge...was. They encountered some mercenary types lead by an Olop guy. The mercs are down. The leader got away and was last seen moving forward."

"Think the six they took out are part of the group we heard ushering folks to the lifeboats?" Cynthia wonders.

Zephyr shakes her head. "Unlikely. Unless they have a way around the lockout, they'd be limited to service stairs, same as us. Lot of ground to cover."

Bennie nods along.

Wil asks, "Mr. Londo, what can you tell us about the lifeboats?"

The Harrith man frowns, then reaches up to rub his chin. "I... what would you like to know?"

"If I remember the safety briefing for—"

"You paid attention to that?" Bennie interrupts.

Wil looks at him, then returns to Londo. "Yes, maritime safety is important. Anyway, they're arranged along evac decks every dozen decks or so." Londo nods. "The passengers' wristcomms or other devices would guide them to their designated escape pod." More nodding from Londo. "Can we reach them on comms?"

Londo shakes his head. "I don't think so. The lifeboat comm systems are designed to talk to each other and broadcast a distress beacon. They don't have a general use transceiver."

"Is there a way to tell who's still on the ship? How many lifeboats are still aboard?" Cynthia asks.

Londo shrugs. "I think so, but that would all go through the main computer and the bridge. With the bridge separated and assuming the computer is offline..." He rubs his eyes. "I don't know. I don't think so."

Wil is rubbing his chin. "So, we can't issue the recall. The ship's computer can, though." Londo nods again.

Zephyr says, "We know that most of the investors and VIPs are locked in a lounge, the one with Chief Vlaruna."

Londo makes a forlorn noise as he makes a slow circle, spinning in place, mumbling about investors dying.

Wil grabs him, pulling him to a stop. "Gabe and Max will figure out what's up. For now, our next move should be to get Chief Vlaruna and the others out and to a lifeboat. Then his people in the barracks."

Cynthia and Zephyr smile. "Reinforcements," they say in unison.

Bennie looks at them, frowning.

Wil motions everyone toward the stairs. "Okay, let's go spring Chief Cranky-Pants."

As they work their way down the stairs, Londo is mumbling to himself. Finally, Bennie snaps. "What are you doing? Speak up!"

The group pauses on the next landing. Londo looks at the others. "Sorry. I was thinking about this whole thing and why it's happening."

"Ransom?" Bennie offers.

"That was my guess," Cynthia agrees.

Londo shakes his head. "I don't think so. I mean, yes, some of the VIPs and investors surely have kidnapping policies, wealthy family, and businesses—but the rest of us, unlikely."

"No one would pay to get him back." Bennie points at Wil. He makes a sickening screech as he falls down the next flight of stairs while Wil brushes his hands on his pants.

"The ship?" Zephyr asks, ignoring Wil and Bennie's antics.

Londo watches Bennie hit the landing below in horror, then turns to the others, shaking his head. "It has to be about insurance. The ship itself is certainly worth a fortune, but a bit conspicuous. Her insurance value, however..."

Zephyr holds her hand up. "But all the investors are onboard, right?" Londo nods. "And locked in the observation lounge with Chief Vlaruna. Wouldn't one need to be alive after this to get the insurance pay out?"

Londo nods, then stops. "Well, not all." He ticks his long thin fingers. "Misters Quistic and Folakshima and Miss Fev'Ti were not in the observation lounge. I was actually going to check on them when all this started. I could not find Fev'Ti but found Mr. Folakshima. He got himself lost and was in another lounge, enjoying the show."

"And Quistic?" Zephyr asks.

"You think the two of them are involved?" Cynthia presses.

Londo shakes his head again. "No. I can't imagine them working together. They barely seem able to stand each other in meetings. Quistic and Fev'Ti have been especially vocal about their investments not returning anything yet. It's been all I could do, keeping them in line."

Wil smiles. "Yeah, Quistic chatted me up to complain about it, too. He really wants a return on this. Guess he lost a ton as a Farsight investor. There seemed to be something he wanted to ask me, but he never got a chance."

Bennie says, "Sounds like motive."

Wil shakes his head. "Okay, let's go talk to Quistic, then find and evacuate the VIPs."

"Oh, wurrin," Maxim says as he and Gabe step into the computer center. The massive sphere of the computing core is dark. Scorch marks and burnt-edged holes riddle the massive sphere. Smoke still wafts from some of them, sparks raining down to the deck below. The bodies of the droid staff are scattered everywhere. Maxim walks further into the room. "They slaughtered them."

Gabe is slowly scanning the area. His gaze settles on a far corner and he sprints off. Maxim on his heels.

The ruined body of Delphine is shoved in a corner. Her roller ball is missing, torn from her torso. Energy weapon burns mar her torso; one arm ends at the elbow, a mess of wires and burnt plastoid. Maxim puts a hand on his friend's shoulder. "I'm sorry."

Gabe turns. "As am I." He looks around the space. "This is not promising." He heads for the spiral walkway that winds up the eight-and-a-half decks of the computer core to the control room.

Maxim gently collects two other mechanical bodies, laying them next to Gabe's friend. The damage to the bodies is horrific. He's worried about what they'll discover in engineering, which, if he recalls, was crewed primarily by biologicals, not droids.

"Maxim," Gabe says from above. It is less a shout and more an increase in volume. "Please join me in the primary interface room."

Maxim looks up. "On my way," he shouts, trotting up the spiraling ramp. As he circles the core, he realizes that whoever shot it up had walked along this same walkway, firing as they went.

The primary computer interface room is a wreck. After shooting up the droid employees and the core itself, the attackers turned their weapons on the control room. Maxim looks around. "Can you make use of anything in here?"

The droid is surveying the room. Finally, he nods once. "Let us find out." He approaches one of the least damaged consoles, extending his hands towards it. Data tendrils extend from all of his fingertips, their glowing ends waving around as they seek entries into the panel. Once the tendrils have dug deep into the console, Gabe looks at Maxim. "Not good."

The big Palorian's jet-black eyebrows creep up to touch his cranial ridges. "Not good?"

Gabe nods. "Almost all the ship's systems are offline. Main power and maneuvering are offline. Sensors are online, but the bridge connections have been severed." His eyes dim. "Attempting to reactivate bridge connections. Oh, someone has jettisoned the bridge."

Maxim's eyes go wide. "Can you reactivate shipwide comms, at least?"

Gabe is silent a moment, then turns to his friend. "No. Our opponents appear to be deeply familiar with this vessel's systems and command codes. The lock-outs are...impressive. Comms in particular. I cannot do much without the encryption keys they used. Without the main computer, everything that is running, is doing so locally at minimum levels."

Maxim rubs his chin with one hand, while the thumbs of his other hand tap against each other, like Zephyr does when deep in thought. "So, this is an inside job."

"Almost certainly," Gabe agrees. He adds, "I have been able to confirm that approximately forty percent of the ship's passengers and crew are locked in their staterooms and berths. The remainder have been evacuated."

"That's probably for the best," Maxim says. Gabe nods. "Do you have access to the ship's sensors? Can you pinpoint the mercenaries?"

"I am afraid not. The ship's sensors are not that finely tuned." Gabe shrugs.

Maxim looks around. "Okay, anything else we can do from here?" Gabe shakes his head. "Then let's get back to our friends."

Walking down the ramp back to the entrance, Maxim says, "I hope we find that little furry bas—" Gabe raises a hand, bringing them to a halt.

A Hulgian man and two Guldraniis enter. The Guldraniis fan out, and from halfway up the ramp, the two *Ghost* crew members hear the Hulgian man say, "Team 8 checking in. We're in the computer center. We'll look around, see if anyone is here."

Gabe and Maxim step back against the wall, as out of sight as they can get. Maxim looks at his friend, whispering, "Aren't those the —" His friend nods, eyes shifting to red. Maxim nods up the ramp, shoving Gabe in that direction.

From below they hear the Hulgian mercenary's comm unit reply, "Hurry. Someone was accessing systems they shouldn't. Dar said he ran into a Palorian and a droid around engineering. Proceed with caution."

"Copy that," the Hulgian replies, then points toward the ramp. The two Guldraniis head up.

"Do you know where their staterooms are?" Cynthia asks.

Mr. Londo nods. "I do, yes."

Wil runs his hands through his hair. "We need a plan."

"That's what I hired you for," Londo offers.

Bennie looks up and opens his mouth but slams it shut at a look from Wil.

"I think we need to talk to Mr. Quistic," Wil says. Everyone nods. He turns to Londo. "Lead the way."

It turns out, not surprisingly, that Paldo Quistic's stateroom is in the luxury suites tower, the floor above Wil and the team's stateroom, in fact. The climb up the service stairs is anything but fun but is thankfully uneventful.

"What if he's not here?" Londo asks, pressing the announcer button on the access panel. The panel is dark; it might not work.

Cynthia looks at the hatch. "You said he told your man he was sick?" Londo nods. "If he is, he's here. If he's not here, well, I guess we know who the villain is."

Bennie exhales and bangs on the wood inlaid hatch as loud as he can. When everyone looks down at him, he shrugs, "What? We're kinda on a timetable here." He points to the panel Londo is still absently pressing on. "That's dead."

Zephyr makes a face but nods her agreement. Wil says, "Uh, won't this hatch be sealed? Isn't that the whole thing?"

"Oh," Londo says. Cynthia makes a face, nodding.

Bennie sighs and pushes past them. "Fake wood doors, easy."

Mr. Londo makes a strangled noise. "These doors are not fake."

Bennie looks over his shoulder. "Even better." His beam saber ignites and plunges into the wood. As he works through the wood, it catches fire.

When the two smoldering pieces of the hatch fall to the deck, a Hulgian man, wearing a terrified expression and a *Galactic Empress* bathrobe clearly made for a much smaller person, is standing in the entry. Whether Quistic wants to secure the robe closed or not is immaterial, as it is very much too small to close. "What?" he grumbles. Looking at the ruin of his stateroom hatch, he adds, "That seems rather extreme. I was coming to the door."

Everyone finds something interesting on the floor or ceiling to stare at. Wil, looking at the ceiling, says, "Oh, you're here."

"Where else would I be? I feel like dren, and someone locked me in my room. Something I ate last night, I suspect." He turns to Londo. "I've already filed a note for the chef and sent a complaint to engineering."

Londo rubs his hands together, finally looking up from the floor to meet the Hulgian investor's gaze. "Yes, well. I'm sorry about that, and good idea on the notes. I'm sure chef will want to know." He looks at the others for help.

Quistic cuts any help off. "What the grolack is going on? The terminals in my suite are all offline, I can't reach anyone on comms, and until now, I've been locked in my room." He points back into his suite. "And, it looks like we're about to enter the nebula."

Bennie leans to the side to peer around the large man. He hisses, "He's right."

"Of course, I am."

Cynthia says, "So if he's not our villain, who?" She turns to Londo. "You said two others were absent from the gathering?"

"What are you talking about? Villain?" Quistic demands. He puts his hands on his hips, drawing the robe open even further.

"Oh, my...yeah, uh..." Wil says, taking a step back.

Cynthia murmurs, "Oh my, indeed," then sees the look on Wil's face and turns to Londo.

Zephyr takes over. "Mr. Quistic, I'm sure you heard the announcement. Someone has hijacked the *Empress*. They've cut all internal and external comms."

He holds up a hand. "The lifeboats."

She nods. "And the bridge. As far as we know, we have zero control of the ship and it is indeed drifting into the nebula. If it continues, the thormic radiation will eat through the hull and destroy the ship."

The big man stammers, turning to look through his expansive viewport. He turns back to face the others, causing Bennie to take an involuntary step back.

Wil holds up a hand. "We're working the problem. Someone has hired mercenaries to take the ship. They've destroyed the computer center, locked out engineering, killed everyone inside, and jettisoned the bridge."

"And the XO was a bad guy," Bennie says, leaning forward.

The uncomfortably still-mostly-naked man looks down at Bennie. "Was?"

"Oh, we killed him," the Brailack says, pride obvious in his voice. Wil looks at him, making a face.

Quistic shakes his massive head. "So, why are you here?"

"Well, we thought you were the bad guy," Wil admits.

"Me?"

Wil blushes. "Well, I mean, you kept complaining about how much this project cost, being behind schedule, how you need this project to start paying returns. You mentioned your losses over Farsight and all that. Then, at the pool, you seemed like you wanted to talk to me about something. You were acting, I dunno, suspicious."

"Suspicious?" the other man replies. "All that is true, but I'm not a monster. I wanted to talk to you about your experience with Farsight. It sounds like a fascinating story. As much as I am unhappy about my losses, I had no idea the company was up to such dastardly things."

Zephyr whispers. "Dastardly?"

Quistic looks at Londo. "There are, what? Three thousand beings on board?" The Harrith man nods, wobbling one hand side to side. "You thought I'd kill thousands of innocents, for money?" He looks like he's getting misty eyed.

Bennie whispers, "Is...is he crying?"

Cynthia plants a palm on his face, pushing him backwards. "No offense. We're piecing things together as we go."

The massive financier snuffles. It sounds like a trumpet. "It's fine. I understand."

"I don't think he does," Bennie whispers from the back of the group.

Cynthia spins. "Will. You. Shut. Up," she grates.

Wil ignores the others. "We're really sorry, Mr. Quistic. Stay here. We'll get this sorted out."

The man looks at Wil, doubt clear on his triceratops-like face. "And if you don't?"

"We all die," Wil replies.

In the stairwell, he turns to Londo. "Okay, that was a bust, and time is running out."

Talara'Vey looks at her employer. "This is going well. The computer and its minders are dead. The bridge is drifting somewhere, engineering is locked up tight, the staff is dead." She smiles. "In two tocks, this ship will be so deep in the nebula no one will ever find the parts the thormic radiation doesn't dissolve."

Fev'Ti bows her head, her long neck arching. "Good. With the lifeboats launched, the clock is ticking."

The Malkorite mercenary's ears move, causing her many jeweled earrings to jingle and jangle. "Are you ready to make your way to the shuttle bay?"

The Burzzad woman nods. "Yes, I am ready to be the sole survivor of this outrageously expensive boondoggle."

Talara'Vey snaps her fingers, summoning a group of mercenaries. "Escort her to the shuttle bay, then make a final sweep. Our ride will be here soon." She turns back to Fev'Ti. "You should hurry, the bow will be in the nebula shortly."

A Malkorite man nods. "On it." He turns to the well-dressed Burzzad woman. "This way, ma'am."

The group hustles out of the small cafe that Talara'Vey has chosen as her command center. She looks at Wirra. "Take a team and see if you can track down our pesky friends. They triggered Quakla's failsafe on the bridge deck, and Dar ran into them near engineering. Also, make sure that compartment is sealed." She snaps her fingers. "Gillum is already down there somewhere with his team."

The Hulgian woman nods and waves over a dozen troops to join her as she departs.

Talara'Vey turns to a pale green Brailack at a table nearby. She has portable computers and PADDs spread across the table top. "What's the status of your project?"

The woman looks up. "Still working on it, but it won't be long." The deck shudders under their feet. "We'll need the secondary core online to finish."

The mercenary commander nods. "Good. Be a shame to let such a valuable piece of equipment be destroyed in a nebula. As long as the insurance company thinks it is destroyed, that is sufficient. Parting this monstrosity out will make us all rich. The finder's fee that the slave brokers on Madrillo will pay for the passengers and crew who didn't get to lifeboats, will be sugar topping." She pulls out a comm unit. "Dar, take a team and get to engineering."

"Copy that."

"Be careful. Those security consultants are still on the loose. Go through one of the secondary access points."

She hears the Olop man growl. "Maybe I'll run into the same two drennogs from before."

"Be. Careful." She drops the device into a pocket.

The other woman grins, baring tiny sharp teeth. "As long as I don't get assigned to cleaning up all the bodies."

The Malkorite mercenary chuckles. "Indeed. Speaking of, how many are left aboard?"

A few taps on the data terminal and the other woman answers, "Hard to be exact. We took the sensors offline. Looks like a couple hundred, at most almost a thousand. Most are security forces locked in their barracks and the other investors and VIP types in the observation lounges. The rest are crew that stayed aboard and hapless drennogs that didn't want to watch the nebula and are locked in their quarters."

Talara'Vey nods, smiling. "Good. We can ransom the VIPs, sell the rest." She walks over to the entry of their makeshift command center. "Figure out if the *Lwolveneer* has arrived."

Another member of her mercenary team, another Malkorite, says, "On it." He grabs a PADD and taps it a few times. "The monitoring team in the aft airlock confirms, they can see *Lwolveneer* on approach."

"Captain!" an officer shouts. She's Trenbal, and if Captain Ramalbong remembers, this is her first cruise with Red Nova lines.

Ramalbong's gaze follows the reptilian officer's extended finger, looking through the massive forward viewport. Off to the side of the bridge module, still making its way toward the cluster of lifeboats several thousand ploriths distant, is a ship. "What the wurrin?" She looks at the other woman. "Who is that?"

The Trenbal woman's head rocks back. "No idea, ma'am."

Ramalbong moves to the transparent hull section to peer through it. The unidentified ship isn't very big or yet very close, but it is clearly approaching the *Empress.* "Pirates," she hisses.

CHAPTER NINETEEN

Gabe and Maxim creep back up the ramp until they're inside the control room at the top. They can hear the two Guldraniis coming closer, chatting amongst themselves about nothing in particular. Maxim looks at Gabe, points to his rifle, then shakes his head. Gabe tilts his head. Maxim pantomimes choking someone. Gabe nods his understanding.

The first Guldranii man comes through the threshold. As he moves further into the space to make room for his colleague, One of his side mounted eyes turns toward Gabe. He opens his mouth to raise the alarm but is snatched by the neck and pulled deeper into the control room. The best he can do is gurgle.

A loud crack echoes, and the other man shouts, "Mola?" The other man steps in, leaning forward to see his friend only to have a powerful blue-skinned fist slam into the back of his head, dropping him with a wet crunch.

"Hey! What are you two doing up there?" the Hulgian man shouts. Maxim vaguely recalls his name is Gilligan or something.

Gabe stands and says, "Hey, Gillum, get up here!" in a perfect imitation of the Guldranii they just took out. Maxim looks at him, eyebrows arched. The droid smiles.

They wait for the Hulgian to make his way up the ramp. It takes a while: Hulgians aren't known for their speed or endurance.

"What the wurrin is wrong? Why'd you make me come all the way up here?" the mercenary demands, walking into the computer center control room. He comes face to face with Gabe. "The wurrin is—" The rest of his question is cut off by a bolt of supercharged plasma burning a hole in his thick hide, then two more for good measure.

The body thumps to the ground. Maxim looks at his friend and smiles. They exit the control center and walk down the ramp to the ground floor.

Maxim taps his earpiece. "Wil, we just ran into three more mercs." He nods. "Yeah, we're gonna make our—" He looks up as another Hulgian, a woman, walks in with six armed men and women on her heels. He stumbles, falling back as shots ring out.

The sound of Gabe's arms transforming and his blasters charging is drowned out by the sounds of weapons fire. Maxim hits the deck in a roll and scrambles back from the hatch.

"Take 'em!" the woman in charge shouts, raising her pistol.

Blaster bolts strike Gabe several times before he falls back against the wall, just out of range of the weapons behind a storage crate. Maxim is behind a console a few meters away.

"Can you jam their comms?" Maxim shouts. He pops over the console, his rifle barking. The console erupts in sparks as return fire shreds the plasti-form frame, exposing the metal support and internal workings of the console. Gabe nods.

Gabe leans out from the crate he's behind, firing. Someone screams. As he leans back, sparks pop from several scorch marks on his torso.

Maxim crawls away from his cover toward an alcove. Shots fly overhead, and the console he was just behind bursts into flames.

Maxim pops up and fires. Two mercenaries fall. The Hulgian woman has two pistols now and is firing each on fully automatic mode. "I'll kill you!" she screams.

Gabe sort of tilt falls from cover and takes aim. He fires, striking the woman in the leg. She bellows, tossing one of her oversized pistols at him as she hobbles for the hatch. Maxim stands again, firing as the last of the mercenaries flee through the hatch.

Maxim makes his way to Gabe, keeping his rifle trained on the hatch. No one comes through it. He looks down. "You've looked better."

"I have felt better," Gabe admits. He holds out his hand for Maxim to help him up. "I have warned the others."

Maxim nods. "Okay, let's go."

The shuttle bay of the *Galactic Empress* is spacious, to say the least. While carrying auxiliary craft isn't the primary function of the ship, and even future ports of call would not require tenders be carried by the massive cruise liner, the designers recognized that certain clientele may prefer to come and go under their own power, discreetly.

The space forms a squat T-shape with small auxiliary exterior doors on the port and starboard sides of the ship, while the much larger primary opening sits forward facing, below the recreation deck. All three sets of heavy bay doors are closed. Small auxiliary craft are plugged into berths along the arms of the T, while the main space is empty, save for the luxury shuttle parked in the middle.

Given the largely non-essential nature of the space, there aren't crew members assigned to regular shifts. A small number of droids and customer service staff are called in when a ship is arriving or departing—assuming, of course, the arrival or departure is scheduled.

Fev'Ti and her escort are very much not scheduled. Her Lorem Shipworks Blasta Mk-5 is sitting exactly where she left it when she came aboard the *Empress*. The sleek craft looks like a swift in flight, wings swept back over two powerful, centrally mounted engines. The Burzzad woman looks around the spacious central bay; three smaller shuttles assigned to the *Empress* are sitting in corrals. No one is around. She looks at one of the beings assigned to escort her to the bay. "Help me prep for departure."

The Trenbal man nods, his tail swishing as he looks around. He looks up near the ceiling, four decks above. "I'll check the control room." His tongue slips out as he talks, tasting the oily air of the bay.

"Max and Gabe are on their way," Wil says as they turn a corner. They're making their way forward through the arboretum.

"This place is nice," Cynthia says, taking in the view. The nebula is now visible through the dome overhead.

Bennie says, "Lots of privacy to be had."

Wil looks down at him. "Uh, do I want to know what that means?"

Bennie winks. "I think you know what it means." He makes a thrusting motion with his hips, forcing Wil to look away.

Cynthia takes a step away from the Brailack hacker. "How are you this gross? You're like those creepers that loiter at night clubs well past the age they should be at night clubs."

Bennie turns from Wil to Cynthia. "Those guys don't get laid." He points to a cluster of trees, shrubs obscuring their trunks. "Great spot, over there, by the way."

Everyone takes a few steps away from their friend.

"So gross," Zephyr says.

"What?" Bennie spreads his hands. "Just because you all shacked up with each other and live boring monogamous lives doesn't make it the only choice." He bares his teeth. "It'd be a crime to deny the ladies all of this." He runs his hands down the length of his body. "I'm in my prime."

Wil pointedly looks at the artificial forest. "So, what kind of trees are these, anyway?"

Cynthia looks at Wil, then Bennie, then the trees. "Good question." She points to a stand of what look like aspen trees. "Those are Rabliso trees." She looks at Zephyr. "Palor?"

Zephyr nods. "Yeah, from the southern region of Holpta."

"Whatever," Bennie says, looking at the stand of trees he had pointed to. "Wonder if she's still onboard?"

Wil looks over his shoulder. "You hoping for a mid-mission booty call?"

Bennie rubs his chin. "I mean, would that be—"

"Yes!" Zephyr and Cynthia shout in unison.

BACK TOGETHER

Zephyr and Maxim exchange a quick kiss as the big Palorian man and droid meet up with the rest of the crew. They're in a buffet near the center of the ship, a few decks below the arboretum. The deck shudders underfoot. It is difficult to tell if it is a lifeboat launching or hull decompression.

Bennie looks at Gabe. "You look like dren." He grabs a tray and makes his way to one of the food warming counters. When the alarms sounded and the pirates told everyone to vacate, trays had been dropped everywhere. There was plenty of food still warming in the trays. Everyone else grabs a seat at a large table.

The tall droid inclines his head. "Self-repair is almost complete." Bennie nods absently as he fills a plate, his back to the group. Gabe sighs.

Maxim looks at the droid, then turns to the others. "These folks brought some serious ordinance."

Cynthia grunts, "You two seem to be magnets. All we got was a minor kerfuffle with the XO."

"The dead XO," Bennie offers from the food counter. He scoops a ladle full of something pale purple with orange bits in it onto his plate. "Am I the only one that's hungry?"

Wil looks at his friends, ignoring the Brailack hacker. "We stopped by a window. The ship is maybe an hour or two from fully entering the nebula." He wiggles a hand. "Give or take. The bow is almost certainly already in."

"That's not good," Maxim says.

Cynthia nods. "Agreed. You can see the leading edge from the arboretum. That means the forward sections are likely already breaking down."

Gabe nods. "The thormic radiation will probably begin damaging the hull immediately, so evacuating the exterior compartments should be a priority. It will not be fast, but still quite dangerous."

Zephyr shakes her head. "How? This thing is massive, and most of the passengers are locked in exterior sections because they wanted to see the nebula. We can't even get most doors to open."

Bennie says, "I can only cut through so many hatches." He drops into a seat at the table.

Gabe inclines his head. "A non-optimal approach, to be sure."

Mr. Londo raises his hand.

Wil says, "We need a way to get control of the ship, or at least partial control."

"With the bridge literally floating off in the distance, that'll be tough," Cynthia replies. Wil nods.

Bennie says, "Too bad we can't listen to what these krebnacks are saying." He shoves a bit of food into his mouth.

Maxim and Gabe exchange a look. Wil sees it. "What?"

Maxim places the comm device he took off of one of the mercenaries in the hydroponics bay on the table.

Bennie looks at the device then Maxim. "Keeping that for just the right moment?"

Maxim reaches over and pushes Bennie hard enough to tip his chair over.

Wil picks up the damaged device, looking at Gabe. "Can you fix it?" He offers it to his mechanical friend.

Gabe examines the comm unit, turning it over in his hands.

Finally, he holds it in one hand while the other extends data tendrils that burrow into the unit. After a heartbeat, the tendrils retract. He looks around the table. "No."

Bennie, back in his chair, upright, chuckles. "That was anti-clamactic."

Wil says nothing, staring at Gabe. The droid adds, "The internal components are too damaged. The encryption module took the most damage. There is no way to repair it."

Londo's hand is still in the air. He wiggles his fingers.

Zephyr looks at Gabe and Maxim. "Computer center—lost cause?" Both nod.

"Excuse me," Mr. Londo says. Everyone turns to him. "The secondary computer core might be an option."

Gabe makes a noise like a cough. "I apologize for not thinking of that sooner." He smiles at Mr. Londo. "You are quite right."

Maxim leans over and snatches something from Bennie's plate, saying, "We checked the hatch. It was pretty well locked up." Bennie bares his teeth. Maxim continues, "Gabe wrote off trying to force our way in." He hitches a thumb at Bennie. "Even with green utility knife here." Bennie makes a rude gesture in response.

Mr. Londo says, "There are auxiliary hatches." He taps his forehead, thinking. "Decks 30 and 42, if I recall correctly."

Bennie licks his fingers. "Gabe and I can go down there and see what we can do." He reaches down and puts his beam saber hilt on the table. "If they're not too thick, or numerous, I can get us in."

Gabe adds. "I suspect they will be secured, but likely not as thick as the main hatch. There may be more than one to accomplish the desired safety feature."

Wil stands and grabs a plate, helping himself to the food counter.

"Okay, what else? That doesn't solve our drifting-into-a-nebula-of-space-acid problem." He winks at Zephyr as she frowns.

"Or address Fev'Ti. She's here somewhere, right?" Cynthia adds.

Around a mouthful of food, Bennie says, "Or explain who's in charge of these mercenaries and where they are."

Zephyr raises her hand. "Maxim and I can work the Fev'Ti problem. The only way she can get her insurance payout is to survive this. I'm thinking that shiny Lorem Blasta we saw in the shuttle bay is hers." She looks at her partner, who nods.

Londo nods. "Indeed, it is. She insisted we make room for it."

Cynthia takes something off of Wil's plate when he sits down. "Okay, we'll go spring the VIPs and security folks." She looks at Wil's plate. "That's good. Go grab more of those." He dutifully gets up and returns to the food counter. Watching him, she says, "I doubt the security force is up to taking on well-trained and well-armed mercs, but if nothing else, they'll be a distraction."

"Dark," Bennie quips.

Wil sits back down. "Okay, we good on tasks?" Everyone nods except Mr. Londo, who shakes his head. Wil asks, "What?"

The Harrith man looks around the table. "What do you want me to do?"

Wil taps his chin. "You come with us." The other man takes a deep breath and nods. Wil grabs one of the snacks from his plate, popping it into his mouth. He claps his hands and around chewing his snack says, "Alwight, team. Bweak!"

Everyone rolls their eyes.

"Good morning. This is your GNO Morning Briefing. I'm Megan," the blonde journalist says, her bright pink eyes alight.

"And I'm Xyrzix," her blue-skinned co-host adds. He continues, "This morning brings good—no, great—news. The mysterious attackers known only as the 'Invaders' seem to be on the run."

Megan leans forward. "Not just on the run, but in every system the Peacekeepers have been engaged in fighting, the Invaders are fleeing."

Xyrzix nods, his cheeks bluer than normal. "This terrible war might be over."

Megan looks to another camera pickup. "We've heard from our embedded colleague, Mon-El Furash, that Peacekeeper Command was able to develop a weapon that made short work of the chitin-like armor the Invaders covered their ships, and ground troops, in."

Xyrzix turns. "We'll keep you posted."

PART 4

CHAPTER TWENTY

BACK DOORS

"This is decidedly less imposing," Gabe says. He and Bennie are standing in front of one of the secondary entries to engineering. He places a hand on the hatch. Turning to Bennie, he says, "It is still quite robust and I suspect there will be another just inside it."

Bennie unclips his beam saber hilt. "Let's get to work." The purple blade springs to life with a snap hiss. He spins the blade twice, then jabs it straight into the hatch. The blade penetrates the metal, burning a molten hole around the blade. Sparks and globs of liquid metal erupt from the wound in the hatch.

The Brailack hacker and Knight of Plentallus, in training, pushes the hilt of his beam saber, dragging the blade up a half inch at a time. Straining to push the energy blade, Bennie looks up at his friend. "This might take some time."

Gabe says, "I find myself rather embarrassed that I did not think to attempt accessing engineering through one of these secondary hatches."

"It happens." Bennie doesn't look up from his work.

"To biologicals, perhaps," Gabe says.

"No offense taken." Bennie looks up just long enough to smile at his friend. He turns his attention back to the task at hand. "Do you need to run a diagnostic? Maybe one of your processing cores is damaged?"

Gabe makes his shrugging motion. "Not that I am aware of, but at the first available moment, I will go into standby to run a level one diagnostic."

Bennie nods absently, not really caring one way or another.

The two work for what feels like hours to Bennie. He is drenched in sweat when he looks up at Gabe. "How long have we been here?"

"Ten microtocks." The droid smiles. "Would you like help?" He extends a hand, palm up.

Bennie frowns as his beam saber deactivates. He hands the hilt to Gabe. "Careful. I didn't think they could overheat, but it's getting pretty warm."

The droid accepts the weapon with a bow. With a familiar snap hiss, the purple blade springs to life. Gabe jabs it into a different section of the thick hatch. Something inside makes a loud twang, like a spring uncoiling. Gabe slides the blade up, faster than Bennie had been able to. Another something inside the hatch twangs.

Bennie watches wide eyed, using his shirt to wipe sweat from his forehead. Another twang and the two sides of the hatch shudder and slide apart just enough to allow the pair to see inside. There is indeed another hatch two meters from this one.

Gabe closes the energy blade down and hands the hilt back to Bennie, who says, "You could have done that ten microtocks ago."

Gabe turns to his friend. "I was scanning the door. It took time to locate the locking mechanisms."

"How much time?"

"Two microtocks."

Bennie scowls, clipping his beam saber back onto his belt. He hitches a thumb toward the hatch. "Open the door." He adds. "Then we can talk about your bypassing my DNA scanner on the activation switch.

Gabe grins and slides his fingers into the gap. The two halves groan in protest as they slide apart, centon by centon.

The second hatch proves to be less of a challenge. Bennie leans in to peer through the widening gap. "At least it doesn't look shot up, like the computer core," he offers. The moment the gap is wide enough, he slips inside.

With a final heave, Gabe forces the interior hatch open, standing with his arms fully outstretched. He steps inside, the hatch remaining open. The reactor complex is silent and cold. Whatever the mercenaries did appears to have shut everything down without causing damage. He points. "The secondary core is down there."

From where he's exploring the space, Bennie makes an *eep* sound. "I think they suffocated everyone," he says. At his feet is a body.

Gabe looks around. He points to the melted form of Hogarth, the Chief Engineer. "They also released a corrosive of some sort."

Bennie gasps, covering his mouth with both hands. Gabe looks down. "We would be dead already if it was still active." The small Brailack shrugs, his cheeks a darker shade of green.

Gabe reaches the secondary processing core, examining it. "This appears to be undamaged."

Bennie joins him, pulling data cables out of the end of his wrist-comm. "That's good." He looks around at the bodies and shivers.

The two get to work.

Dar and his team reach the main entrance to engineering. He has eight beings with him, some of the last foot troops aboard the *Empress* until their support ship arrives. He looks the hatch up and down, his mechanical eye whirring as it moves through its various scan modes. "Doesn't look like they got in," he says.

A Quilant woman steps forward. "Sorry?"

The Olop mercenary turns. "What?"

"Were you talking to us?" she asks.

His furry face scrunches. "What? No. I was...never mind." He turns to the hatch controls and connects his own wristcomm. Even without the main computer, the access codes that Fev'Ti gave the mercenary team can operate most regular ships' systems, like hatches. Her codes, plus Dar's own code slicing skills used earlier to secure engineering, have kept the space locked down tight. Sucking the oxygen from the large space, and piping in a specially designed corrosive that targets the most common elements in droid chassis' was child's play.

The main hatch to engineering emits a series of heavy clicks, then slides apart.

Dar and his team walk in and across the space come face to face with a Brailack and a weird-looking droid. "Who—?" Dar starts to demand.

"What's taking so long?" Fev'Ti demands from the base of the luxury shuttle's ramp. The lithe craft remains secured to the deck, and the automated umbilicals are still connected to the spine of the ship. Her trio of eyes is united in glaring at the control console and its inept operator.

"Sorry, ma'am," one of the Brailack mercenaries shouts from a control console near the back of the space. "Without the computer..." He trails off.

The Burzzad woman sighs and walks toward the stables where smaller auxiliary craft are stored. The short-range shuttles are meant to ferry passengers of the massive cruise liner to and from a planet's surface or to a nearby space station.

Maxim and Zephyr are watching from a secondary control room, at the far end of the starboard side of the T-shaped hangar.

Zephyr whispers, "Glad her hired guns aren't good with tech. Looks like they haven't figured out how to manually disengage the secure clamps holding her ship."

"Dummies." Maxim smiles. "I count six, plus the long neck."

"Dear," Zephyr chastises.

"Sorry. The Burzzad."

Outside their hiding place, the group of mercenaries is doing everything it can to free the wealthy investor's shuttle. One is standing near the forward landing gear with a heavy duty cutting tool in his hands.

"I got it!" the Brailack at the console shouts. Orange lights throughout the space begin strobing as the forward bay doors ponderously slide apart. The blue glow of the force field that holds in the atmosphere lights the end of the tunnel. The umbilicals connected to the Lorem Shipworks Blasta click in sequence, then release from the ship, retracting into the ceiling. The last series of clangs is the locking mechanisms in the deck releasing the shuttle's landing gear.

The Burzzad investor turns from the small transport shuttle she was absently examining. When she reaches her ship, she looks to the forward hatch, now almost fully open. She whips around to the Brailack at the console. "You krebnack! I can't fly into the nebula!" She points to the orange and green gas swirling beyond the static atmospheric barrier. "Open the starboard hatch!"

"Oh! Sorry, ma'am!" the mercenary shouts, working his console.

A moment later, the starboard shuttle bay doors slide apart.

"Time to go," Maxim says. Zephyr nods. They crawl back to the hatch and exit their small control room. The corridor outside leads to a matching room on the opposite side of the ship, with an open staircase between the two that leads down into the rather glamorously appointed waiting area.

Descending the stairs, Zephyr says, "How many people do you think they figured would use this?" She gestures to encompass the waiting area they're entering and the spacious hangar complex beyond. "Seems like a tremendous waste of space."

Maxim shakes his head. "No idea, but can't be many. I mean, most folk don't have the funds to fly their private yacht to a cruise ship."

"And it's still fancier than anything I've ever owned," Zephyr says, running a hand along the bottom of a framed work of art. "I bet this isn't even a reproduction." She tuts.

Ahead of them are the wood and glass doors that lead out into the shuttle bay, each bearing the Red Nova Lines logo. Maxim slides his acquired rifle off his back, checking the charge. He looks to his partner, who does the same. She winks. He grins.

The doors slide apart. "Hi, losers," Maxim says, firing on the nearest mercenaries. Two drop before any of them even realize they're in trouble.

The two Palorians dive behind a console as return fire reaches them. Maxim stands, snapping off a few shots before ducking back down. "Still six," he reports.

Zephyr looks around them. The console they're behind won't last long, but there are some storage crates that some *Galactic Empress* crew member didn't stow, a few meters away. "Cover," she says. Without waiting for an acknowledgment, she bolts from their meager cover. Several energy bolts strike the bulkhead behind her as she moves.

The throaty rumble of engines powering up drowns out the sound of weapons fire. Zephyr looks over to Maxim, who points past her. She looks to where he's pointing. Her cover is right next to one of the auxiliary craft corrals. Inside it is a small transport. She turns and nods.

Maxim stands, his rifle barking on automatic, the barrel glowing white. Two more mercenaries fall to the ground: one unmoving, the other screaming and clawing his way toward the powering up shuttle and still lowered boarding ramp.

While Maxim keeps the remaining mercenaries busy, Zephyr boards the small support vehicle. It's barely half the size of Maxim's and her berth aboard the *Ghost*. The rear is open with a long bench running along each bulkhead, seating for a dozen or so beings. Twice that, if people stand in the center. The forward section is a small cockpit with seating for two.

The controls, thankfully, come to life the moment she sits down.

WHAT'S IN A NAME?

"What about Super Friends?" Cynthia asks as she pulls open the hatch to the service stairs.

Wil looks at her. "I mean, we have folks with blue skin, which is close to purple." He steps into the corridor. "And Bennie is kinda like Gleek, but no. Taken. And James would make fun of us."

"All the good names are taken," the feline-featured woman complains, her tail swishing behind her. "The Fixers," she offers.

Wil tilts his head. "That's not terrible." He looks at his wrist-comm. "Should be up ahead around that bend." She nods.

"What are you two talking about?" Mr. Londo asks.

Cynthia looks over her shoulder, smiling. "Working on a team name."

The other man nods. "Ah, yes, you do need one. Your building is hard to find without a name over the door." Wil tilts his head, nodding.

They round the bend in the corridor.

The hatch to Observation Lounge 10, despite being on one of the first-class decks, isn't that fancy. Wil looks at the hatch. "This is it?"

Cynthia looks at him. "You thought it'd be platinum plated?"

"At least gold."

She sighs and plugs her wristcomm into the access panel. "You know, I wish little green's apps didn't all have his face on them." She executes the software, watching lines of code she doesn't understand scroll across the small display.

Wil taps a foot as he waits, until he sees the look Cynthia is giving him.

The access panel beeps, and the animated Bennie on Cynthia's wristcomm pumps his fist.

The door slides open.

"It's about time!" several people shout as they file out of the lounge into the corridor.

"Woah!" Wil shouts, pushing several people aside. "You all need to get to lifeboats, like now!" This elicits a few startled shouts.

"Starboard side!" Cynthia adds.

Chief Vlaruna walks out. "What took you so long?" He looks to Londo. "Hello, Mr. Londo." The lanky businessman nods.

"You're welcome," Wil snaps.

The Trollack man waves a webbed hand. "Sitrep?"

Cynthia pushes past the pair as Wil opens his mouth.

"The situation is that we have this," Wil retorts.

"Have what?" Vlaruna's barbels twitch, his irritation growing.

Wil waves his arms. "This, all of this." He makes air quotes. "The situation. We got this."

The Trollack man grunts. "We saw the lifeboats launching. Is everyone off the ship?"

From inside the lounge, Cynthia shouts, "No, we don't know for sure how many are locked in lounges or their staterooms, or got off the ship."

Each of Vlaruna's eyes tilt in opposite directions before turning to Wil. "Let's get these people to a lifeboat." He starts down the corridor. "Everyone, this way!" The various investors and other VIPs begin to shuffle along after him.

Wil looks at Cynthia. "Maybe we should have left him in there."

She laughs, guiding a straggling pair of Guldraniis out of the lounge. "This way. Please hurry." The pair rushes to catch up to the others.

"Hey, Vlaruna," Wil shouts. "We should cross to the other side of the ship, so the lifeboat isn't launching toward the nebula."

"I know that!" the other man shouts, a webbed hand waving dismissively.

As the group of important passengers files through the access hatch to the lifeboat, a Sylban woman asks, "Will we be safe? What's been happening?"

Vlaruna opens his mouth to answer, but Wil puts a hand in front of the small fishlike man's face. "The lifeboats all have transponders. Help is probably already on the way. It shouldn't be more than a day or two." She nods, the foliage on top of her head drooping.

The chief of security comes over, eyeing the rifle Wil has strapped to his back. "Where'd you get that?"

"Dead bad guy," Wil deadpans. He peeks through the hatch, seeing that everyone is settled in. Slapping the hatch, he and Cynthia turn and start away as the hatch slides closed. Beyond the hatch, the rumble of the lifeboat cycling into its launch system vibrates the deck.

The chief frowns, his barbels twitching. He holds his hand out, fingers wiggling. "Give it over."

Cynthia and Wil exchange a look, the latter asking, "What now?"

The small Trollack man pulls himself up to his full meter and a half height. "I am the head of security. Passengers aren't supposed to be armed."

Wil stares down the other man. "I'll assume you bumped your head somewhere." He looks at his wristcomm, pulling up a map of the ship. "Your barracks are this way."

"I know where they are."

"Good, we're going there to let your folks out. Come or don't." Wil and Cynthia walk away as the other man splutters and swears before he trots to catch up to them.

The image wavers, static artifacts lingering. Finally, Mon-El Furash appears. She's covered in dirt and other things. Dried orange blood traces a line from her right ear down her cheek. She looks at the camera. "I'm Mon-El Furash. This is a GNO Breaking News Alert. The culprit behind the Invader attacks on the GC is now in custody. I'm on Grindflon Four, where the Peacekeepers have surrounded the last remaining vestiges of the Invader fleet in orbit." She takes a deep breath. "The last several days have been a flurry of activity. The GC forces and their miracle weapon turned the tide with astonishing swiftness." Another deep breath. "But at great cost."

Behind her, a squad of Peacekeepers in the latest black combat armor jogs past.

She continues, "The Peacekeepers, after obliterating the orbital defense, landed an invasion force on this planet. The colony here, originally Multonae, appears to have been wiped out—used as slave labor, or worse. We aren't sure yet." An explosion in the distance causes her to flinch, ducking down. After regaining her composure, she says, "While elements of the Invader forces are still fighting, I'm told a commando team was successful in breaching a bunker that was set up in the governmental building of the colony." She takes a breath. "Ex-Peacekeeper Janus, one of the senior-most officers responsible for what has been dubbed the Harrith Incident, has been captured and by all appearances is the leader of this entire force." She looks off camera, nodding to someone, then takes several steps to her right. The camera following her reveals the smoking ruins of the capital city of the colony.

"I'm told Janus was no longer recognizable, having been mutated into something similar to his own mutant ground troops. It is unknown if the mutation is self-inflicted or not. The new biological agent that has turned the tide was used to subdue the rogue Peacekeeper. Janus has not been seen since his rogue task force was routed over Harrith Prime severl cycles ago. He and his senior staff were tried in absentia alongside their co-conspirators. It was assumed Janus and his forces left GC space to find a planet to settle." Another explosion, farther away. The journalist shakes her head to clear her thoughts. "I'm told that Peacekeeper command expects the fighting to be over by the end of the day tomorrow. They have already removed Janus from the planet under high security."

CHAPTER TWENTY-ONE

"Oh, shazbot," Bennie says, falling back from the console as energy bolts strike it.

Gabe spins on his heel, both of his forearms shifting, making the familiar whirring noise of his combat mode.

Bennie scrambles for cover as the Olop man and his crew fire at him. He barely gets behind a rack of parts before the shots home in on him. He scrambles for his beam saber, his hand closing around empty space. He turns and looks back the way he came. His beam saber hilt is lying on the deck. "Well, dren."

Gabe is standing behind another console, one already dead and riddled with scorch marks. He leans out, returning fire, causing two mercenaries to scream in pain.

"You annoying krebnacks are gonna die!" the Olop man shouts as he runs across the open space of the main engineering work area. Two of his troops fire as they run in and find cover.

"My beam saber is out there," Bennie sends over comms.

"Yes, it is," Gabe replies.

Bennie frowns at his friend from across the space.

Gabe makes an exaggerated sighing motion, then leans out, firing as he dashes across the space, snatching the metal cylinder as he passes. Several angry red bolts of energy slam into his side as he crosses the distance, forcing him to stagger the final few paces.

Gabe skids to the deck, crashing against the bulkhead, sparks erupting from the new and old wounds in his torso. He hands Bennie the beam saber. He has multiple glowing wounds along his side. His arm twitches as smoke wafts up out of his shoulder joint.

"You should work on getting shot less." Bennie smirks, taking the metal cylinder and grinning. Gabe's torso twitches. The purple blade springs to life a moment before the snap hiss of the beam saber igniting. He peers out from behind cover, spotting one of the mercenaries.

From somewhere deep inside the small Knight of Plentallus, in training, a war cry comes forth. He leaps over the crate, his beam saber humming as it burns through the air. He sweeps the blade, absorbing first one, then two, bolts of energy. Another passes by his blade, almost hitting him in the face. He leaps into the air, blade slashing down to remove the gun and arm of the mercenary in front him.

"You almost shot me in the face!" he screams at the man.

"You cut off my arm!" the mercenary retorts.

"Fair." He slams the hilt of his saber on the top of the man's head, rendering him unconscious. Another bolt of energy flashes past his face. "Hey!" He turns, then stumbles and falls backward behind the crate.

Gabe reaches up and returns fire from his cover. His undamaged arm is still capable of transforming into a blaster. Bennie uses the covering fire to creep to another console. He spies the nasty little Olop man with one of his goons. Growling, Bennie leaps from behind the console he's using for cover, and charges, a blood-curdling scream coming from deep inside him.

The Olop mercenary, focused on Gabe's position, turns to see Bennie changing his position. His eyes go wide as the Brailack rushes towards him. He turns his pistol toward the new threat, nudging the woman next to him to follow suit.

The two mercenaries fire on their attacker while trying to avoid fire from the droid elsewhere in the engineering space. The Brailack leaps up, his energy blade humming as it moves through the air, blaster fire flying past him.

Bennie hits the ground, driving his blade through the nearest mercenary. She grunts, falling to the ground. He lashes out with a kick, forcing the Olop man to stumble backward, right into Gabe's sights. A single bolt of energy strikes the small furry man, sending him flying backward, his fur singed and smoking.

Bennie stands up. "Good shot!"

"Thank you," Gabe replies weakly from his place of cover.

Bennie rushes over. "You look like dren. Stay there." He heads back to the secondary computer core; it has been shot several times. "Dren," he hisses. He taps his ear. "The secondary core is shot. Literally."

Gabe looks around. "I have an idea. I will need your assistance."

Bennie smiles. "Of course. What's the plan?"

Gabe puts a hand on the ruined secondary processing core.

"Uh, boss," the Brailack woman at the terminal says, her voice a croak.

Talara'Vey walks over. "What is it?"

The hacker looks up, pointing to a list of operatives. Each of Talara'Vey's lieutenants has a bio monitor installed. Dar's is blinking red.

She swears, then asks, "Did he get the secondary computer core online?"

The other woman shakes her head. "No. Without it, I can't bring the ship online. We're pretty much stuck. Should I send another team?"

The mercenary commander runs a hand along the edge of one of her elephant-like ears, thinking through options. She looks at her hacker. "Is *Lwolveneer* ready?"

The Brailack woman nods. "Yeah, they signaled a few microtocks ago."

Talara'Vey sighs. "Have them grapple us and line up a docking tube. Warn the team in the aft airlock. They can send over a few more troops and tow us out. We can do with the hard way."

The pale green hacker clears her throat. "There's one other

thing." She shrinks a little, fearing her boss's wrath. When she looks up, Vey is looking at her expectantly. "Someone overrode the hatch at the lounge with the VIPs."

The Malkorite mercenary commander growls, her earrings jingling. "Time to go." She looks around her makeshift command center. Most of her people are out walking the ship, rounding up stragglers, forcing them into lifeboats, and looking for the increasingly annoying security consultants. She pulls out the comm unit from her pocket. "Wirra, head to the security barracks. There's going to be trouble."

"Why?" the Hulgian woman asks from the small speaker. When her boss doesn't explain herself, the voice says, "On our way."

Talara'Vey adds, "Use whatever force you deem necessary."

The other woman's grumbling laugh comes through the tinny speaker on the encrypted comm device.

Maxim is firing more or less blindly. The four remaining mercenaries are doing an exceptional job of keeping him pinned down.

Fev'Ti's luxurious shuttle is moments, at best, from being ready to launch. The portside shuttle bay door is wide open, the black of deep space beckoning.

The sleek Lorem Blasta lifts from the deck, its landing gear folding as they retract. The repulsor lifts thrum as the ship turns.

Maxim leans out from his scant cover to fire on the ship, his plasma bolts doing little beyond scorching the paint. Several energy bolts strike near him, driving him back behind cover.

"My love, she's about to get away," Maxim calmly says, after tapping his earpiece.

The mercenaries, their job done in escorting the architect of the entire scheme to her ship so she can escape, fall back, covering each other. Maxim peeks over his cover, firing. One of the retreating beings falls to the deck, unmoving. The others round a corner, exiting the bay.

The large personnel shuttle powers up, and the throaty roar of its power plant is deafening. It turns to line up for the exit, a hundred or so meters directly ahead of it now. The engines at the rear of the ship flare to life. It begins moving forward.

Maxim stands and opens his mouth to check on Zephyr when a small transport shuttle rushes past overhead. It collides with the larger luxury shuttle, smashing an engine cowling and knocking the entire craft sideways, to collide with the side of the bay. The crunch of metal is louder than the whine of the remaining functional engine. Two ships, now fused into one gangly lopsided thing, twist and groan, their repulsor lifts competing. The larger ship dips enough that one of its stubby wings gouges the deck, leaving a two-meter furrow. Maxim winces.

As the merged vessels drift away from the wall and back toward the open bay doors, the smaller of the two powers up its engines, forcing the larger against the bulkhead again. Sparks erupt as a piece of overhead catwalk breaks loose, falling onto the two shuttles. The sound of metal rending fills the shuttle bay.

Maxim runs over to the console the Brailack mercenary had been playing with. He looks over the controls, then pulls his rifle around and fires two shots into it. The console bursts into flames, then goes dark. The shuttle bay doors slide closed. "Faster to close than open." He shrugs.

He turns his attention from the massive door just in time to see the two shuttles crash to the deck halfway to the now-closed doors. The impact dislodges the smaller vessel. It skips a few meters, then tips on its side as it hits the opposite bulkhead.

Maxim picks his way through the wreckage of the small personnel shuttle. "Zephyr!" He pushes and pulls pieces of metal out of his way. He shouts her name again. Finally, he finds the rear hatch of the small craft, pulling on the emergency release. The inside of the small craft is mangled. One bench has come completely apart from the bulkhead and is lying across the opening to the cockpit.

Zephyr is strapped into the pilot's seat, unconscious. When Maxim reaches her, he takes in the scene, checking her for blood and obviously broken bones. As he is checking her over, her eyes flutter open. "That hurt," she murmurs. He beams. "Did we stop her?"

Maxim nods. "We did."

He helps her out of the pilot seat, then out of the wreckage. The two make their way to the boarding ramp of the mangled Lorem Blasta. The ramp is bent at an odd angle, the edge of the hatch visible.

"I'm not sure that's going to open," Zephyr says.

Maxim grunts, "Yeah, that looks pretty mangled." He looks around the hull. "There should be an emergency release...there." He points.

Zephyr clambers over some debris to reach a recessed panel forward of the ramp panel. She presses the panel, which pops down and falls away to reveal a manual release lever. She turns to Maxim. "Here goes," she says, pulling the lever down.

Something in the shuttle makes a loud clunk sound, then several explosive bolts fire, forcing the bent boarding ramp away from the hull.

Maxim leans down to peer inside the ship. "Can you just come out? I don't want to have to come in and get you."

From inside the damaged ship, a haughty voice replies, "I'll be right out."

The deck shudders, causing bits of debris to shift and clatter. The two Palorians exchange a look.

CHAPTER TWENTY-TWO

GRATITUDE, OR LACK THEREOF

After winding through interminable service stairwells, Wil, Cynthia, and Head of Security Vlaruna reach the security barracks.

"This ship didn't seem so big when the lifts worked," the portly Trollack complains.

Wil drops his hands to his knees, breathing heavily. "On that, we agree." He turns to Cynthia. "You good doing the Bennie thing?"

She smiles, turning to the access panel. "Yup." The hatch to the security barracks is heavier than those around it. Down in the lower section of the massive luxury vessel, the decks have no carpeting, and there isn't a speck of wood grain to be seen. The security barracks, like engineering and other sensitive areas, has a thick door set in equally thick bulkheads.

Cynthia looks up. "Okay, this might take longer than the lounge."

The deck rattles underfoot. Wil looks around.

Chief Vlaruna cranes his neck to look over Cynthia's shoulder. "Why? What's that?" He points at the cartoon Bennie on her wrist-comm screen. His barbels twitch next to Cynthia's ear. Clear eyelids flutter.

She swats him away. "If I understand this little animated drennog correctly, it's saying the locking codes are more advanced."

A web-fingered hand reaches for the screen. "What if you—"

Cynthia slaps the hand away and turns to glare at the Trollack man. "I will kill you," she hisses.

Wil plants his hands on the other man's shoulders, pulling him back. "She will, and I'll laugh." He guides the man to the opposite side of the corridor next to Londo, who is doing his best to ignore the banter.

"Boom." Cynthia stands. The access panel bleeps twice.

The hatch slides open. Wil looks from Vlaruna to Londo to the open hatch and the several dozen blaster muzzles pointing at them.

"Woah!" Wil shouts, his hands reaching for the ceiling. Cynthia steps back away from the hatch, out of line of sight.

"Stand down!" Chief Vlaruna shouts, stepping into the entryway, webbed hands waving.

"Chief?" a voice asks. The blasters lower. A Hulgian man in a security uniform, his horns filed to dull ends, steps out looking from the Trollack to Wil and back again. "Who's this?"

Vlaruna pushes Wil aside. "Doesn't matter. We have to retake the ship." He looks at Wil. "That'll be all. Thank you." He turns back to his people. "We need to get the bridge open. We also need to find the attackers. Suit up!"

Wil's mouth hangs open. Cynthia walks over, pushing his mouth closed. "Come on."

Their earpieces crackle. Bennie says, "Uh, I think we've got company."

"What do you mean?" Maxim says from wherever he and Zephyr are.

Wil looks at Cynthia. "Yeah, what're you talking about?"

"Those rumbles. Gabe says they aren't decompression," Bennie says. "The computer core is shot, so he's currently..." he turns to look at the secondary core—and Gabe, connected to it by dozens of wires and data cables, plus his own data tendrils. His optic sensors, normally yellow, are glowing a bright blue. "...Acting in that capacity, I guess you'd say."

"He's doing what?" Wil demands.

Bennie shrugs, then looks around, realizing no one can see the gesture. "He's acting as the core so we could get access to the sensors."

"There is a ship directly astern," Gabe says, his voice coming from the speakers in the ceiling.

Bennie looks around. "Did you hear that?"

"Yeah," Cynthia says.

"What's it doing?" Maxim asks.

"It has a name. Rude," Bennie says.

"I mean the ship," Maxim grates.

"Oh."

Gabe's disembodied voice answers. "It has attached tow cables and is pulling us out of the nebula. It is also extending a docking tube to an aft airlock."

"So, what now?" Bennie asks.

Wil looks at Cynthia, opening his mouth to answer when a blaster bolt scorches the bulkhead next to him. "Shit!" he shouts, stumbling back toward the barracks hatch, knocking down Londo, who shrieks on his way down.

A Hulgian woman and half a dozen assorted beings are marching down the corridor. All of their weapons are drawn and pointed at Wil and the team.

Wil pushes Cynthia through the hatch as he fires his rifle blindly behind him, barely holding the weapon.

"What are you two doing?" Chief Vlaruna comes forward, now wearing some type of light tactical armor. Most of his people are similarly outfitted. Each has a stubby rifle strapped to their back and a stun baton clipped to their belt.

The two *Ghost* crew members continue into the barracks, Wil shouting, "Mercenaries," as two Trenbals step inside the hatch, weapons firing.

"Uh, hello?" Bennie says, as the sound of blaster fire and confused shouting comes from his wristcomm.

Bennie looks around. "Uh...They hung up on me."

The cables and data filaments connecting Gabe to the ruin of the secondary computer core fall away. "I have a plan," he says. The damage to his torso is now just a discolored section of his chassis, looking like nothing more than a metallic bruise.

Bennie inhales. "Lay it on me."

"We board the mercenary vessel and disable it."

Bennie waits a beat. "And?"

"That is it. Do you not think that is sufficient?" Gabe asks, rotating his arm. The damage there, too, is now nothing more than a rust-colored patch of metal skin.

Bennie shrugs. "I mean, just a little light on execution." He takes a deep breath. "More of a Wil plan than a Gabe plan."

The droid tilts his head. "No offense is taken." He turns and heads for the hatch. "We should hurry." Bennie shrugs and follows.

To speed things up, Bennie is riding on Gabe's back as the droid climbs the stairs from the main entry of engineering up more than twenty flights. While connected to the ship's systems, Gabe found the emergency airlock that the mercenary ship had connected to.

Internal sensors were still spotty. Apparently, the contractor who installed them used substandard components.

The pair stops at the landing, looking at the hatch. Bennie hops off his friend's back. "Can you detect anyone?"

Gabe stares at the hatch, then says, "Two."

Bennie rolls his shoulders, then rolls his head in a slow circle. He unclips his beam saber hilt. "Let's do this." He taps his wristcomm. "We'll be back in a bit."

"What? Where are you going?" Zephyr asks over the comm link.

"We will explain when we return," Gabe replies. He places a hand on the hatch controls, his other arm shifting into a lethal blaster. He pulls open the door to allow Bennie to leap through into the corridor.

Bennie's war cry drowns out the sound of his beam saber activating. The two beings Gabe has detected are a pair of Malkorite mercenaries. Each has a plasma rifle, and neither is ready for an attack from the service stairs. Nor are they ready for an attack from a small laser sword wielding Brailack, screaming at the top of his lungs.

Gabe steps into the corridor, ready to fire, his other hand now a blaster, as well. Both Malkorites are falling to ground. Smoke is wafting up from their bodies. He steps up to the airlock hatch, looking down at his friend.

Bennie looks up. "What? Did you want me to leave you one?"

Gabe tilts his head, extending an arm for Bennie to take the lead. The Brailack hacker heads through the airlock hatch into the semi-rigid boarding tube beyond.

The other ship has fired four magnetic tethers that have latched onto the rear section of the cruise ship. Firing its reverse thrusters at full power, the much smaller ship is dragging the much larger vessel out of the nebula. The hull plating along the first third of the *Galactic Empress* is warped and corroded. Several breaches line that section, lounges that vented when transparent hull panels failed. Corridors opened to space when a seam in the hull gave way.

From the nose of the mercenary vessel, a boarding tube runs to the *Empress's* aft airlock. Bennie steps into the enemy ship, beam saber at the ready. The receiving airlock is unguarded. "Clear," he says, stepping further into the ship to make room for Gabe.

Gabe looks around. "The bridge is this way." He starts down the corridor, Bennie falling in behind him.

The ship is laid out like a military transport, a central corridor with bunk rooms and cargo hold branching off. The command deck and living spaces take up the upper three decks. Gabe and Bennie don't encounter any mercenaries as they move from the main compartment to the decks above.

"Their entire force must be aboard the *Empress*," Bennie says. They're outside the hatch that, if Gabe is right, is the main community space outside the command deck. Gabe nods.

Several *Empress* security personnel fall to the ground, many screaming, most silent.

Vlaruna is shouting orders; his people are forming up and returning fire. Their lack of real training shows. Their weapons' fire seems to be mostly ineffective. Wil watches several energy bolts hit the mercenaries dead center, their armor absorbing the bolts. The shipboard weapons of the security department—even the rifles—are, at best, meant for crowd control. They aren't lethal or powerful.

He leans out from the overturned bunk bed he and Cynthia are behind to fire. A mercenary falls to the deck as two more rush through the door, seeking cover.

Cynthia looks at the head of security. "Your weapons aren't doing anything."

The Trollack man's barbels twitch, his wide mouth in a frown. "I see that!" He turns. "Kuil! You and Fryt try to get around them!"

An Olop man nods and shoves the Trenbal next to him. They fall back and crawl to the side of the room.

The bed Wil and Cynthia are behind bursts into flames, forcing them to scurry backward. Several security people fall to the deck. Cynthia looks at Wil. "This isn't going well."

He pops up from their cover to fire. The Hulgian woman, apparently the leader of the group, shouts orders as she ducks behind a crate of supplies. Two of her troops rush forward to the nearest set of bunks. Their fire forces the security personnel back. "Why are there so many crates just lying around?" He ducks as energy bolts race overhead.

Chief Vlaruna crawls over to Wil and Cynthia. "They're slaughtering my people," he warbles. The two he sent to try to flank the intruders, Fryt and Kuil, are lying against the wall, smoking wounds in what is left of their heads and torsos, their armor doing nothing to protect them. "We're not trained or equipped for this!"

Wil's eyes go wide. "Then what the hell are you trained for?"

"Bar fights, minor riots, pacifying unarmed passengers, that kind of thing," the walleyed man replies, his eyes darting independently in different directions. "This is a luxury cruise liner. Our weapons are for dealing with passengers in leisure wear, not armored mercenaries."

Cynthia taps her earpiece. "Max, Zephyr, are you all done with your thing? We could use some help at the barracks." Several shots ring out overhead, scorching bed frames and other pieces of furniture in the large open barracks.

"On our way," the Palorian couple replies in unison.

Wil looks at Cynthia, then Vlaruna. "Backup is on the way, but they're in the shuttle bay, I think, not a short walk."

"We'll be dead by then!" the smaller man whines.

Wil slaps him. "Get it together!" He pops up and squeezes off a few shots, pretty sure he got a mercenary that was crouch-walking towards them. "You're the one that didn't even want us here."

Cynthia leans out from their shared cover, firing. Someone screams. She looks at Wil. "I don't have a good feeling about our position." Something overhead explodes, sparks raining down on the trio.

More and more security personnel fall to the more powerful weapons the mercenary team is bringing to bear. Wil pops up to fire and takes a head count. He looks at Cynthia, "I think there's three or four left."

"Maybe we should charge them?" Vlaruna asks, hopeful.

Wil makes a face. "By all means. We'll wait here." The other man frowns.

Over the sound of the mercenaries' powerful plasma rifle fire and the much weaker crowd control weaponry that the security officers are firing comes a new sound.

Screaming.

Wil and Cynthia exchange a look and peek over the top of their cover. The Hulgian woman is waving her people away from the hatch as several plasma bolts lance into the barracks from the corridor outside. Two mercenaries fall back into the barracks, returning fire.

Cynthia shrugs, standing. Wil follows suit. Both open fire on the now distracted mercenaries, mowing several of them down. The Hulgian woman turns, scowling, in time to take several plasma rounds to her chest armor, the final few burning through.

The woman falls against the bulkhead, dropping her rifle. The last mercenary throws down his rifle, screaming about surrendering.

Chief Vlaruna waves to several of his people, then points to the last mercenary standing.

Maxim and Zephyr step into the room. Both are out of breath. Maxim has his hands on his knees, his rifle slung over his back as he takes deep breaths, trying to steady his breathing.

The *Ghost's* first officer smiles. "Miss us?" She walks into the barracks and looks at the Hulgian woman. "How many?"

The much larger woman spits blood. "Grolack off."

Zephyr quirks an eyebrow. "Okay." She shoots the mercenary commander. Several security officers and Mr. Londo scream.

"Why did you do that?" Vlaruna screams, running over.

Londo joins him. "I don't think killing them needlessly is called for."

Zephyr turns. "It was set to stun, calm down." She looks around. "You have a brig?"

Vlaruna makes a face. "Not one that will hold her."

Zephyr sighs, handing her weapon over. "Keep someone on her. Every time she wakes up, stun her."

Vlaruna claps his hands, a wet slapping sound. "Grogu, come here."

"This afternoon I'm here with good news." GNO newscaster Klor'Tillen's face is split by an ear-to-ear grin. "The *Galactic Empress* is safe."

He turns to another camera. "A scout ship dispatched by Red Nova Lines has arrived at the Tallgese Nebula and has confirmed that the *Empress* is still there. Another vessel appears to be rendering aid but is not answering hails." He walks over to a large display with a grainy image on it. "The unknown vessel appears to be towing the *Empress* out of the nebula. How she ended up in the nebula in the first place, is unknown." He gestures to several dots. "We believe these are lifeboats, and this," he gestures to a larger object, "is the bridge module." He sighs. "The scout ship has thus far been unable to make contact with either ship or the lifeboats. While it's great news to find the ship intact, it raises many questions that we, as yet, don't have answers to." He smiles. "But we will."

PART 5

CHAPTER TWENTY-THREE

NOT ALL PLANS ARE GOOD

"Get everyone back here," someone says from behind Gabe and Bennie, in the ship's main corridor. They've crept out of the primary hold area into the forward section of the mercenaries' ship. "We'll take care of the survivors once we get the ship somewhere out of sight. Where's Wirra?" the voice from behind them says.

Gabe and Bennie exchange a look. They are in the central living space of the ship, an open lounge area with seating, tables, and a small kitchenette in the corner. A little TLC and a lot of bleach, and Bennie thinks it could look like the common area of the *Ghost*.

"Uh..." Bennie says. Gabe turns toward the opening the voice came from. His optic sensors turn crimson at the same time both of his forearms whir and click, blasters sliding into place as his hands fold in and out of the way. One of the blasters still looks damaged to Bennie.

Bennie shrugs, thumbing the activator on his beam saber, the purple blade igniting. "I guess the hard way is fine."

A Malkorite woman and four beings—two Trenbals, a Quilant, and a Tleb—walk in. The woman stops. "Who the wurrin are you?" She eyes Gabe. "You're that droid from the..." She spots Gabe's blasters and dives for the nearest cover, a ratty chair. "Kill 'em!" she shouts as she moves.

Gabe opens fire as he steps back toward the corridor that probably leads to the bridge. One of the Trenbals yelps, falling to the deck. Bennie's saber hums as he attempts to intercept the blaster bolts. One gets through, striking his leg and causing him to grunt and fall to his knee, his saber still swishing back and forth.

Gabe snatches the back of Bennie's shirt, pulling him into the narrow corridor. His blaster barks nonstop, charged plasma streaming from it. The return fire hasn't yet dialed in on him this far down the short corridor. Bennie drops and hobbles forward, slapping an access pane. The hatch slides open.

Bennie comes face to kneecap with a startled Sylban man. Before the much taller being can react, Bennie lashes out, severing the man's leg at the knee. As the big bark-covered pirate falls, Bennie leaps up to land on the man's chest, his beam saber close enough to the pirate's leafy crown to set the nearest leaves to smoking.

Gabe follows Bennie in, slapping the access panel. Once the hatch closes, he presses the lock icon, then his data tendrils slip out into the panel. The mechanism makes several beeps, then sparks pop out of the top.

The bridge of the mercenary ship is laid out unlike any bridge Gabe has seen before, not that he's spent a lot of time on ships' bridges. There is no command chair, just a well-worn section of carpeting where someone has paced, a lot.

Bennie is standing on the Sylban pirate still. "I don't really want to kill you, but won't lose any sleep." The pirate puts both hands on his head. "Good call."

Gabe immediately moves to a different console, his blaster shifting and morphing as it folds back into his forearm. Once he has both hands, data tendrils snake out of his fingertips, probing the console. The thin tendrils find their marks, and their glowing ends burrow into the electronics.

Several loud thumps come from the locked hatch. Bennie joins his friend. "That hatch won't last long."

Gabe turns to his small friend. "I am done."

Bennie makes a face. "Great, and then?" Gabe stares, his optic sensors spinning. Bennie flaps both arms. "You didn't think about the step after this one?" The hatch thumps twice more. A section of it begins to glow.

"If it helps, I did signal the others," Gabe offers, his eyes shifting to red as his combat mode engages. This time something deploys from his shoulder.

Bennie looks around the bridge. The only cover is the chairs secured in front of each workstation and their sole prisoner. He looks at Gabe. "Oh, good. They'll be able to find our bodies while they're still warm." He makes a face and turns to the glowing hatch. His beam saber ignites again with a snap hiss, bathing the space in a faint purple glow.

"We gotta go. Gabe and Obi-dumb need us," Wil says, looking up from his wristcomm. Everyone else's device is displaying the same text message. They turn to leave, stopping near the hatch where Vlaruna is shouting orders at his people.

"Go deck by deck, clear the ship!" Chief of Security Vlaruna orders, waving his arms emphatically at his remaining security personnel as they file out of the barracks, over and around the bodies of the mercenaries.

A Quilant officer is standing over the Hulgian woman. The ship shudders and she tips over, causing the anxious security man to jump and fire a stun blast at the prone form.

Maxim shakes his head at the officer.

Zephyr snaps her fingers at a passing Trollack man. "Oh, and swing by the shuttle bay. We left the primary culprit tied to a pipe in a storage room. She's got a lot to answer for." Turning to Wil. "I can't believe my people never knew how to do this." She snaps her fingers a few times. "Ingenious."

Wil beams. "Finger snapping and tacos. Gonna put Earth on the map."

The head of security nods to the Trollack officer and another.

"Go." They take off at a run. He turns to the others. "Do you need backup?"

Wil tries to keep his reaction under control. "No, we're good, thanks. You secure the ship, we'll get the mercenaries." He turns to Mr. Londo. "You should stay here." The other man nods his agreement.

Maxim removes his wristcomm, handing it to Londo. "You can keep in touch with us with this." He indicates the communications sub-menu. Londo bobs his head.

Jogging through the corridors of the ship, Maxim says, "I still can't believe you didn't tell me you were going to ask Cynthia to be your life mate."

Wil stumbles. "What?"

"You heard me."

"Is..." Wil looks around. The two women are ahead of them. "Is this the time for that heart to heart?"

Maxim shrugs. They reach a service hatch. He begins taking the stairs two at a time. "We've got twenty-odd decks to go. You have other plans?"

From a few stairs up, Cynthia looks at Zephyr. "He's particularly worked up over this."

The Palorian woman rounds a landing, heading up the next flight of stairs. "This is a side of him I honestly didn't know existed. I'm used to the 'kill everything around me' Maxim. This one is..."

Cynthia sniggers. "Your joining is going to be a mess."

"That thought has kept me up at night more than I'd like to admit lately," Zephyr says.

Behind the women, Wil says, "Honestly, dude, I didn't think—"

"Exactly," Maxim interrupts.

Wil sighs. "I didn't think it was that big of a deal."

The big man's deep voice cracks. "You're one of my best friends. Why wouldn't you taking the next step in your relationship with Cynthia be a big deal to me?"

Wil feels his cheeks burn. "Best friend?"

Maxim speeds up the stairs. Wil rubs sweat from his brow. He doesn't have the breath right now to think about Maxim's issues.

The emergency airlock is unguarded, but evidence of Bennie and Gabe's passing is clear. The boarding tube and airlock aboard the mercenary ship are equally unguarded. Cynthia is the first to exit into the hostile ship. She looks over her shoulder. "Security is obviously not a priority."

Zephyr and Maxim follow her in, fanning out. The sounds of weapons fire comes from somewhere above them.

"Oh, my God!" Wil wheezes as he finally joins the others. "I'm getting jet boots."

"Working out more would cost less," Zephyr points out. Wil replies with his middle finger.

"Come on," Cynthia urges, pointing to a hatch leading deeper into the ship.

Outside the bridge, Talara'Vey and a dozen mercenaries are firing their weapons on the hatch. The glow has moved from faint orange to bright white. The hatch won't last much longer.

Maxim and Wil walk in. The former says, "Hey, everybody."

When the assorted mercenaries turn, the two *Ghost* crew members open fire. They rush back into the lounge space, taking cover behind a chair. As the mercenaries follow, abandoning for now the bridge hatch, Cynthia and Zephyr lean into the open hatch, firing their weapons.

After much screaming and shouting, a single voice rises above the sound of weapons fire. "We surrender!"

Wil and Maxim stand up from behind the flaming ruin of the chair they are hiding behind. Wil looks around. "Smart." There are three mercenaries left, the woman who appears to be in charge and two others. Their weapons are already on the ground.

NEWSCAST

"Hello, I am Belzar."

"And I am Gulbar' Te."

Both journalists are somberly staring straight ahead, hands and tentacle-finger parts folded on the desk before them.

The Burzzad continues, "Disgraced Peacekeeper Janus is in custody aboard the Command Carrier *Lancers' Hope.* During the final fighting on Grindflon Four overnight, our colleague and friend Mon-El Furash was killed."

Belzar takes over, his solid black eyes glossy as he blinks several times. "She was with a forward infantry squad clearing a laboratory where it was discovered that the Multonae colonists were being experimented on by that criminal monster, Janus." His voice catches in his throat.

His colleague looks over, then takes over, triplet eyes blinking in succession. "The squad was attempting to find survivors, as there have been rumors of such. When they got to the lower levels, a researcher who had not fled opened the holding pens containing several experiments—er, people."

Belzar inhales deeply, nodding to his friend. "The Peacekeeper unit was met with overwhelming opposition. When reinforcements were able to clear the lower levels, they found the Peacekeepers and…" He sobs, putting his face in his hands, finger-like tentacles wrapping around his head.

Gulbar' Te stands and puts a long thin arm around his colleague. He looks up. "There were no survivors." A fluttering flute-like noise comes from the man. "As a journalist, it is important to remain neutral and detached from the stories we report on, but I am hopeful that Janus suffers greatly for what he has done."

CHAPTER TWENTY-FOUR

CLEAN UP, AISLE 42

After securing the few remaining mercenaries, Wil comms Bennie and Gabe to let them know it's safe to come out of hiding. After several choice words are exchanged, he and the others work on securing the rest of the ship.

Bennie cuts through the hatch once it cools down. He walks up to Wil, looking around. "Good job." Wil makes a face. The hacker looks around. "You even kept a few alive." He points back into the bridge. "We did too."

"You are remarkably dark for someone who's supposed to be a champion of light and virtue or some shit."

Bennie shrugs. "I'm complex."

"You're not," Zephyr says without looking up from the chest she's digging around in.

Gabe exits the bridge, a Sylban man with one and a half legs held in his arms. Wil raises an eyebrow but doesn't ask.

Against the nearby bulkhead, the Malkorite mercenary commander is sitting with her two surviving goons. She says, "I can't believe this was all undone by the five of you."

"You mean us pesky kids?" Wil says, trying to stifle his chuckle.

"What?" The woman replies. "No. You five adults." She looks around. "What kids?"

Bennie looks at Wil, his face flat and expressionless as he slowly shakes his head.

Gabe says, "I have tied myself into this vessel's control systems. The *Galactic Empress* will be clear of the nebula in just under a tock. I have instructed the autopilot to remain at full burn until then. Once the *Empress* is clear, this vessel will go into station keeping. I have encrypted all controls." He turns to look at their prisoners, smiling. "A Red Nova Cruise Lines vessel is also on approach. I have filled them in so that they may relay our current status."

Maxim nods. "Good job."

Gabe inclines his head. "The scout ship will be docking with the *Empress* in ten microtocks."

Zephyr adds, "With the fighting, I'm guessing most PK forces are stretched pretty thin right now."

"Janus. You know, I'd forgotten he was trying to invade the GC," Wil says. He adds, in a whisper, "Hate that guy." He turns to Gabe. "Can you do your magic thing with the *Empress*'s computer again? Recall the lifeboats? Activate her systems?"

The droid makes a noise like sucking in a breath. "I would prefer not to." He holds up a hand. "However, the scout ship on approach has a perfectly good computer core we can make use of. It will not be perfect but should be sufficient to get the *Galactic Empress*'s main systems online."

While Bennie, Gabe, and Maxim work on scrounging up enough data cable to connect the two computer cores, Wil and the others escort their captured mercenaries to the *Empress*'s brig.

Chief Vlaruna's barbels twitch as he watches them approach. He rubs his stubby-fingered hands together. "So, she's the leader?" He and Mr. Londo are standing near the watch desk. Wil called ahead to have them meet the team there.

Wil nods. "At least the leader of the hired guns."

"I'll make a deal," Talara'Vey says.

Mr. Londo looks past the woman to Wil, then back. "For what?" He extends a hand toward one of the cells. Inside is an angry-looking Burzzad woman. Her already thin mouth is pressed into a tight line. All three eyes are squinting through the bars. Her long arms are folded in front of her. He expensive pantsuit is torn and covered in smudges of unknown origin and more than a few burn marks.

The Malkorite woman looks from her employer to the crew of the *Ghost* to Londo and Vlaruna. "Dren."

Maxim smirks. "In you go." He pushes her toward the cell next to Fev'Ti's.

The overhead speaker crackles. "I don't think it's working...No... How would I—what? Oh! Attention, everyone, the ship is safe now." It's Bennie. "You're sure it went shipwide? How would I know?"

Wil puts a hand over his eyes, sighing.

Cynthia taps her earpiece, looking at the ceiling. "Yes, you little drennog, we can hear you."

From the overheads, "Oh? Great! Thanks, Cyn. The Captain of the scouth ship is looking for you."

She looks at Londo, shrugging. Her tail twitching, she says, "Can you issue the recall on the lifeboats and bridge module?"

"Already done," the ceiling replies.

PUTTING THE PIECES BACK TOGETHER

The recall command works as expected. Mr. Londo, Captain Worworu of the scout ship *Eyes Wide*, and the crew of the *Ghost* are standing outside the combination bridge anteroom and airlock. Several loud clangs echo through the space as the multi-story bridge module locks back into place on the command tower of the ship. The sound of mechanical locking mechanisms doing their job echoes through the space.

Wil looks at Bennie. "You good?"

The team hacker nods as he moves to the hatch and the access panel next to it. He kneels next to the console, connecting his wrist-comm to the panel. A few minutes and a few choice expletives in both galactic standard and Brailack normal later, and the hatch slides open.

Mr. Londo spreads his arms. "Captain Ramalbong, welcome back!"

The blonde woman walks through the hatch, her bridge crew clustered behind her. She looks at Wil and the others. "You earned your fee, I guess," offering her arm.

Wil shrugs then takes her forearm in his hand.

The captain looks around the gathering before her. "Your droid friend is missing."

Wil nods. "He's managing our jury-rigged computer." The captain's eyebrows arch. "The main and secondary core aboard the *Empress* got shot up. We patched in Captain Worworu's ship."

"A lot shot up," Bennie quips. Cynthia chuckles, nodding.

Wil continues, "The mercenary ship is pulling the *Empress* away from the nebula." He shrugs. "It's ugly, but it's got this bucket back up and, mostly, working."

"Captain!" someone shouts from inside the bridge. Everyone turns. The crew of the *Ghost* all raise their weapons.

A Tleb trots out and yelps when she spots the weapons trained on her. She bares her teeth.

"What is it?" the captain asks.

The diminutive officer turns her attention from the crew of the *Ghost* to her captain. "We're clear of the nebula."

Ramalbong nods. "Good."

Maxim smiles. "Hopefully, reinforcements are coming. That merc ship won't be able to tow us far, and not at FTL."

Captain Worworu nods. "The *Eyes Wide* lacks the power as well."

Ramalbong dismisses her officer and urges the rest of her people back to their stations. Turning to Londo, "Now what?"

THAT'S A WRAP

"Well, this isn't the joining party I would have preferred to throw you, but such is life," Maxim says. The crew of the *Ghost*, as well as Captains Ramalbong and Worworu plus a few assorted investors and passengers, are gathered in the *Galactic Empress's* main dining room. What remains of the forward section of the *Empress* is a wreck from the nose to almost a hundred meters back. The forward recreation deck is open to space, the thormic radiation having burned through the transparent hull. That section will not be reopening any time soon. The shuttle bay is equally wrecked, the forward doors having failed, letting the toxic nebula deep inside the ship.

"I'm just glad you two thought to lock Fev'Ti up in the storage room," Wil says to Zephyr and Maxim, each holding a flute of what Mr. Londo assures them is the most expensive alcohol on the ship. "The entire shuttle bay decompressed when the forward doors failed."

The big Palorian grunts, "It would have been a fitting end."

His longtime partner looks up. "No justice in that." She takes a sip of her drink. He shrugs.

Cynthia slips an arm through Wil's and says, "Are all human engagements like this?"

Wil laughs, then takes a sip of his drink. "No...well, sometimes, I suppose. There was this family, the Kardashians. So much drama."

Ankpol walks over, Nic perched on his back. The former dips his white furry torso, the latter clinging to him. "My congratulations, again." He makes a show of rising to his full height. "And my thanks for keeping us safe."

Nic leaps off the big Xelurian's back. "You guys are amazing! I wish I coulda been here."

"You would have gotten in the way," Bennie says, offering her a drink.

Cynthia intercepts the glassware, clucking, "No."

Bennie makes a noise. "Spoilsport." He turns. "Oh, those look yummy." He walks toward the forward section of the dining room and a large table loaded with food.

Since the *Empress* can't continue on, the captain and Mr. Londo are giving Wil and Cynthia a party to remember. Outside the transparent ceiling a pair of tugs moves into position trailing thick tow cables behind them.

Mr. Quistic stomps over. "It appears that you and your team are quite good at destroying my investments, Mr. Calder."

Wil smiles. "We're good at what we do." Maxim chuckles and nods.

Near the table of food, Security Chief Vlaruna is next to Gabe. "Tell me, is it always like this with you people?"

Gabe looks down at the stout, walleyed man. "Indeed. It can be exhausting at times. I am considering politics as an alternative."

The aquatic-featured man laughs, a sound like he's choking on something. "Then I am glad you will be leaving us. Also, I don't think politics is any safer."

Gabe makes his sighing noise. "You are likely correct."

Vlaruna opens his mouth, but stops to point out the transparent hull. "Our saviors." He points.

Gabe turns. The captured mercenary ship has towed the *Galactic Empress* several thousand ploriths from the nebula, but that is extent of its capabilities. Working with another cruise line, Red Nova was able to get another cruise ship dispatched to offload passengers and crew while the tugs made their slow way back to the Hub.

From the overhead speakers a voice says, "May I have your attention, please? The *Nebula Princess* has arrived. You'll need to make your way to the aft embarkation center. Your floor stewards will direct you."

Quistic looks at Wil and Cynthia. "Congratulations." He bows and heads for the exit.

The crew of the *Ghost* gathers near the forward section, Bennie shoveling food into his pockets. He looks up. "Guess we're done here."

Wil nods. "Yeah, time for ... Rogue Enterprises to head home."

Maxim purses his lips. "I like it."

Bennie holds his hand out, wiggling it. "It's okay."

Cynthia rests a hand on Bennie's hairless head. "Yeah. It's us." She tilts her head toward the rear of the dining room. "Let's get out of here."

Bennie turns to Zephyr. "We got paid, right?"

The End

Thank you so much for reading this latest Space Rogues adventure

If you enjoyed it I'd love it if you left a review. Seriously, reviews are a big deal. They help readers find authors. They help authors show how awesome they are.

Reviews are social proof and go a long way to encouraging other readers to take a chance on an unknown author.

OFFER

As they say, there's no harm in asking, so here we go.

If you can help connect me with someone who can get Space Rogues on a screen (Big or Little) I'll cut you in for 10% (Up to $10,000) of whatever advance is paid.

Send me an email and we can discuss.
rights@johnwilker.com

**Want to stay up to date on the happenings in the
Galactic Commonwealth?**
Sign up for my newsletter at
johnwilker.com/newsletter
You can also join my Patreon page for all
sorts of awesome goodies!

Visit me online at
johnwilker.com

If you like supporting things you love by sporting merch, well you're
in luck! I've launched a Space Rogues Shop. Take a look.

ACKNOWLEDGMENTS

I couldn't do this without an amazing group of people who sign up to beta and/or ARC read for me. The Beta readers in particular have to suffer through an early draft to help shape the story.

Below are some of these awesome people (If I missed your name, email me and you'll be in the next one :D)

- Chris Boyd
- Alice
- Jim Stiles

Thank you so much, all of you!

OTHER BOOKS BY JOHN WILKER

The Space Rogues Series. Wil Calder and a bunch of alien misfits somehow keep finding themselves in the thick of it. No one ever checks qualifications when it comes to saving the galaxy!

The Grand Human Empire Series. Jax, Naomi and the droids are just trying to get by. New droid parts ain't cheap after all.

www.ingramcontent.com/pod-product-compliance
Lightning Source LLC
Chambersburg PA
CBHW051205190726

48288CB00006B/1818